LOVE
ME
Deeper

NATALIE Sadè

More from Natalie Sadè

Cut From The Same Cloth 1&2
Money By Any Means
Cut From A Different Cloth
Friends Are Foes 1&2
InstaFamous 1&2
Legendary Love 1-3
Unapologetically Yours
And So We Hustle 1-3
You and I: A Murderous Love Story
I Came Back for You
Money Making McCoys

∞

Connect with me @

Facebook: www.facebook.com/AuthorNatalieSade

Instagram: @ natalie_sade_edits

Twitter: @NatalieSade

www.october15thpublishing .com

Prologue

Geechi stood in the middle of the VIP section at V-Live. Beautiful women were all around him, but he could only focus on one. She'd had him captivated since the very first time she walked into his office.

Currently, her body was wrapped around him like a snake to a tree. Her legs straddled his waist, her arms fell to her sides; one holding a bottle of D'Usse as she grinded against him so seductively that the women on stage watched her. She requested that the DJ play *Go* by Alex the Kid, Rapsody and H.E.R.; her body moved slowly, her ass bouncing with the beat. She told him he couldn't touch her with his hands, he could only watch and feel as she grinded, snaked, and allowed her body to caress his.

"Fuck this, we leaving," Geechi said. He let his people know they were leaving the club with a peace sign and a head nod, but he didn't put her down until they were at the exit. Maleek, Geechi's best friend, was busy getting a lap dance but managed to throw his head back in acknowledgement of Geechi's departure.

The parking lot was packed; some people saw Geechi leaving and followed him outside.

"Hey Geechi!" a woman called out to him.

"What's up, Geechi!" People yelled as Geechi made his way through the crowd pulling Gotti's hand. Everyone had their phones out recording and asking questions as if he was the world's biggest celebrity.

"Congratulations," a few men Geechi knew in passing said, walking up to him and dapping him up. Geechi knew they just wanted to be captured in a picture with him.

"Is it true, Geechi?" a woman with red, 28-inch bundles dressed in a red bandage dress, yelled out. Geechi knew what she was referring to; everybody wanted to know if he had really done the unthinkable. Someone from the courthouse had leaked the information revealing that he had come in for a marriage license and since then social media had been going crazy. Girls were DM'ing Gotti left and right with lies. Thank God she was solid and didn't let any of it faze her.

"Is what true?" Geechi asked, looking back at Red. He was ready to officially claim his woman; they had moved in silence for far too long.

"You married her?" she asked.

He stood before Gotti, towering over her. Gotti was on the shorter side; 5'4 with skin the color of carob; Gotti wore white fitted pants that laid across her body as if they were painted on and a white bralette.

"Did you marry me, baby?" he asked making her blush as he bore deep into her eyes.

"Did you marry me?" she shot back; her joy impossible to hide.

"Hell yea," Geechi said and pulled Gotti to him. When her body crashed into his, he kissed her so succulently that she was out of breath, yet craving more, even as she pulled back.

Chapter 1

"**I**'ve done it before...I mean it doesn't happen every time," Troy said with a slight shrug as she tucked her shoulder length hair behind her ear.

"It's not that big of a deal; the shit is nasty to me," La'Shea fussed, using her fork to pick up a nacho and stuffing it in her mouth.

"It has never happened to me," Gotti said matter-of-factly. "I mean...I want to I..." Her sentence trailed off when sex moans traveled from La'Shea's phone.

"Oh Daddy," a seductive voice moaned. Fright sent shockwaves through Troy's body; she was so flustered she couldn't speak; her walnut toned skin burned with embarrassment.

"Look," La'Shea said, shoving her phone into Gotti's face. "It's pee," she informed her. Gotti was humiliated too; her mouth dropped open and she looked at La'Shea bewilderedly.

"Turn that shit off," Troy demanded through tight lips which were painted dark red. She looked around the restaurant to see if anyone from the surrounding tables had heard the commotion.

"I know what it is," Gotti hissed. La'Shea, who was unbothered, took a moment to look at the video. A woman was being fucked by a chocolate brother with a vicious stroke and squirting everywhere.

"Yea," the man panted as he drilled inside of her. "Come for daddy."

"Oh my god," the woman moaned as La'Shea clicked out of the video. She looked up at her two best friends and saw looks of disgust on their faces.

"Oh so you two are virgins now?" she quipped.

"How we virgins if we talking about squirting?" Gotti sassed, rolling her neck and eyes as she swirled her Alfredo pasta on her fork.

"Y'all don't watch porn?" La'Shea shot back.

"La'Shea, you turned me on to the shit in college," Gotti reminded her. The threesome met during their years at Spelman. La'Shea was in school to become a lawyer, Gotti had dreams of being a brand consultant, and Troy, who loved money, went for an accounting degree.

Now the three women were successful in their perspective careers, although Gotti was going through a transitional period. They all dressed to the nines, but Troy was more of a designer whore; she had turned both ladies on to fabulous pant and skirt suits as they entered the professional world. While Gotti loved wigs and weaves, Troy and La'Shea opted for their natural hair.

La'Shea was half Native American, from the Navajo tribe, and had spent her childhood living on a reservation in New Mexico. Her mother moved them to San Antonio, Texas when she was ten. She bore a cinnamon skin tone and hair that fell to her bra strap which she always wore parted down the middle.

"Yea to help you since you couldn't ride dick," La'Shea teased. Truthfully, it wasn't that Gotti couldn't; it was more about her being too scared to try.

"I *hadn't* rode dick; there's a difference," Gotti replied.

"Bitch, you stayed on your back," La'Shea said.

"That's why you couldn't orgasm," Troy added with the lift of her eyebrow.

Gotti laughed. "Oh but bitch, I bust like a firecracker now! Anyway, I didn't know much about squirting, so I looked the shit up. I read that it's only two percent pee," Gotti explained.

"Yes, it's pee, but it's mixed with—" Troy began, but was cut off by La'Shea's big mouth.

"No, the fuck it ain't. It's pee. Some freaky ass woman wanted to pee on her man—" Now it was Gotti's turn to cut her off.

Gotti huffed and rolled her eyes. "You swear you went to school to become a sex-pert and not a lawyer."

"You've done it!" Troy reminded La'Shea.

"And I'm a freaky bitch," La'Shea countered. Gotti threw her head back in laughter and then high-fived La'Shea. Troy couldn't contain the chortle that exploded from her mouth. La'Shea was the sex-pert of the group; she was honest with her experiences and unashamed by her uninhibited trysts. Although in this moment, she was putting on a humorous show for her friends.

"Women are smart as hell, and we're quick on our feet," La'Shea said. "A woman was fucking and peed on her partner; he probably jumped up like, 'Yo, what the fuck'. Then she was like, 'oh baby you fucked me so good I squirted'. She probably made the word up on the spot. And y'all know men are stupid; all you gotta do is stroke their ego," La'Shea said, making up a story about how squirting became a thing.

"I can't disagree with the part about men," Gotti said, raising her glass.

Troy laughed. "Me either."

They all knew there was more to it than that, but the story was funny.

"So now women just pissing on men and making them think they doing something major?" Gotti asked concluding La'Shea's theory.

"Yup," La'Shea said, taking a big swig from her wine glass. "I missed y'all so much; thank y'all for coming to see me," La'Shea said, in a more serious tone.

"How is our god daughter?" Troy asked, referring to La'Shea's daughter La'Bella, as she dug into her salad.

"She hates it here; sometimes, I just want to pick up and go back home." La'Shea had moved to Dallas for the job opportunity of a lifetime. She felt guilty because it was only a few months after she divorced La'Bella's stepfather, Kyle. La'Shea wasn't the type to harp on things, so she was happy for the distraction. But she had soon realized the toll it had taken on La'Bella and her stepdaughter, Kelsie...and maybe even Kyle.

"She's a teenager; she'll adjust," Troy said to comfort her.

"That's what I'm hoping. It's just hard...she seems depressed," La'Shea revealed. She had tried to talk to her mother about it, in an effort to get strength that she could pour into her daughter. Her mother, at sixty-five, couldn't grasp the concept of a fifteen-year-old girl with no bills being depressed.

"Depressed?" Gotti questioned, sitting up straight in her seat. She'd had a small bout with depression and took the accusation very seriously.

"Yes. When we were coming up, I don't remember being depressed and shit, but we can't dismiss what this generation goes through."

"Depressed as in..." Gotti asked needing more clarification on La'Bella's actions.

"As in no friends, she goes to school, comes home, gets in bed..."

"Her grades?" Troy asked.

La'Shea laughed. "Oh she keeps those up."

"It's just the readjustment period," Gotti said.

"Yea. Y'all are probably right. It's just hard to see her like this," La'Shea said. The ladies got back to discussing their favorite topics, men, clothes and their careers as they enjoyed their food and drinks.

●●●

"Babbbby!" Troy screeched when she turned the corner entering La'Shea's living room. La'Bella ran into her arms and squeezed her tight. Before long La'Bella felt another set of arms around her and knew it was Gotti.

Twenty minutes later, they were sitting around the living room. La'Bella was eating the takeout her mother brought her from The Cheesecake Factory while her mother and aunties drank wine and talked about the past. La'Bella loved their friendship; they had been through a lot together including her mother unexpectantly getting pregnant her senior year of college. No matter what, they always had each other's backs. La'Bella had never experienced that; it was different in San Antonio because her family was there. They had to get along or Granny would hand out ass whoopings. Here, in Dallas, no one had to like her, and they didn't.

"Oh Gotti," La'Shea said, "I have someone for you to meet."

"I don't want no country ass man from the south. I'm not riding horses, living on a ranch; none of that shit."

"First off, have you seen any horses around here? Stop the dumb shit. But it's not like that, he's my client...he owns a car lot...young, black, successful dude and I handle contracts and things for him. He's trying to rebrand and you're trying to rebuild; it could work for both of y'all," La'Shea reasoned.

"I'm not doing shit for free," Gotti said. Even though she was happy her best friend was looking out for her.

"I didn't ask you to," La'Shea said with an attitude. Gotti was two years younger than her so they had a little sister/ big sister relationship and normally Troy was the referee.

"Or a discount," Gotti said, knowing she was annoying La'Shea.

"You know what, I thought this could be a good look for you, but—"

"Thank you," Gotti said, rolling her eyes.

"Y'all are crazy," La'Bella said, standing up and grabbing her empty to-go box.

"You going to bed?" La'Shea asked.

"Yea," she answered.

"It's Friday! You're fifteen and you're going to sleep?" Gotti questioned.

La'Bella laughed. "Yea, I'm tired." Troy, La'Shea and Gotti shared a quick glance.

"Good night," they all said, and each took turns giving her a hug.

"So anyway, what's his name?" Gotti asked after La'Bella was gone.

"Geechi Koran; look him up. He's a star in Dallas and known throughout Texas."

"Why does he want to rebrand?"

"Get that information from him," La'Shea said, doing something on her phone. "Can you meet him tomorrow?" she asked a few minutes later.

"Yea; where?"

"His office."

"Cool; send me the address," Gotti said.

"So you gon' work on *our* weekend?" Troy questioned. She was the workaholic of the crew but knew that on their weekends none of that was permitted.

"She has no choice; she quit her job," La'Shea replied.

"I have savings; I'm good."

"How long will that last with rent and shit?" La'Shea questioned.

"Oh I forgot to tell y'all, I moved back in with my mom," Gotti revealed.

"What!" Troy screeched almost spitting out her wine. Gotti had moved out when she attended college and swore she would never live under the same roof with Helen again.

"Yup. I'm serious about getting my own shit off the ground. They didn't see my talent," Gotti told them.

"They saw it; they just didn't want to pay you for it," Troy clarified.

"Hell yea 'cause they sure didn't mind stealing your shit," La'Shea chimed in.

"We think Johnathan could present this better but thanks for giving us something to build on," Gotti said mimicking her old boss. "Lying asses."

"The pot is yours," La'Shea told Gotti, then looked at Troy, "My bad. Is that cool with you?"

"Hell yea; I was about to say it." The women shared a bank account where they made monthly deposits for times like this.

"Aww, you guys; thank you! Y'all know I'm good for it."

"Yea we know," Troy and La'Shea agreed.

"We still going out tonight?" Gotti asked.

"Our old asses ain't doing shit," La'Shea said lazily.

"We'll go tomorrow after you wow old dude," Troy said, and the ladies agreed.

●●●

"Hi, I'm Gotti Lexington, here to see Mr. Koran," Gotti announced, stopping at the front desk of Koran Motors. The ambience of the lobby read more as a high-end boutique than a car dealership. Both the location and outside appearance was lowkey, so Gotti figured you had to be invited in order to ever see the inside of the business. The waiting area was all white: white couches, tables, the two doors on either side of the reception area were white, the countertops, the Mac computer and the desk behind the counter, all white.

The receptionist was the only piece of color. She had an olive complexion and blonde, shoulder length hair. It was parted diagonally, and her natural curls flowed freely. She was 5'6 and cute, dressed in a hot pink, short skirt displaying her toned legs.

"Do you have an appointment?" she asked, looking at the calendar.

"Yes."

"Because he doesn't see walk-ins." Blondie continued to talk as if she hadn't heard Gotti's reply. "I can get someone else to help you. What are you looking for?"

"Mr. Koran." Gotti tried to sound as polite as possible but chick was getting on her nerves. "The appointment was last minute...orchestrated by La'Shea Yarborough. If you'd contact him, he could tell you—"

"I don't need to contact him. I know his schedule better than he does, and like I said..." Before she could finish, Gotti placed her business card on the counter.

"Just tell him Gotti stopped by. I'll also have Ms. Yarborough to call him, ya know, in case you forget."

"Look, let me double check with him; I can see when he is available and make an appointment for you," Blondie offered. She still didn't believe Gotti, but she knew Ms. Yarborough and figured not just anyone would know to mention her.

"Thanks," Gotti said sarcastically. She waited with her arms folded across the counter. Gotti could tell that Blondie was fighting hard to bite her tongue. When she finally walked out of the door on the left, Gotti walked around the lobby. Old magazines were on the table more for decoration than to pass the time. Long stemmed, tulips flowed out of the big white vases positioned around the sitting area, and a floor to ceiling mirror was in the corner.

Gotti didn't have anything to wear to a business meeting so she borrowed a red pantsuit from La'Shea; she paired it with black Red Bottoms and a black Chanel tote.

"Uh-huh," the receptionist said announcing that she had returned. "He'll squeeze you in; make it quick, he has another appointment right afterwards. It's the room straight to the back," she said without looking at Gotti.

"He asked for a meeting with me, love, so he can make it long or short," Gotti said just to fuck with her head. Blondie was obviously fucking her boss, and as a result, she didn't know how to conduct business. Gotti allowed her legs to take long, model like strides to the door that Blondie had just come out of. When she pulled it, it wouldn't open. Gotti turned to Blondie and leered, burning holes into Blondie's hot pink blazer.

"I need to let you in," Blondie said. She tossed her hair and waited a few moments before she pressed the button.

"Bitch." Gotti mumbled.

"Hoe," Blondie returned before the door closed behind Gotti. She pulled out her phone as she stomped down the hall.

Gotti: *These muthafuckas are so unprofessional!*

La'Shea: *Geechi? Hell no.*

Gotti: *His receptionist slash baby mama or whoever the hell she is...*

La'Shea: *He doesn't have kids.*

Troy: *You sure know a lot about him.*

La'Shea: *Bitch I work with him. Relax!*

Gotti looked up as she started her next text and was stopped in her tracks. He was caramel complexioned with a low fade, waves for days, and a beautiful smile. He was dressed in black jeans and a collared Louis Vuitton shirt with matching shoes. Baller Belly, beard, Rolex, diamonds in his teeth and a pair of Versace square framed glasses completed his look. The teeth and the glasses were a contradiction, hood and smart, but he was the definition of perfection.

"Gotti?" he questioned.

"Mr. Koran," she said, extending her hand. He took it, turned it and shook it gently.

"Geechi, please," he told her.

"Geechi," she agreed with a smile. He led the way through the door and into a conference room. He sat at the head of the table and she sat beside him.

"This is a nice location," she complimented.

"You know Dallas?" he questioned. La'Shea hadn't told him much about Gotti other than she was a good friend, from New York and perfect for the job. Because of all the great work La'Shea had put in, he trusted her.

"No...I—"

"Researched," he finished. "I like that."

"Where are the cars?" she inquired.

"In the back," he let her know. She nodded.

"What? You want to see them; you think I'm bullshittin'?" He laughed. He was used to being judged, his look confused people. Was he a businessman or drug dealer? Most pretended not to know they were the same thing.

"No, I, no," Gotti said, shaking her head. She opened her tote, pulled out another phone and dropped her personal one inside. "La'Shea says you want to rebrand; why?"

"It's time. We're getting bigger. We have a new look."

"Rebrand in what ways?" Gotti asked, taking notes in her business phone.

"I thought you would figure that out," he shot back. Geechi had a few ideas, but he wasn't going to share them just yet. He wanted to see what Gotti could do.

"What do you want...out of your business?" she questioned.

"For the police to stop fucking with me. I'ma be honest, they think what you thought," he let her know.

"I didn't think anything," she lied. Gotti hated that she thought it, but she did. This location screamed money, but it didn't even whisper dealership. If he was selling cars, why weren't they visible?

"They think we sellin' drugs out this bitch. We not; we're legit." His country drawl was sexy, disarming and endearing to her.

"And you want me to let them know that..." Gotti said more as a question.

"La'Shea said you're the best...I'm skeptical, 'cause you're based in New York and shit—"

"I travel," Gotti quickly blurted out. She was trying to be cool, but the truth was, she needed this job.

"So you're up for the job?"

"La'Shea speaks highly of you..." she said trying to maintain her cool.

"How long will you be in town?"

"I'm leaving tomorrow, but I can come back in a week...you can show me the ins and outs and we can go from there," she suggested.

Geechi nodded his head in agreement, "Lemme walk you out," he said, standing up. Gotti stood up too. "Email me your prices, so I can send them to my lawyer." He smiled.

"She's going to give me whatever I ask for," Gotti replied, following him out of the conference room.

"Nah, she good business; she gon' look out," he joked.

"We've been best friends since college."

"So you went to Spelman too?" he turned around to ask her.

"Yea."

"What was your major?"

"Communication with an emphasis in marketing and advertising."

"Good," he said and started back walking. The southern gentleman opened the door that led to the lobby for her and she walked out. He was right behind her.

"Bye Blondie," Gotti said over her shoulder. "See you next week." She smiled as Geechi followed her to the double doors. He opened one for her and she walked out.

"Which parking lot?" he asked.

"That one," she said and pointed across the street. "I can get there." She laughed.

"I got you," Geechi replied and followed her to the crosswalk. At her car, he opened her door and she slid in. "I'll be in touch," he said.

"Okay," Gotti smiled, and he closed the door. She was only five minutes from La'Shea's condo, but she still called to fill them in.

"You're on speaker," La'Shea announced.

"Where's Baby?" she asked using La'Bella's nickname.

"In her room," Troy answered.

"Good. Did you fuck him, La'Shea?"

"What? Hell no!"

"He knows you went to Spelman."

"Bitch, I'm his lawyer; that's important information."

"He opened every door I walked through...walked me to the parking lot across the street and made sure I got inside the car before he closed the door for me." Gotti gushed. Troy and La'Shea looked at each other; Gotti's attraction to Geechi was evident in her voice.

"Hahaha! That's a Texas boy for you! You're used to those mean ass 'You my bitch, shorty, now shut the fuck up' New York niggas!" La'Shea teased.

"Whatever, I like his teeth," she said.

"Are they pearly white?" Troy asked.

"No, he has permanents," La'Shea told her.

"I thought it was a grill...so he can't take them out?" Gotti asked.

"Yea, but not by himself."

"A grrriillll?" Troy questioned.

"Not no cheap shit. It's like diamonds in his teeth...it's expensive and it looks that way," La'Shea said.

"I don't know," Troy said, turning up her nose. She always liked a man in a suit, clean cut and polished.

"I like his belly," Gotti said in a childlike voice.

"Bye bitch," La'Shea said and hung up in her face.

●●●

Gotti was back in Texas for her meeting with Geechi. She was supposed to return last week, but he had other business and luckily for her so did she. Now she was at La'Shea's Uptown condo hopping on one foot trying to hurry and get dressed.

"Are you going to work or on a date?" La'Bella asked from the doorway of the guest bedroom.

"Hush, auntie baby, go in your mama's room and get me some gold earrings. I must have left mine at home."

"Yes ma'am," La'Bella said and walked away. Gotti was dressed in hot pink, wide legged slacks and a navy blue, silk button down.

She paired the ensemble with a pair of plaid, Chanel pumps that matched her outfit with the double C's in gold.

"Here Auntie," La'Bella said, walking back into the bedroom.

"I like these," she said, admiring the earrings. "I might have to…"

"I'ma tell," La'Bella threatened, walking out of the bedroom and laughing.

●●●

As soon as Gotti walked into the lobby of Koran Motors, she was greeted by Blondie who was dressed in a baby blue dress. The sleeves stopped at her elbows and the hem clung to her thighs. Without speaking, Gotti headed to the door that led to the back.

"Hot pink," Blondie called out from her desk. "Let me find out you were inspired."

"Glad you noticed, but don't flatter yourself. I'm trying to show you what business professional looks like!" Gotti was now at the door but hadn't reached for it because she knew she had to be buzzed in. She turned to face Blondie who was sitting in her chair; she looked up at Gotti with a smirk on her face.

"Where are you going?" she finally asked.

"Am I not on the calendar? Buzz me in," Gotti said, refusing to play her game.

"He's in his office," she revealed.

"No shit," Gotti shot back.

"That's on this side." She pointed to the other door. Gotti huffed and walked sound the front desk to the other side and Blondie buzzed her in.

"Bitch," Gotti said again.

"Hoe!" She heard Blondie say. Gotti rolled her eyes.

"What's up," Geechi said, greeting Gotti in the hallway before she could walk into his office. They hugged, he smelled delightful; his body against hers felt good. Gotti pulled back; she'd had a talk with herself. The one thing she could never do was mix business with pleasure; it was hard enough for women in business and that type of shit...a reputation like that, would only make it harder.

"I'm heading to the back...put your stuff down, if you want, and follow me."

"Okay," Gotti said, grabbing her phone and setting her purse in his office chair.

The well-trained PR consultant tried to maintain her composure, but she was in awe. The showroom floor was white marble with crystals in it. Twelve luxury cars were strategically placed around the room. There were Lamborghinis, Bentleys, and Ferraris just to name a few. The cars ranged from brand new to classics and even they were striking.

"We rebuilt this one," Geechi said, pointing to a Bentley. "It's an '86," he let her know. "We keep ten to fifteen cars here, but we can get anything sent in from around the world." Gotti nodded her head in amazement. "You know what this is?" he asked as they approached a car in the back. It was the shiniest, most flawless silver she had ever seen, and flowed into crimson in the back. The Skyview was beyond impressive and the interior matched the exterior even down to the rims that nearly made Gotti gasp.

"Expensive," she answered.

"Hell yea." Geechi chuckled. "It a Chiron," he said. Gotti nodded.

"It's made by Bugatti," Geechi said knowing that name would resonate with her. Gotti was impressed, he could tell, but he liked that she didn't get overly excited. "People come to us because we're exclusive, professional and we know our shit," he told her.

"I can work with this," she said as ideas ran through her mind. She pulled out her phone and started typing her thoughts.

"Speaking of professional, your receptionist is rude and very unprofessional," Gotti said. Geechi laughed; Tione was a lot of things but unprofessional she wasn't. Thorough, yes...by the book, okay—but unprofessional, nah. She brought money into the business and gave sales to people to build their confidence. She was usually the first one in the office and the last one out; she knew everyone's schedules, strengths and their weaknesses. Because of that, she knew who to give what customer. So nah, lil mama was tripping Tione was the profession.

"That's not funny; people are spending a lot of money with you."

"She's not unprofessional...she has to deal with a lot. People finding our location and coming in here knowing they don't have the money. Or coming to see me..."

"Groupies?" Gotti laughed.

"I guess." Geechi shrugged. "I forgot to put you on the calendar, so her antennas went up."

"She called me a hoe."

"You called her a bitch," he pointed out. Tione had already ran down the chain of events to him.

"Are y'all together?" Gotti asked. He laughed again.

"She's my sister. Our grandfather was into cars...luxury ones. He taught us the game; we turned it into this. You don't get along with women?" he asked.

"Yes I do," Gotti said looking at him side-eyed. "I love women," she expressed thinking about La'Shea and Troy. He looked at her amused. "Not like that. I have two best friends; we've been locked in since college. I employ women, I support women...so yes I get along perfectly fine with women."

"Cool, so make that shit right 'cause you ain't going nowhere, and she ain't either." Gotti took in Geechi's statement and then took a deep breath.

"So how do y'all advertise?" Gotti asked, walking around the bronze Lamborghini Aventador.

"We don't. If you know, you know," Geechi said.

"Hmm," she said, "I like that."

He spent an hour going over the details of the cars with her. She could tell that he really loved cars and was extremely knowledgeable on the subject. They headed inside and sat in his office to discuss ideas.

"What's that?" Gotti asked, looking over his head at the framed watch.

"My grandfather's watch. He was known for it...gave it to me on his death bed."

"I'm sorry for your loss," she said.

"He lived a good life. Come on," he said, standing up. "It's lunch time," he said. Moments later, they walked out of the office and down the hall to the lobby. Tione and two others stood there waiting.

"Eric and Lark, this is Gotti; she's going to be working with us," Geechi said introducing them.

"It's nice to meet you," Eric and Lark took turns saying as they shook her hand.

"Likewise," she said, with a polite smile.

"Carl and Tina are staying back; they haven't met their quota yet, but I told them I would bring them lunch," Tione informed Geechi.

"They haven't met their quota, they don't eat," Geechi said. Gotti couldn't tell if he was joking or not. And before she could truly dissect it, Geechi was pulling her in front of him so that she was face to face with Tione. "You've met Gotti," Geechi said to Tione.

"I have," she replied with a fake smile.

"Louboutin?" Gotti asked taking in Tione's striped pumps.

Tione smiled. "They are. Your bag is fire. I'm not going to lie I'm going to get one when I get off." She shrugged and then laughed.

"Oh now who's inspired?" Gotti joked, following everyone out of the office. Geechi led her to a white G-wagon and opened the door for her. He grabbed her hand and helped her climb in.

"Where you going?" Geechi asked looking back at Tione.

"We gon' smoke," she yelled over her shoulder, following Eric and Lark.

"You don't smoke?" Gotti asked Geechi once he was seated in the car, and they were pulling out of the parking lot.

"Do you?" he asked. She smiled a little and tilted her head left to right. "You a pot head?" he asked.

"No. I will smoke, though. Not every day or even every week. But if I feel like it, I smoke," she admitted.

"I smoke, just not in my cars," he revealed with a laugh.

"How many cars do you have?"

"Just three," he answered.

"Just three?" she mimicked.

"To love cars like I do, that's not a lot," he told her.

"I guess," Gotti said looking out the window as they drove. She liked Downtown and Uptown Dallas because it reminded her of New York.

"You good with Spaghetti Warehouse?" he asked.

"Yea," she answered.

●●●

After eating, the ladies excused themselves to go to the bathroom.

"You like my little brother, huh?" Tione asked as they were washing their hands.

"What? No," Gotti said.

"He's handsome, charming...rich," Tione said.

"I have my own money," Gotti shot back.

"Yea, but him having money doesn't hurt," Tione said.

"Agreed!" Lark said, walking out of her stall.

"I don't like him. That shit sounds so childish. How old are y'all?" Gotti said now fingering through her 24-inch bundles.

"How old are you?" Lark asked as she washed her hands.

"35," Gotti answered.

"I'm 32," Tione said.

"I'm 30," Lark said.

"How old is he?" Gotti asked, reapplying her lipstick.

"Who Eric?" Tione teased.

"Yea," Gotti said, rolling her eyes.

"Like 40...Geechi is 31 though," Tione said as Lark exited the bathroom. "Carl is her husband," Tione whispered after the door swung closed.

"Damn, and she left him at work hungry?" Gotti said. Tione made a face as she pulled the door open.

"I said he is her husband; I'on really know if she is his wife," she said.

When they walked back out, the bill had been paid and Geechi held a to-go bag.

"You ready," he asked Gotti.

"Yup," she answered and headed to the door.

Chapter 2

Three Months Later

"This looks good," La'Shea said, looking around the lobby of Koran Motors. Gotti had done a lot of work for Geechi over the last three months, but this was her first big event. It was the unveiling of their new logo and a way for the public to get acquainted with Koran Motors.

"How many potential buyers are you expecting?" Troy asked. She was dressed in a white dress with a Louboutin belt and shoes. La'Shea wore a silver, metallic, one strap goddess dress with black Gucci accessories and heels.

"It's not about that. It's open to the public," Gotti told them. A server walked by with a tray of drinks and La'Shea and Troy grabbed a champagne flute.

"You not drinking?" La'Shea asked Gotti.

"I'm on the clock," she said, holding up her phone and walking away.

●●●

"You see this shit?" Tione said to Geechi with a fake smile on her face. They were posted by the front desk trying to take a break from fake smiles with the Who's Who of Dallas.

"I see that slimy muthafucka," he said. The server smiled and stopped in front of them. They both grabbed a champagne flute from the tray. Geechi downed half of his while Tione held hers.

"We shouldn't have had it open to the public," she said.

"Gotti thinks it's best. She's been doing her thing, so I'm going with it," he replied. In the few months they had been working together, Gotti had managed to get him on the list of some exclusive events. Those banquets allowed him to obtain more clientele.

Tione beamed after the Moet glided down her throat. "The logo looks good."

Gotti had taken two things that represented the car dealership and capitalized on them in a way neither Tione nor Geechi had ever considered. Geechi couldn't respond to her because his eyes were locked on Donny as he casually strolled to them.

"This muthafucka got the nerve to approach me," Geechi fumed through tight lips. Tione followed his eyes and saw Donny approaching them. He was dressed in a wrinkled, pickle green suit. The oversized polyester fabric did nothing for his six-foot, 200-pound frame.

"Keep your cool," she warned.

"Always," Geechi said, standing straight up and smoothing out his Brioni suit.

"Tione," Donny said. Sarcasm oozed from his tone as his thin lips formed into a smile.

"Donny," she replied with a big smile, patting his shoulder condescendingly.

"Everyone calls me Costa," he reminded her.

"That's business. We're family," she retorted with a wink.

"I see you've remodeled the place," he said to Geechi. Donny looked around the lobby but refused to acknowledge Geechi by name or eye contact.

"Who are you talking to?" Tione asked, although they all knew he was talking to Geechi.

"Where is Lorenzo?" Donny asked Geechi instead of answering Tione's question. "Or," Donny said as if he were in deep thought. "What about Orlando?" he asked. Geechi simply laughed and waved Maleek over. "This shit is crumbling around you. It won't last long," Donny hissed. "Just throw in the towel."

"What's up?" Maleek asked Geechi. Maleek owned a security company and Geechi used his connections to help him secure jobs with popular clubs and top party promoters. Now, his company had expanded, and he had a full staff. But Maleek still worked all of Geechi's events. Maleek was dressed in black pants and a black shirt with his security company's logo on it. His locs were braided and rested on his back.

"Will you please show Donny out," Geechi requested with a pleasant smile. Embarrassment rushed over Donny's pale face painting it red.

Maleek placed his hand on Donny's back. "This way," he said, motioning toward the door.

"Don't fuckin' touch me!" Donny said with a low growl.

"You got it, big man," Maleek said, throwing his hands up. Maleek followed Donny as he walked past the step and repeat backdrop, to the door and then watched him disappear into the night.

Gotti was making her rounds when she saw the tension on Geechi's face. She politely ended her conversation with one of the ex-head coaches for the Dallas Cowboys and made her way to Geechi and Tione.

"Did I miss something?" Gotti asked.

"No," Geechi said with a smile.

"You sure?"

Tione cheesed. "We're sure. Stop worrying." Gotti nodded her head. "This is a nice turn out," Tione said. She was dressed in a flower print Carolina Herrera dress with black pumps.

"Y'all ready to move to the showroom?" Gotti asked, rubbing her hands together.

"You more excited than us," Geechi said. He took in her beautiful smile and the way her eyes lit up. He liked that she was so passionate about Koran Motors.

Gotti made the announcement that the party was moving to the showroom to unveil the logo. Five minutes later, Geechi stood in front of the crowd reciting the speech that Gotti insisted that he read. It was hard for people to pay attention to Geechi's speech about his grandfather's watch and the calculated effort to create a low-profile presence for the dealership, because they were mesmerized by the cars. Finally, he tied those two things into the new logo before he removed the red covering. There was a portrait of his grandfather's watch with the words *If you know, you know* floating around them.

The crowd cheered and toasted before Geechi went on to answer questions about the cars. The night finally came to an end as Gotti ushered people toward the door with goodie bags.

After everyone was gone and the lobby had been cleaned, Geechi found Gotti in his office gathering her things.

"We going out to celebrate," he told her.

"I can't," she said, shaking her head. "I have a red-eye to New York. I need to interview a potential employee and pay attention to my other clients," she told him.

"Man, fuck them," Geechi said standing before her. She looked up into his eyes and smiled. "Thank you. Tonight was lit as fuck," he said, pulling her into a hug. Geechi's embrace felt so good, Gotti melted into him. Before she could let out a peaceful sigh, the door flew open.

"Geec—" Gotti jumped back as if she had been doing something wrong, which caused Lark to raise her eyebrow.

"What's up?" Geechi asked Lark.

"We still going?" Lark asked him.

"Damn, the whole squad going?" Gotti asked Geechi. Now she was sad about not being able to attend.

"Carl can't make it. He has an early morning," Lark said, leaning on the doorway.

"Oh okay, well I don't feel too left out," Gotti said, putting her purse on her shoulder.

"Can you give us a minute?" Geechi asked Lark.

"Oh, it's fine. I'm on my way out. I have to pick up Troy and go straight to the airport," Gotti told Geechi.

"Let me walk you out," Geechi said, following her. They headed to the small, employees-only parking lot outside of the building

At her rental car, Gotti placed her purse and briefcase in the backseat and then made her way to the driver's side door. Geechi grabbed her arm so that she'd turn around and face him.

"Congratulations," Geechi said. She was lost for a moment and it showed on her face. He chuckled. "You're about to hire your first employee," he said. She blushed. No one had congratulated her on that, so it made her feel special. "Your business is growing," he said to her.

"Yea," Gotti said and looked at the ground. She was so proud of herself but never sat in her joy because she felt like she was behind in life.

"Congratulations," he said again. She looked up at him, the dark sky decorated in stars was the perfect backdrop for his wide smile filled with diamonds. *New York doesn't have stars like this*, Gotti thought as she leaned in.

"Geechi!" Someone yelled causing her to pull back.

"What the fuck," he fussed. Every time he got close to her, someone sensed it and sabotaged it.

"Damn. What car are we going in?" Tione asked.

"Goodnight Geechi," Gotti said.

"Wait mama," Geechi said to her.

"I'm gonna miss my flight," Gotti said, easing by him. He huffed and opened the door for her. When Gotti was inside, he closed it. She smiled and started the car.

On the drive to pick up Troy from La'Shea's, Gotti thought about how lax she had become around Geechi and how much she needed to tighten up. At the club, Geechi thought about how much harder he needed to go to get Gotti.

Chapter 3

The next several months flew by so quickly, Gotti sometimes lost track of the days. Gotti's business was booming thanks to the recommendations and results from Koran Motors. She had hired a small team of employees and was working with a couple of college interns at her headquarters in New York. Geechi was her top priority and in working so closely with him, they had developed a tight bond. While they kept things very professional, she still considered him a friend and respected him as a man. Those things made her work harder for him.

Not only did she create a plan for rebranding the car dealership, she also set up fundraisers and galas to highlight Geechi's philanthropic efforts. While he had always given back, he had never done so in such a public way. It felt weird to Geechi, like he was begging for attention or validation, but Gotti knew it would soften his persona to outsiders. It also helped the boys involved in Young Kings Academy, a mentorship program Geechi had developed for young men. Through these galas he was able to present them with awards, which looked good on college applications, and show the mentees a different way of life.

When Geechi pulled up to Tione's apartment complex, he parked under the carport and headed for her front door. Gotti and Tione had become like sisters over the last year. Tione looked up to Gotti's fashion sense and business mind. She felt like Gotti moved like a boss and it inspired Tione to step her game up.

"You look good," Tione said to Geechi. She moved out of the way to allow him to step in. He was dressed casually in black jeans, a black Fendi shirt with the logo on the collar, and sneakers. His jewelry was light, but the gold Cartier watch made a statement.

"Thank you," he said. He walked toward the bar. "Where she at?"

"Getting dressed," Tione told him. She walked over to the plush leather sectional and had a seat.

"Man y'all had all damn day. And she rushing me," Geechi fussed as he poured a shot of Hennessy.

"Those new?" Tione asked referring to his oval shaped bronze glasses.

"Nah, but this my first time wearing them," he told her.

"Tione, you act like he's your man," Gotti said, standing in the hallway. Geechi looked up the hall at her. A Herve Leger bronze dress adorned Gotti's physique. The smooth fabric contoured her body with the hem slightly cuffed at her knees. Open toed, Fendi, strappy heels made the simple outfit pop. Geechi's eyes danced all over Gotti's body making him lick his lips as Gotti clasped her watch around her wrist.

"And yet you're dressed like him," Tione said with a laugh. Gotti looked up for the first time and her eyes roamed the length of Geechi's six-foot-one body. He looked good. So good that Gotti wanted to stare longer, but she felt his glare on her. Gotti took a deep breath and reminded herself that she was at work. Geechi was her boss no matter how close they had gotten.

"You look nice," he told her. The innocence in his tone and eyes made her swallow hard.

"You too," she said and walked into the living room. He downed his drink as she grabbed her purse.

"You coming back here or staying with him?" Tione teased. She didn't care how hard or long they fought their attraction for each other, it was evident. Seemingly to everyone except them.

"I'm going back to my hotel," Gotti said, rolling her eyes and turning up her nose. When Gotti came to Dallas, she always booked a room, but sometimes she would end up staying with Tione, if they were going to a nice lounge or bar. Or La'Shea so she could spend time with La'Bella.

"Oh you big mad," Tione replied with a hearty laugh.

"Why you sitting down?" Gotti asked Geechi.

"It's early as fuck. You act like we meeting Obama," he said.

"This is an important meeting, Geechi. Aligning yourself with politicians makes a statement and lowkey it gives you some power," she told him.

"Man, them muthafuckas gon' do what they wanna do."

"Whatever. Come on." Gotti pouted. When she hopped up and down her titties jumped, and one eased out of her bra. He licked his lips and zoned in on her chocolate breast.

"Ugg!" she said, stuffing it back in her bra. "Sir, we need to go," she said with an attitude.

"Yes ma'am," he said. The lazy drawl in his speech made her nipples hard. She headed for the door so he wouldn't see.

In the car, they hopped on the highway heading North. A few minutes into the ride, Geechi's phone rang interrupting the music. When he disconnected it from the Bluetooth, Gotti figured it was one of his women and looked out of the window.

"Hey Lucindi," Geechi said answering the call. "Okay," Geechi said in a rushed tone. Gotti heard the worry in his voice and looked at him. "Don't worry, Lucindi; I'll handle it," Geechi said before disconnecting the call. He and Gotti were on Highway 75 in route to a dinner meeting she had set up with Councilman Chandler. When Geechi turned off the GPS and took the next exit, Gotti started to panic. After a few minutes, she realized they were headed back toward Interstate 35.

Gotti had been working hard to build connections for Geechi. While he had been doing great work in his community, she felt that being connected with certain individuals would give him a bigger platform.

"Geechi, we're gonna be late," she said.

"You had us early as fuck, Gotti. I gotta handle this," he told her.

"Handle what? What's more important than this?"

"My young kings," he said, speeding down 35. Gotti knew this meeting couldn't compete with Geechi's nonprofit, Young Kings Academy. He helped middle school and high school boys with the equipment they needed for sports, tutors for school and life lessons.

Geechi took another exit and a few turns later, Gotti could tell they had entered the hood. They pulled alongside a curb where a group of young men stood, their eyes danced around the rose gold Bentley Mulsanne with gold rims. Geechi parked the car and hopped out. The boys' faces lit up as they rushed to dap him up and say hello. He put his arm around the neck of a young man with locs.

"Come ride with me," he said. The young man slapped hands with a few friends and hopped in the backseat.

"This is Gotti," Geechi introduced when he got back in the car. Gotti looked back at the young man with a smile.

"What's up?" he said.

"That's how you greet a woman?" Geechi asked him, looking at him through the rearview mirror. The young man chuckled and extended his hand to Gotti.

"Terrell," he said when she placed her hand in his. He lightly shook it, turned it and kissed the back of her hand. Gotti grinned and looked at Geechi. Geechi smiled and his teeth sparkled; he winked at Gotti. She felt her heart jump.

"You dirty?" he asked. Terrell's face dropped; he looked uncomfortable as he shifted in his seat.

"Nah." After Terrell finally answered, Geechi pulled off from the curb.

"Why am I getting calls from Lucindi?" Geechi asked Terrell. His tone was serious letting Gotti know this wasn't a social call. She thought back on how Geechi had hopped out of the car and greeted the boys. That showed respect for them. When he draped his arm around Terrell that showed love. Geechi didn't embarrass Terrell by confronting him in front of his friends.

"She trippin'," Terrell said and looked out the window.

"She's worried. Why you on that shit now?" Geechi asked.

"I'm sixteen, Geechi. In the hood I been grown. I look dumb as hell letting my granny struggle," Terrell said.

"And you think this is the way? You stressing her out. You're the oldest; this the example you want your little brothers and cousins to follow?"

"We barely have money for shoes, Geechi."

"Shoes? You doing this shit for shoes? You know it's young boys out here with no lights, no damn water? That's why they get on the block, but you doing it for shoes? That shit sound dumb," Geechi said.

As he cruised through the streets, Geechi honked his horn at people on their porches or kids playing in the streets. He threw up his hand to greet them as they stared inside the car. They smiled and returned the gesture.

"I'm taking some of the stress off her," Terrell said.

"You got two more years of school left. You know you're gonna get a scholarship; why risk all that for this?"

"I'm not. I'm just tryna make some easy money."

"Easy? You think that shit is easy, standing on the block all damn day? That shit is going to cut into the effort you put into school; shit, you fuck around and start missing school," Geechi said.

"I ain't that dumb," Terrell replied.

"This shit is pretty fuckin' dumb. If your grades drop, you gonna lose ya fucking scholarship. Then what? You want this shit for the rest of your life?"

"Nah."

"Look, struggle builds character. You gotta be able to see the future; see what you can be if you keep going down the path we put in place for you. You wanna be the first one in your family to graduate high school, right? That's what you said, not me and not Lucindi; that's what you promised the woman that raised you." Geechi pulled in front of a worn house and put the car in park. He

35

looked up at Terrell through the rearview mirror. "Be a man of your word," he said.

A wire fence wrapped around the property but wouldn't do much to keep intruders out. Two young kids were on the porch playing with toys. An older woman walked out on the porch staring at the car.

"Hug your grandma. Thank her for her sacrifices, and make yours," Geechi told Terrell. Terrell nodded his head.

"It was nice to meet you, Gotti. You look nice, and I hope this knucklehead shows you a good time tonight," Terrell said.

"It was nice meeting you too, Terrell. Listen to the knucklehead," she said and laughed as she looked over at Geechi. "He knows a thing or two."

Geechi squeezed her thigh as he rolled down his window.

"Hey, Ms. Lucindi," he said.

"Hey, baby, come on in," she said.

"I can't. I'm on my way to a dinner with Councilman Chandler; he gotta get these potholes fixed and create more jobs for our youth," Geechi said.

"I know that's right. Stay on him," Lucindi said.

"And you stay on him," Geechi said, nodding at Terrell.

"You know I ain't giving him no leeway," she said just as Terrell approached her.

Gotti watched them hug as Geechi pulled off.

● ● ●

When they walked into Saltgrass, the hostess showed them to their seat. The councilman stood to greet them and complimented Gotti on her dress. Thirty minutes into the dinner, their food had been served and they were knee deep into a conversation about Geechi publicly endorsing him. Councilman Chandler knew the power Geechi held within the community, so he was using a new program for business owners to entice Geechi into voting for him and to encourage others to do the same.

"I'll telling you, Geechi, this will help business owners to cut taxes."

"I see how it helps me. I just don't see how it helps my community. What about people who want to start a business? This seems to discourage them," Geechi said. He knew Gotti wanted him to play nice and get the councilman on his side, but he wasn't going to sell out his people to do it.

"What we have to remember is that most small businesses fail. Twenty percent in their first year," Councilman Chandler stated. "And then we have to consider our community and the likelihood of the residents starting businesses."

"They start businesses," Geechi corrected him. He thought about the gambling houses, women who sold plates and the ladies who ran daycare centers out of their houses. "They just don't have the backing; they can't get loans. Couldn't you rework this program so that it benefits the people? More businesses in our community means more jobs for its residents. You're a democrat, right?" Geechi said with his eyebrow lifted.

"Of course I am," Councilman Chandler said, leaning back in his seat. He looked over at Gotti for assistance.

"What Geechi means is that y'all can evoke more change by working more closely with the residents. Geechi's vote alone can't ensure that you will remain in office. But, if you give him something to take to the townhall meetings and the barbershops, you stand a better chance," Gotti explained.

"Umm," Councilman Chandler said, taking a bite of his bread. "You're right. Let's rework this and meet again," he said with a smile.

"Let's do that," Geechi said. He looked over at Gotti who was beaming from ear to ear.

Chapter 4

It was late, and Koran Motors was closed but Gotti was still there. She was in the conference room going over the numbers for Koran Motors' social media activity and preparing an email to follow up with guests from their recent gala. The gala was to raise money to improve the conditions at the high school Geechi had attended. People pledged money but not all the money had come through, so she was creating an email to send out the next morning as a friendly reminder.

"Hey, I'm gon'. You wanna walk out together?" Tione peeked her head in the conference room to ask.

"I—um," Gotti said, then paused to quickly proofread the last paragraph of her document. She looked up at Tione. "No, I'm fine. I have a little more work to do; I'll catch Geechi on his way out. But let me walk you to the door, so I can watch you run to the car," she said. She saved the document and stood up.

"I'm not running in these heels," Tione said. They walked up the hallway and through the lobby.

"If someone was chasing you, you would," Gotti said.

"Nah, I got hands," Tione joked and got in a fighting stance. They laughed and continued walking to the front door.

"Girl run!" Gotti said. She stood at the door watching Tione sashayed through the parking lot. "Jason!" Gotti yelled. Tione laughed hard as she ran to her Lexus and jumped in. Gotti locked the door and went to check on Geechi. He was normally the first one gone, but he had been held up in his office all day and even had a bit of an attitude.

When she opened the door to his office, he was seated on his couch drinking out of a bottle of Hennessy. A scowl covered his face as he glared at the door trying to see who had interrupted his thoughts. He noticed her and sat up in the seat. Geechi placed the bottle on the table and adjusted his clothing.

"What's up?" she said.

"What you doing still here?" His speech was slightly slurred.

"I came to ask you the same," she said, entering the office.

"Just finishing some shit."

"What, that bottle of Hennessy?" she joked and took a seat beside him. "What's on your mind?" she asked.

"Nothing that I can't handle," Geechi said, leaning back in the seat. He rested his head on the back of the couch. Geechi knew Gotti liked to fix things. It was her job and she prided herself on being the best at it. And she was, but this was a battle he had to fight solo.

"I can't fix a problem I don't know we have. I can't stop something from happening that I don't know is on its way, Geechi. You gotta trust me." Gotti pleaded with him because she could tell this was major. She didn't want his business to suffer because he was too proud to ask for help.

"I trust you, Gotti," he said, placing his hand on her knee and gazing into her eyes. She smiled. "To handle what you're supposed to handle." Geechi grabbed his bottle and stood up. He stumbled at first then gathered his bearings and walked to his desk.

"I'm supposed to handle whatever can affect you," she said and stood up. "You are the face of this company; you know that. My job is to handle everything that has to do with this dealership," she said, standing in front of his desk.

He took a deep breath. She was smart, thorough; he figured maybe she could see something that he couldn't, so he trusted her with what had the potential to bring the company down.

Unbeknownst to her, she had been an accomplice in the matter, but he assured her that it would never touch her. And she believed him.

Gotti had known Geechi for about a year and she had fallen in love, not with him, but with his hustle, with who he was and how he was with the people he loved. Working with him had provided leverage for her newly formed PR company. It showed the results she was able to produce in a short amount of time and garnered more clientele. Those were the reasons why, to protect him, them, and everything they had worked for, she married him a month later in an impromptu wedding at City Hall. And it was why she paid the receptionist to leak the story.

●●●

Geechi stood in the middle of the VIP section at V-Live. Beautiful women were all around him, but he could only focus on one. She'd had him captivated since the very first time she walked into his office. Currently, her body was wrapped around him like a snake to a tree. Her legs straddled his waist, her arms fell to her sides; one holding a bottle of D'Usse as she grinded against him so seductively that the women on stage watched her. She requested that the DJ play *Go* by Alex the Kid, Rapsody and H.E.R.; her body moved slowly, her ass bouncing with the beat. She told him he couldn't touch her with his hands, he could only watch and feel as she grinded, snaked, and allowed her body to caress his.

"Fuck this, we leaving," he said. He let his people know they were leaving the club with a peace sign and a head nod, but he didn't put her down until they were at the exit. Maleek, Geechi's best friend, was busy getting a lap dance but managed to throw his head back in acknowledgement of Geechi's departure.

The parking lot was packed; some people saw Geechi leaving and followed him outside.

"Hey Geechi!" a woman called out to him.

"What's up, Geechi!" People yelled as Geechi made his way through the crowd pulling Gotti's hand. Everyone had their phones out recording and asking questions as if he was the world's biggest celebrity.

"Congratulations," a few men he knew in passing said, walking up to him and dapping him up. Geechi knew they just wanted to be captured in a picture with him.

"Is it true, Geechi?" a woman with red, 28-inch bundles dressed in a red bandage dress, yelled out. He knew what she was referring to; everybody wanted to know if he had really done the unthinkable. Someone from the courthouse had *leaked* the information revealing that he had come in for a marriage license and since then social media had been going crazy. Girls were DM'ing Gotti left and right with lies. Thank God she was solid and didn't let any of it faze her.

"Is what true?" he asked, looking back at her.

"You married her?" she asked.

He stood before Gotti, towering over her. She was on the shorter side; 5'4 with skin the color of carob; she wore white fitted pants that laid across her body as if they were painted on and a white bralette.

"Did you marry me, baby?" he asked making her blush as he bore deep into her eyes.

"Did you marry me," she shot back; her joy impossible to hide.

"Hell yea," he said and pulled her to him. When her body crashed into his, he kissed her so succulently that she was out of breath, yet craving more, even as she pulled back.

Gotti stared at Geechi for a few moments after the kiss; momentarily she had forgotten about the people surrounding them and recording their embrace. Geechi's cocky smirk sent tingles dancing through her body.

"Congratulations," the red head in the red dress said as she watched their interaction. "Y'all need help celebrating?" she offered with a laugh. Without responding, Geechi grabbed Gotti's hand and they trekked to the car.

As soon as they were in the car, Gotti pulled out her phone to follow the social media buzz surrounding their club appearance. She glanced up to see where they were a few minutes later and noticed that Geechi had passed her exit.

"Hey, where are you going?" she said with her hands up in confusion.

"To my house," he stated.

"You need to drop me off at my hotel first," she reminded him.

"Man, you my wife," he said, placing his hand on her knee.

Laughing, she pushed it off. "Yea on paper," she replied with a wink.

"That shit gon' look crazy...You gotta come to my house."

"Who's going to know? You ain't that big of a deal. ...What? You think people are following us?" She laughed. "Take this exit and make a U-turn," Gotti instructed.

"Stop acting like you know my city; you're from New York, remember?" he joked. "I don't feel like turning around; I have five bedrooms, you can sleep in the guestroom," he told her.

"Nah homie," was all Gotti said as she got back to tracking the hype on Instagram. Reluctantly, Geechi made the next exit and headed to her hotel. He looked over at her thinking she would notice his attitude, but Gotti was so focused on her phone that she didn't even feel Geechi's glare. He liked Gotti; he had since he first met her, but she was one of those overly independent, married to her job types. Still, she was beautiful, smart, loyal and a hustler; in his eyes that was a deadly combination. One he wasn't sure he could live without.

When they pulled in front of the Omni Hotel, she removed her seatbelt and started grabbing her things. "Meeting in the morning at eight," she told him. She opened the door and placed her foot on the ground.

"Ten," he said. "I'm tryna celebrate my wedding night with Red," he let her know. He figured he had time to go back by the club and find the sexy red head.

"Geechi, what the fuck!" Gotti said, turning to face him with her nose turned up. "That shit is going to look crazy. Chick with the red hair can't wait to use this shit for clout," she preached. He looked unfazed. "Please," Gotti said lowering her tone and adding puppy dog eyes.

"Man, my wife is staying at a hotel on our wedding night; I need love," he replied.

"You gon' fuck the plan up, Geechi; we need this shit to work or both of our asses are going to be in jail," she hissed.

He placed his hand over hers, "You know I wouldn't let that happen."

"No strippers tonight, please," she said in a sultry tone. Her eyes were low, and a sexy smirk adorned her face.

"I'm horny," he told her, using his hand to push a stray hair out of her face.

"Jerk off," she suggested.

"In Texas we say jack off. And fuck no; handle your wifely duties," he retorted. He was no longer facing her, now he was looking straight ahead with his hand on the gear shift.

"You promised you wouldn't make this hard for me, Geechi," she whined. His nostrils flared and his jaw clenched.

"Book me a flight tomorrow for after the meeting; I guess I'ma have to go out the country to get some pussy," he stated.

"Ooohh," she said, easing back in her seat, "I should go too...we can post honeymoon pictures," she told him.

"Pay ya own way," he said unapologetically.

"Seriously?" she questioned with her nose turned up.

"On my mama," he said, putting the car in drive. She rolled her eyes and climbed out.

When Gotti got to her room, she stripped out of her clothes as the jacuzzi tub filled with hot water. She dug through her bag and pulled out her essential oils to ensure that the bath would be relaxing; she added Epsom salt, lavender and eucalyptus to the water and used her hand to swirl it around.

Chapter 5

Gotti woke up to the sound of her phone vibrating on the nightstand. She reached her hand from under the warmth of the comforter and quickly grabbed it, bringing the phone under the covers with her.

"Hello?" she said groggily.

"Biiiitttttch!!!" La'Shea screamed. "Hold on let me click Troy in," she said and did so before Gotti could speak.

"Oh so you married?" Troy screeched.

"Yea, I love him," Gotti lied. Maybe she'd watched too may gangster movies, but she was not about to be caught slipping on a wiretap. She had purposefully not told her friends about the marriage to see how long it would take them to find out through social media.

"Where did y'all see it; Instagram?" she questioned.

"Bitch, you're on Channel 8 news!" La'Shea informed her.

"What!" Gotti gasped, sitting up in the bed like a dead person sitting up in their casket. She hopped out of bed and ran to the TV. While it was coming on, she searched social media on her second phone.

"How many times have they reported the story?" Gotti asked La'Shea.

"I just saw it once and was about to call you when Troy sent me the viral video of y'all dancing at the club."

"I knew your ass was feeling that man," Troy sang into the phone.

"That kiss bitch...he still sleep? I know you put him to bed." La'Shea joked.

"It's fake," she mumbled, too consumed with the TV and social media to remember to stay in character.

"What?" La'Shea asked.

"It's...fate," she quickly replied. "Y'all I gotta go...we leave for our honeymoon later today, but I want to see you two when I get back," she told them.

"Y'all gotta come to me...well I guess Troy has to come to us," La'Shea said figuring Gotti would be moving to Dallas to be with Geechi.

"I won't be in Texas," Gotti said, not picking up on why La'Shea said that.

"He's going to move to New York?" La'Shea questioned. "You can adapt to Texas, Gotti; he's going to be like a fish out of water in New York."

"He's..." Gotti caught herself again. "We're trying to figure that part out," she said.

"Don't start off fighting, Gotti," Troy warned.

"Yea, Gotti, give a little," La'Shea stated.

"Y'all are right. I love you guys but I gotta go...bye."

"Bye," they said in unison as she hung up. Before she could call Geechi, he had sent her the story on Channel 8 News with the caption, '*Yes I'm that big of a deal*' in reference to her comment the night before. Gotti clicked the link.

"We have exciting news," the news anchor reported. "Businessman and philanthropist Geechi Koran had reportedly tied the knot to Gotti Lexington. This comes a month after the couple was spotted at the gala thrown by Koran Motors to raise money for our inner-city youth."

Gotti: *I did that for you!*

Gotti: *Be on time for the meeting!*

Geechi: *I'll come get you. We need to pull up together...*

Gotti: *I'll be ready in an hour.*

He was right, no one at the office knew this was a farce so they needed to keep up appearances. She took a quick shower and then got dressed in a white pantsuit with colorful Versace heels and a matching purse.

"Morning wife," he said when she opened her room door.

"I need help with my stuff."

"Why didn't you call the bellhop; we need a cart."

"It's not that much. I'm trying to move as lowkey as possible," she told him. After she did a once over of the room, they both grabbed her luggage and left the hotel.

"Were you good last night?" she asked once they were seated in his car.

"What do I get if I was?"

"To stay outta jail," she sassed.

"I used to wonder why you were single," he said and pulled off; before she could respond, the horsepower of the Hellcat caused her head to jerk. Geechi laughed and turned up the music. As they got on the freeway, she turned the music down causing him to look over at her. His honey brown eyes hypnotized her for a moment; he usually wore glasses but today he wore his clear contacts.

"What?" he asked because she didn't say anything.

"The hotel was a bad idea."

"Ya think?"

"I didn't know how big this would get," she admitted.

"So what, you moving in?" he smiled; the diamonds in his teeth glistened in the sunlight.

"Yea when I'm in town. After Fiji—"

"I knew your ass would pick a beach. I can't wait to see that fat ass in a—"

He stopped because of her glare; she was on some feminist type shit where she didn't want to be objectified by men. She wanted to wear tight ass pants or blazers that showed the roundness of her breasts, but she expected men to look her in her eyes when she spoke.

"My bad," he said to appease her. Truthfully, he wasn't sorry; she was beautiful, and he was a man. It wasn't in his nature not to notice.

"After Fiji I have to go to Chicago for a week and then I'll be in New York."

"Chicago? For what?"

"It's the home office for Girls In Media. They are offering classes for production, hosting, things like that. We need to come up with a plan for the roll out," Gotti told him. "And I have meetings and things with potential clients in New York."

"Nah, I need my wife by my side. The potential clients need to fly to Texas."

"You need to chill," she said, shaking her head at his antics.

"You like that shit," he said and turned his music back up. Soon they pulled into Koran Motors and climbed out of the car. Tione wasn't at her desk, which was cool because they weren't open yet. The reason everyone came in early was for a sales meeting.

"Congratulations!" the staff yelled when Geechi and Gotti walked into the conference room. Everyone cheered as Tione popped open a bottle of champagne. It overflowed and spilled onto the floor before she could grab the champagne flute to catch it.

"This was all I could do on such short notice," she told them, handing the champagne to Geechi and hugging Gotti.

"Thank you, this is good," Gotti said looking at the decorations around the office; they even had a table with gifts.

"I want to plan something bigger...a reception," Tione said, "with the family," she told them. *Shit*, Gotti thought. She hadn't thought that far ahead. "I'ma need that black card," Tione told Geechi.

"Anything for my baby," he said, pulling Gotti into his arms and kissing her lips. She tried to peck him and turn away. "My baby is so shy; kiss me like you did last night," he said and went back in for a more succulent kiss. Gotti was pissed but plastered on a big smile anyway.

"I knew you liked my little brother," Tione said as Geechi made his rounds saying thanks to everyone. Tione loved to announce, even to those who already knew, that Geechi was her baby brother.

"Girl please, your brother likes me," Gotti shot back.

"Loves you," Tione corrected. "Geechi said he'd never get married," she said, sipping her champagne and watching Geechi finesse the room. "I'm happy for y'all."

Gotti felt bad about deceiving Tione. She already knew she was going to tell her girls the truth and now she decided she needed to tell Tione as well. They spent thirty minutes celebrating the couple and then moved into the meeting. Geechi discussed his expectations and what they needed to do as a company to reach their end-of-year sales goals. Later he would have individual meetings to discuss personal sales goals.

After the meeting, Geechi and Gotti headed to his office.

"You doing too much," she seethed, thinking about the kiss and the fact that he kept his hand on her leg throughout the meeting.

"Man, we have to sell this shit." He laughed. "When's the last time you was fucked right?" he asked staring into her eyes.

"When I did it myself," she answered, truthfully; no man, no matter how cocky, could touch her the way she could.

"That's sad," he said, shaking his head. Quickly, he reached out, grabbed her hand and pulled her to him.

"Sorry to interrupt," Tione said, peeking in the door. Gotti wiggled out of his embrace and smiled at her. "Are y'all about to christen the office?" She giggled. "Have y'all already?" she asked.

"We need to tell her," Gotti said looking at Geechi. While the relationship between Gotti and Tione started off rocky that was her little sister now; in the same way that La'Shea and Troy had taken Gotti under their wings.

"Come in and close the door," he said. Tione's face turned serious. She walked into the office and closed the door behind her.

"What?"

"We're not really married," he revealed.

"What!" she screeched.

"Keep your voice down. We are, but not for the reasons you think," Gotti said.

"Y'all love each other," Tione told them.

"No, we don't," Gotti said with an attitude. "I know too much, and I don't want to have to testify. I wouldn't tell shit anyway, but still, this protects him."

"Wait the investigation is that serious?" Tione asked, walking closer to Geechi. She placed the papers in her hand on his desk and glared at him. Even she wasn't fully aware of what Geechi was facing. He tried to keep it from everyone but Gotti knew. She sensed something was wrong, got him to talk to her and began to work to clean up his mess. As his publicist, it was her job, but the extent she was willing to go proved that it was more than that.

He told Tione that there might be a possible investigation. He had to, because she was the eyes and ears of the office and he needed her to be paying attention in case the detectives were getting information from an employee.

"No," he said still trying to protect her. He didn't want her to worry.

"But it could turn serious," Gotti told her. Tione relaxed a little.

"You love him, whether you know it or not," Tione said and hugged her. Gotti looked over Tione's back at Geechi who had a gigantic smile on his face.

"This is top secret," Geechi informed Tione after their hug. "We only trust the people in this room with this information. Don't go snooping and coming up with plots and shit. We got it; just hold us down."

"Always," she said with a smile.

"I'm telling my girls," Gotti looked back to inform him.

"Why?"

"'Cause...they ain't gon' say shit...you know La'Shea don't move like that."

"Yea, aiite." He agreed because he knew nothing and no one came before her girls.

"So no reception? I was trying to book Reunion Tower," Tione whined as the fact that this really wasn't real hit her.

"We can still do a reception, but scale that shit back...she won't even give a nigga no pussy."

"Y'all never fucked?" Tione asked looking back and forth at each of them.

"Never," Geechi confirmed.

"Not ever?" Tione said.

"Anyway," Gotti said, rolling her eyes at them. "We need to be ready to go by 6," she told Geechi.

"Aiite," Geechi said.

"Go where?" Tione asked.

"Fiji for our honeymoon."

"I wanna go...y'all might need me," Tione expressed.

"Nah I need you here; watching muthafuckas," Geechi said.

"Please don't hype her; you know she already thinks she's your bodyguard," Gotti said.

"Is!" Tione joked.

"We gotta go," Gotti said looking at her watch. "I need to hit the mall," she let Geechi know.

"Me too," he said.

"Cool, let's go to the one you took me to a while back," Gotti said.

"NorthPark," he said. "I'ma pay while we there but keep track of your expenses so you can pay me back," he said.

"No." Gotti simply stated. He never made her pay for anything, and he wasn't about to start doing it now as a punishment.

"You gon' pay one way or another," he stated.

"Another," she joked, looking at him seductively.

"Tione, get out," he said, pulling Gotti to him.

"Sike!" Gotti said, pushing him back. "I'll pay for your shit since money is tight for you," she told him.

"My money good," he responded.

"Apparently not! We'll just say it's tied up in legal fees, so you won't feel bad," she said, grabbing her purse and heading for the door.

Chapter 6

"Can you believe this heffa is married?" La'Shea asked Troy as she drove home from work.

"Girl, I'm still in shock. I was so happy for her that I couldn't be mad that she didn't tell us," Troy mentioned.

"Now that was fucked up...like damn, we could have been witnesses," La'Shea stated.

"All that talk about not liking him..." Troy laughed. Gotti wanted to be so tough but they had been friends for too long not to see through her shit.

"Gotti is delusional. She probably didn't know she loved the man until she was saying 'I do'," La'Shea said.

"My baby is just scared of being hurt again."

"I know, but Geechi will be different; he really is solid," La'Shea said vouching for him.

"He better be," Troy stated.

"Or else," La'Shea said and then changed the subject. "What are you doing?"

"Getting ready to pull up on Dominic."

"With his fine ahh!"

"Whatever," Troy said dismissively.

"You can't even admit that the man is fine?" La'Shea questioned.

"I don't look at him like that."

"Well how do you look at him?"

"Like he's my son," Troy joked. Truthfully, she couldn't describe the relationship with Dominic.

"Bitch bye, unless you step-mama!"

"Nah, but I mean I taught him the game...that's my lil man." She continued to joke in her thick New York accent. She had met Dominic when he was in graduate school and had become his mentor.

"Have you seen him lately?" La'Shea questioned thinking about his business page on Instagram. He used it to give helpful tips about investing and managing money, but he also posted a few pictures of himself. "That's a full-grown sexy ass, successful man ain't nothing lil...well I hope not."

"It's not..."

"Wait, what? How you know?"

"I...he, one night we were drinking and went dancing."

"And what?" La'Shea questioned, stopping at the yellow light instead of zooming through. She wanted to hear this groundbreaking news.

"And nothing...really...we were on the dance floor at a Jamaican club."

La'Shea gasped. "And he rocked up?"

"Man," Troy sighed, thinking back on that night. "I'll admit I was doing too much, but I was drunk. Soon as I felt that shit, I sobered up." Troy laughed.

"Haha!" La'Shea yelled into the phone.

After another twenty minutes on the phone, they hung up so La'Shea could perform her motherly duties.

"You can smell money 1000 miles away," Dominic said, looking up at Troy. She stood in the doorway of his office and he sat behind his oak desk. Dominic dropped his pen, leaned back and took a few moments to take her in. She was dressed in an off white, silk Carolina Herrera skirt suit with snakeskin, heeled booties.

He stood to make his way to her. Dominic was 6'5, with a two-hundred-and-twenty-pound frame. He was beautiful with long eyelashes that shaped dark, piercing, deep-hooded eyes, pronounced cheekbones and juicy lips. His Armani cologne wafted through the air and reached her before he could.

"To what do I owe the pleasure?" he asked after their hug as he directed her to have a seat. He knew why she had popped up; it was almost a test. Dominic hadn't told Troy about the acquisition he was working on because he knew her, in the same way that she knew him. He knew whether she was in New York, LA, Miami or any other place, she was watching him.

"I can't check in?" she asked.

"You normally do that with a phone call," he shot back.

"Whatever; we have lunch and dinner often," she stated and took her seat.

"We have lunch and dinner," he nodded in agreement, "but not often," he replied.

"Not as often as we should," she agreed. She wasn't sure what, but something was in the air; something that hadn't been there before, or maybe it had but she had been too busy or he too ambitious.

"What about dinner tonight?" he asked.

"Sure," she replied and fumbled with the fringe on her purse. "Let me see the proposal," she finally asked.

"See, I knew it," he exclaimed.

"We work best together, and you know it."

"You going in with me or just critiquing my work?" he inquired.

"Whatever you want," she said with a smile "...If the proposal is good," she added. He went to his desk and pulled up the proposal.

"Get comfortable, read and critique. When I get back from my meeting, we'll discuss it," he said. Troy dropped her purse and removed her beige, floor length, cashmere coat. Dominic pulled out the chair at his desk and waited for her to come to him. She sat in the chair and the proposal was on the computer screen.

●●●

A few hours later, he was back from his meeting. Her heels had been removed; her blazer was tossed over the arm of his couch with his. And the silk camisole she wore was easing out of her skirt. The top buttons of his shirt were undone, his tie was gone, and he was reading the ending of the proposal. He sat at the desk now while she paced the floor carefully listening to each word he read.

"I think that's it, Mr. McCoy," she said, turning to face him with a big grin.

"I do too," Dominic said with a smile. He grabbed her hand and kissed the center. Troy froze, laughed and discreetly pulled it away from him.

"You promised me food," Troy said, walking towards her heels. He smiled at the rejection but didn't let it faze him.

"What are you in the mood for?"

"Something good," was her only reply. Troy grabbed her purse and went into the bathroom. After freshening up, she came out looking brand new. Dominic had fixed his clothes, straightened his office and was ready to go. Claudia, his receptionist, was already gone for the night, so Dominic locked up the office and got in the car with Troy.

Troy whipped through the streets of New York like only a true New Yorker could and effortlessly slid into a parking spot that she was sure others were trying to get.

"They gon' flatten you tires," he joked, climbing out of the car.

"I'll ask for a table by the window," she said.

Forty minutes later, they were seated, sharing calamari and discussing business.

"Writing a proposal to become the accountant for Locke & Marks is big," she told him.

"I know. He needs me though. You read the write up in Forbes; he is losing money left and right. It has to be his money guys. I can help with that."

"We," Troy corrected, "can help with that." The conversation died down as the focused hunter studied his prey.

"I have a speaking engagement at Rutgers tomorrow; if you want to tag along," Troy offered.

"Stop tryna lil brother me," Dominic said, shaking his head as he chuckled.

"What are you talking about?" Troy asked looking around the restaurant for their waiter.

"Stop pretending like you don't see how I'm looking at you and stop acting like you don't look at me like that too. Stop tryna change the subject."

"I'm not changing the subject; we were talking about proposals and clients," she told him. "So I brought up Rutgers; you said you wanted to get into speaking engagements."

"You told me I should," he retorted. Those eyes would be the death of her; Troy diverted her attention once again.

"I'm your mentor," she said slowly looking into his eyes. Troy hadn't meant for that to sound sexual, but it did. Or maybe she did; today, for some reason, she didn't know what she wanted.

"Our mouths were," Dominic said getting back on the subject of what they were talking about. "Our eyes were having a deeper conversation and our vibe was even deeper than that." Dominic reached across the table and grabbed Troy's hand. It sent tingles up her body. *When's the last time I had sex?* Troy wondered. Four months ago...Alex; it was okay. He could eat pussy but his stoke needed work. Troy pulled her hand from his and tucked it in her lap under the table.

"You're my protégé," she reminded him. Dominic was a baby when they met. Twenty-three, seven years her junior and in an on again off again relationship with someone. Troy couldn't lie, at thirty-one years of age, her protégé was a grown ass man. From his broad shoulders to the way he dressed; Dominic could pick a suit, and always got them tailored to perfection. And the ambitious money man handled his business...was professional, proficient... a quick learner, easy to teach...shit, he loved to be taught.

"Teach me something new," he said as if he had read her thoughts.

"You'll start acting crazy...it'll fuck up the money." Troy dismissed his suggestion as the waiter returned with their food. Troy ordered a loaded baked potato with shrimp and grilled chicken; Dominic ordered steak, broccoli, and mashed potatoes.

"I'm your protégé, so I know that rule number one is don't fuck up the money," Dominic said once the waiter was gone. He unrolled his silverware and placed the cloth napkin across his lap. Troy looked up at him as she gulped down her wine. This was her second glass and its magic had started to flow through her body.

"It's not that I don't want to..." she admitted, then cut into her chicken.

"I know. You just don't want to ruin the relationship, because even though I started off as your protégé, I've become a good business partner and a sounding board for your ideas. You won't have to worry about that."

"What happened to that girl," Troy asked.

"What girl?" Dominic asked.

"The one who was getting married?"

"She got married," he said nonchalantly.

"You're really this confident, but it wasn't powerful enough to stop her from marrying a white boy?" she teased and drank the rest of her wine. Moments later the waiter was back refilling her glass.

"Oh that's what you think? Nah," he said and laughed. "She had a plan; I respected it. I didn't ask for or try to manipulate the situation to fit what I wanted. That just goes to show you that I stick to the plan. I can compartmentalize," Dominic explained. "Business relationship, friendship and... whatever else."

"So," Troy said and took a moment to swallow her food. "You wanted more with her but didn't go for it because she wanted him?"

"I have an ego, everybody does. It wasn't about wanting her, it would have been more about proving, to myself I guess, that I could have taken her...from him. But honestly, no, that's not what I wanted."

"I don't know," she said after ten minutes of silence.

"Think about it," he said, "and let me know."

Chapter 7

otti was laid out in a beach chair dressed in a white one-
piece swimming suit. It exposed her thick hips and the
lining of her freshly waxed vagina. A big white hat shielded
her from the sun as she sipped on a margarita and watched the
beautiful waves thrust to and from the shore. Gotti's pussy
suddenly tingled; it took her a moment to realize that it came from
fingertips trailing up her legs. Gotti jumped, prepared to go off on
the only person that would be so bold.

"You look so sexy," he said with a lazy smirk, silencing her.
When he smiled his eyes squinted into sexy bedroom eyes and that
sent her heart into overdrive. She steadied her breathing as her
heart thumped against her chest.

She finally sneered. "Keep your damn hands to yourself."
Geechi grinned but didn't respond. "I figured you'd be tied up all
day," she stated as nonchalantly as she could.

"I did too," he admitted, sitting at the foot of her lounge chair.
"I can't fuck women with you here," he said looking up at her.

"Oh really." She laughed, not believing a word he said.

"For real," he said gazing out at the water with his hand on her
shin.

"Stop touching me," Gotti said, playfully kicking her foot.

"You don't know how this wife shit works I see."

"I saw you," she said. "Last night. I came to the lounge. I saw you," Gotti let him know more firmly this time.

She had love for Geechi, not in that way, but it was love nonetheless. If she didn't, she wouldn't have married him. It was to save Geechi because Gotti respected him. Geechi gave the kids a superhero that they could touch. He was a dream that was tangible to them; shit to her. And too important to serve even a day in prison. But he was a ladies' man. Effortlessly. Almost as if it wasn't by choice. Ladies just chose the charismatic entrepreneur even if Geechi walked in a room with men who were richer, more well-known, more attractive; ladies chose Geechi. It was his aura, his smile; even with a laid-back persona, he still knew how to connect with people. Geechi wasn't distant, his presence was felt and because of that women craved his attention.

"Saw me what?" Geechi asked with his eyes on Gotti. She watched the waves instead of answering because he knew what she saw. It was cool; they were only married on paper, but Geechi needed to chill with the extra shit. They had flirted in the past; the ladies' man had taken his shot but never with the persistence he had since they had decided to get married.

"What you see me doing?" Geechi asked again. Gotti finally looked at him.

"I saw you doing you and I respect it. You don't have to do this. I'm in it; I'm not going to switch up or flip on you. Our bond isn't solidified because we got married, Geechi, and you know that. We were solid before. Stop playing with me," she told him with a little laugh to lighten the mood.

"Thing is I ain't playing."

"You didn't start this shit until we agreed to get married. It's like you feel you gotta come on to me to keep me. It was my idea; it's business. This protects the both of us," she let him know. Gotti had a company and employees to consider; people whom she had promised a future if they believed in her. This mishap would be a stain on her reputation, a big one that Gotti wasn't sure she could scrub away. She worked with sister companies of large organizations and start-up companies who only had one chance to get it right. Even the implication that her success was built illegally could end her, and she couldn't start over again.

"I was always going to protect you," Geechi let her know.

"I know 'cause you the homie," Gotti said, kicking her foot again to get his hand off her ankle. Geechi wanted to say so much but couldn't articulate his words. He wasn't the mushy type, but he fucked with Gotti on a deeper level than "homie". He had confided in her in ways he hadn't with his homies. Geechi trusted her beyond her being his PR, brand strategist or whatever the fuck she called herself.

"Hang with me tonight," Geechi suggested. Words escaped him but maybe he could show her what was in his heart. Gotti looked at him like he had lost his mind wondering had he heard anything she had said.

"On some homie shit," he said; her body relaxed and she smiled. "I wanna get to know you better. I know you businesswise like the back of my hand. But like you said, we're homies. We gotta get to know each other on a more personal level."

"I know you personally."

"You think you do because of Tione."

"She don't tell me much." Gotti laughed, knowing Tione told her more than she should. Geechi gave her a look that said he thought she was lying. "For real. She don't have to though, because even though I don't know all the facts of your life, I see how you move in business. If you were grimy, you'd be that way in business too," she let him know. Geechi stared into her eyes allowing his ambience to float around them. It was deep and could easily penetrate a person. Her heart jumped; her soul stirred. She coughed and looked away taking a sip of her drink.

"What you wanna do?" Geechi asked.

"What about dinner and maybe a lounge," Gotti suggested.

"That shit sound boring, I'm not ya homegirl; do that shit with La'Shea," Geechi said. Whereas Gotti liked lounges, he preferred clubs. Loud music, bottle service, beautiful women dancing and a

VIP section was his idea of a good night. "The resort has a casino; we can go over there."

"I am not about to throw my money away," Gotti said.

"Come on man that shit will be fun."

"We gotta eat too though. Dinner and then the casino?""

"Nah, I can't be full at the table. The casino and then dinner," Geechi suggested.

"Cool," she agreed, relaxing in her seat.

●●●

Later that night, Geechi and Gotti were at the casino. He was a bigger gambler than her so while he was at the blackjack table, Gotti was on the slot machines. She had eaten a small snack before leaving her hotel suite because she would be drinking at the casino. Periodically, Geechi would join Gotti at the slot machines but would easily get bored and leave her alone.

Finally, she'd had enough and sent Geechi a text message letting him know she had won $500 and was ready to cash out. He was up $1600 and figured that was a good time to cash out. The casino hadn't been good to Geechi and it had taken him forever to win back the $4000 he was down.

"Oooh, I want to do that," Gotti said, passing by the crap table that offered big winnings on the way to cash out.

"Hell nah, the odds are 30 to 1," Geechi informed her. She was looking at what she could win and how easy it could be, but he was looking at her chances of actually winning. Geechi knew his words had fallen on deaf ears by the way Gotti's eyes were still beaming. "You gon' lose ya lil 500," he warned her.

"So what." Geechi shook his head and threw down $500 worth of chips to match her. The dealer shot the dice, and before it could register to Gotti that she won, bells were going off and Geechi was hugging her as he spun her around.

"You just won $30,000, bro," Geechi told her. Gotti looked up at the screen in awe then back at him. "You so fucking lucky," he told her.

"Nah I'm just always right," Gotti teased. Geechi's hand fell from her back to her hip; in a swift motion, he pulled her to him. Instantly his lips met hers, then his tongue parted Gotti's lips and she opened her wanting mouth inviting him inside. When her pussy began to purr, Gotti quickly pushed him back.

"Geechi!" she screeched, fixing her dress.

"My bad man, my bad," was all he could say as he walked to the table. The dealer tried to get them to try again but they refused. Once everything was squared away and Gotti had set up her back account with the casino so her funds could be transferred, they headed to the restaurant.

Geechi had reserved a table on the terrace that overlooked the beach. The sun had set, the mood was serene and the sound of the water crashing against the shore was calming. Liquor flowed through Gotti's body plastering a constant smile on her face. She was drunk and she knew it, so she triple-checked the information on the napkin before she slid it across the table to Geechi.

"Fuck is this?" he asked, studying the I.O.U for $500.

"Your money back. Well, when I can get to an ATM," Gotti replied nonchalantly.

"Bullshit, you owe me fifteen thousand."

"I didn't tell you to put money down," Gotti said with a giggle as she sipped her red wine. She lifted her fork, picked up some asparagus and then a piece of steak and put it in her mouth.

"You good man," Geechi said, ripping up the I.O.U.

"Nooo," she whined, "because you're going to try to come back later and get my money."

"We're married," he reminded her. "In Texas that means what's yours is mine," Geechi smirked.

"We gotta get the post-nup done," Gotti said. The idea to get married came to Gotti about a month after Geechi told her what was going on. She had planned on a prenup, but they didn't have time to iron out the details, so she proposed a post-nup.

"I researched that shit; it doesn't really hold up in court," Geechi told her. She thought that he was insinuating that she might try to take his money. Gotti only wanted what was hers; she would never try to take something that someone worked hard to build.

"I'm not going to take any of your money or try to get half of your business," she told Geechi looking up in his eyes with sincerity.

"I know that," Geechi told her. "I'm only mentioning it because I want my fifteen. I don't have the morals you have." He laughed.

"Whatever," she said finally laughing too.

"You want dessert?" Geechi asked as the waiter cleared the table.

"I do, but I'm full," she said, rubbing her stomach through the black, skin-tight dress. "I don't have no more room."

"Okay, we can change and get some at the hotel," Geechi suggested, sliding his card into the black folder for the waiter.

"Okay." Gotti agreed even though she wasn't sure. The waiter came back with Geechi's credit card, he signed the slip and then stood, holding his arm out for her. They walked over the wooden bridge and down the shore on the way back to the hotel.

"I wanna be clear," Gotti said.

"About what?"

"I just want dessert. I don't know if that was a sexual innuendo or..."

"Bro, it's dessert. Like real dessert, like chocolate cake or some shit," he told her.

65

"Cool. I just wanted to be..."

"Clear," Geechi finished for her.

●●●

"How many people are we telling that it's not real?" Geechi asked as they looked over the dessert menu. He was dressed in Nike shorts and a white T-shirt and Gotti had on a thick robe provided by the hotel. His imagination had been in overdrive since she opened the door as thoughts of what was underneath took control of him.

"We had to tell Tione and I have to tell La'Shea and Troy. Is there anyone else you think needs to know?" Gotti asked.

"Nah, I really think that's too much, but it's cool," he answered.

"How is that too much?"

"I might be paranoid; I just like to do my dirt solo," he said.

"I know," she said with a playful smile. "But see how telling little ol' me helped the situation," she joked. Geechi looked at Gotti but didn't reply; he only liked to talk about certain things when he had to. "I want the chocolate cake," she let him know.

"We can share," Geechi said and went to the hotel phone to order their treat. Gotti sat on the couch and searched movies.

"So my ma wants to meet you," Geechi revealed once he took his seat on the couch.

"Why?" she asked, settling on the movie *Love Jones*.

"That's why I asked who all we telling; she thinks a nigga married," he said.

"Oh yea. Damn. I don't want to lie to her," Gotti said cringing at the thought.

"Maybe this wasn't a good idea," Geechi said. He was a little frustrated by her need to be so honest about some shit that was illegal.

"No, I," she stammered a little. "I know we can't, and we won't, but I still feel bad."

"She may not even like you," he admitted, "she's one of those moms."

"Shit, I don't wanna cuss out Mama Gina," Gotti said pretending to be hurt.

"Bro, I will put hands and feet on your ass," he threatened.

"Ha!" she said and rolled her eyes. "What's our story though?"

"About what?"

"How we met and shit."

"Our story," he said. "We don't have to lie about shit. Tione been telling her about you. Plus, she's seen pictures of us at events. Even though you choose to ignore it, a lot of people see our chemistry."

"Whatever," she said with a bashful smile.

"You want me to meet ya people? Ya mama gon' be excited?" Geechi asked. He knew how important marriage was to women and figured Gotti's mom might be pissed that she wasn't a part of it. There was a knock at the door, and he got up to retrieve their order.

"Why'd you get wine. I'm already tipsy," Gotti asked when he reentered the living area.

"Learn how to say no," Geechi teased.

"Whatever, just pour me a little." He shook his head but did what she asked.

"Ohh," Gotti moaned as she put a piece of the chocolate cake with chocolate icing in her mouth. It was so moist and chocolatey that she had to do a little dance. Geechi watched her close her eyes and roll her body and couldn't help but laugh. They were quiet for a few moments as they enjoyed the dessert and wine.

67

"I was married once," Gotti admitted, using her fork to cut another piece. Geechi was surprised to hear that; she had never mentioned it before, and he figured any woman would.

"Oh yea; what happened?" he asked.

Gotti picked up the juicy strawberry that had been on the cake and bit into it. Thoughts of Jeff and the bullshit he put her through ran through her mind. That familiar lump formed in Gotti's throat. She was over him, had been before they signed the divorce papers. But the shit Jeff did to her still hurt.

"He didn't know what he was getting into. He wanted somebody to cook his food and wash his clothes," Gotti said and shrugged her shoulders. They were young and fresh out of college with big dreams and high hopes. Things didn't happen as fast for him as they did for her; Gotti was on top of the world career wise, but Jeff couldn't find a job in his field.

"I mean, it's nice..." Geechi said pulling Gotti from her thoughts, "to have someone that caters to you... but I can cook and wash my own clothes," he said. That made Gotti look up at him. "That's not what I want from a woman," Geechi added. And there was that debonair aura again diving into her longing and pulling down her panties.

"What you want from a woman?" Gotti questioned seductively. She bit into another strawberry, its juice oozed out and she slurped it up before completely removing the strawberry from the stem.

"I would have to show you," Geechi said. His hand was on her thigh now moving up her robe. Gotti placed her hand on top of his then gripped it to stop him.

"It's late, Mr. Koran," Gotti said. Her eyes were closed tight as she tried to will her professional side to emerge. Finally, she had it; Gotti opened her eyes and removed his hand.

"Oh it's late now?" Geechi questioned when she stood from the couch.

"It is," she said, pulling him up from the couch. "I'll see you tomorrow," Gotti said with her hands on his back as she pushed him to and then through the door that connected their suites. Geechi turned to protest but without looking at him, Gotti closed and locked the door. Then she sank to the ground, shoved her fingers into her love box and pounded them in and out until her love coated her fingers and relief covered her body.

Chapter 8

"**I can't believe y'all made me come all the way to New York,**" **La'Shea fussed, dragging her suitcase into Troy's Manhattan apartment.** She was on the phone with Troy who was supposed to be at home but claimed to be stuck at work.

"I'm happy we came," La'Bella said with a smile as she pulled her suitcase behind her. La'Bella headed straight to the window that provided a view of the Hudson River.

"Yea so stop complaining. I should be home no later than six," Troy rushed to say.

"Six!" La'Shea shouted. La'Bella turned around to walk to her mother. "So we have to decorate and cook by ourselves?" La'Shea continued to fuss.

"Have a good day at work, Auntie," La'Bella said, grabbing the phone from her mother. "We got it from here," she said and hung up.

"Umm, I don't know who you think you are but—"

"I'm the daughter of La'Shea Yarborough; you know who I am," La'Bella teased. "Come on; this is going to be fun. I haven't been to New York in a while," La'Bella said. La'Shea had to admit she was happy to see the genuine smile on her daughter's face. Because of that, she quickly changed her mood. La'Bella had finally found a couple of friends at school and even had a little boyfriend. Knowing that she was happy and adjusting well brought peace to La'Shea. She was no longer second guessing her decision to move.

La'Shea and La'Bella spent the next couple hours walking up and down the busy streets of New York. They got decorations, ordered a cake and went to the market to get Gotti's favorite foods.

"Why we getting all this?" La'Bella asked as La'Shea moved around the store getting everything she would need from pots and pans to milk and eggs.

"Did you look in her kitchen? She doesn't even have flour. Troy doesn't cook, and she's never home."

"I wanna travel like that for my job," La'Bella revealed.

"Have you decided what you want to do?" La'Shea asked as nonchalantly as she could muster. She tried not to pressure La'Bella but feared that she and her aunties had spoiled her, and it took away La'Bella's motivation. La'Shea came from humble beginnings and it was that upbringing that gave her the ambitious spirit she possessed. La'Shea wondered if her laid-back parenting style had ruined La'Bella.

"No. Sorry; I know you and my aunties had it together by my age."

"It's fine, Baby. I was just asking," La'Shea said not wanting to ruin her mood.

Back at the apartment, La'Shea started cooking while La'Bella started decorating. They called to tell Troy to pick up the cake on the way home.

●●●

"Oh my goodness it smells so good in here," Troy said, entering the apartment with the cake in her hands. "This looks good," she said taking in the décor.

"I did it!" La'Bella bragged.

"Hey Baby," Troy said, setting the cake on the table and meeting La'Bella in the middle of the living room. They hugged and

Troy kissed La'Bella's face before she released her and went to La'Shea.

"Hey sis," Troy greeted with her arms out for a hug.

"Hey honey," La'Shea said, hugging her.

"You bought me pans?" Troy laughed.

"I knew you wouldn't have any," La'Shea replied.

"I was going to order food," Troy let her know.

"I know," La'Shea said, rolling her eyes.

"She'll be here in about an hour." Troy said as she kicked off her heels.

"Okay, well try to remember how to cook and watch the food while I shower," La'Shea said.

"La'Bella..."

"Can't cook either," La'Shea said, handing Troy the big spoon. La'Shea laughed as she walked out.

An hour later the food was set up, the decorations were perfect, and they were awaiting Gotti's arrival.

"Congratulations!" They screamed when she walked inside the apartment. She took a moment to observe the white and silver décor. They had balloons, streamers, tablecloths, center pieces, and a gift table. The food was set up to the left and it was all her favorite dishes that La'Shea made from greens to meatloaf to cornbread and red beans to corn casserole and ribs.

"Oh my..." Gotti said, and they all rushed to hug her. "Y'all shouldn't have," she added.

"Whatever bitch. We had to do something since we couldn't plan a bachelorette's party," La'Shea blurted out.

"Maybe we can have a post-bachelorette's party," Troy said. "Invite some girls from school."

"Oh wow," Gotti said. They finally picked up on her sarcasm.

"What?" Troy asked.

"Did you leave him already?" La'Shea said.

"Oh Auntie," La'Bella sighed.

"No, I didn't leave him," she said with a chuckle. "I'm trying to decide if Baby should hear this," Gotti said.

"Hear what?" La'Bella asked. Gotti looked from La'Shea to Troy as a way of asking them should she talk in front of La'Bella.

"Is it bad?" Troy asked.

"Illegal? My baby don't need to know shit that can get her time," La'Shea joked.

"I think it's illegal but not that illegal."

"The fuck," La'Shea fumed.

"That's all you need to know," Gotti told La'Bella.

"What? No! It's just getting good," La'Bella complained.

"Fix your plate, Baby, and go eat in my bedroom," Troy told her.

La'Bella huffed. "This is not fair."

"Get your cake too," La'Shea said.

"So I can never come out of the bedroom?" La'Bella said, rolling her eyes.

"We don't know, maybe not tonight," Troy said.

"If she ruined the marriage already can I have her Chanel bag?" La'Bella asked as she fixed her plate.

"Hell no!" Gotti replied and turned to La'Shea. "You got me a Chanel bag?" Gotti said, her eyes lit up like a kid on Christmas.

"Let me fix my plate and get a stiff drink so we can hear this shit," La'Shea said after La'Bella left the room.

They fixed their plates in silence then sat at the table and stared at Gotti.

"We're not married," Gotti blurted out.

"What? It's a hoax?" La'Shea questioned.

"We're married legally but we're not in love," she told them.

"Baby can have the Chanel purse," La'Shea said.

"I can't believe you got me Chanel!" Gotti beamed.

"Bitch, I thought you were married! It's all white like a bride," she said.

"And I got you the matching briefcase and heels," Troy said.

"Baby can have that too," La'Shea said.

"What Baby need a briefcase for?" Gotti questioned.

"True. Save that for me," Troy said.

"Y'all serious?" Gotti asked sounding like a child.

"Dead ass," Troy confirmed.

"Why, Gotti?" La'Shea asked.

"I can't say too much," she replied.

"Bullshit!"

"You know the legal troubles he's having," Gotti said to La'Shea.

"Bits and pieces."

"What legal troubles?" Troy said.

"They're saying he was illegally exporting cars overseas," Gotti said.

"Like a straw buyer," La'Shea said. Typically, someone with money would hire a straw buyer to purchase a car. All the straw buyer needed was a driver's license; they would go into a dealership to buy the car with the other person's money. Then the car would be shipped to its destination.

La'Shea knew that in previous cases people lost the money they spent on the luxury vehicles, which could go up to a hundred thousand dollars or more and got probation. The worst case she had heard of the guy got six months in prison.

"What's that?" Troy asked.

"Cars in China are a lot more expensive than in the US," La'Shea said. "I don't know why—"

"China has a high tax on imported cars so manufacturers up the price of the car to offset the high tax," Gotti explained.

"Why have the high tax though?" Troy asked.

"To make manufacturers build their cars in China," Gotti said.

"Ohhh," Troy said, nodding her head.

"So anyway," La'Shea said. "People buy them in the US and have them shipped to China to avoid the high prices but there are laws prohibiting that. In the cases I've seen, there isn't a big penalty for it," La'Shea said.

"No, they want to charge him with bigger shit. I guess to make an example out of him. Racketeering, fraud, shit like that," Gotti said as if it were no big deal. "As if he built an entire operation doing this." Gotti loved to solve problems and could always strategize and think out of the box to get people out of trouble. It was what made her a good friend and a good brand strategist, but La'Shea felt like she had taken this too far.

"What!" La'Shea screeched.

"That's major," Troy said.

"I married him so that I couldn't testify."

"You don't know shit," La'Shea said. Gotti made a face and La'Shea's eyes bucked.

"You know shit?" Troy asked.

"A little. Geechi is not going down for that shit, though. It ain't like he's killing people or even stealing money. He takes care of a lot of people; they're not about to railroad him and take all that he's worked for. Meanwhile that damn white boy raped that girl and got no time."

"Which one," Troy said referring to the numerous white men who had gotten off on charges of rape and molestation.

"How much do you know?" La'Shea asked.

"That's between me and him," Gotti said. It felt weird to not tell them everything. It came naturally to spill her guts to them but now she had to protect Geechi.

"Shouldn't you know about all this; aren't you his lawyer?" Troy asked La'Shea.

"I'm his corporate lawyer… for business shit. He told me about the possible criminal charges, but I thought it was minor. He has a criminal lawyer for that," La'Shea explained.

"True. I didn't think about that," Troy said. "So you need a lawyer?" Troy asked Gotti.

"No, well not yet, but in the meantime, I had to make sure we were safe."

"So it was your idea?" Troy questioned.

"Of course it was her idea," La'Shea stated.

"I should have known," Troy said, shaking her head.

"I like fixing shit; that's why I'm in public relations," Gotti said.

"You sure that's all it is?" La'Shea probed.

"Positive," Gotti answered ignoring the looks on their faces. "Y'all really giving away my shit?" she asked laughing.

"Girl fuck you," La'Shea said, rolling her eyes.

"I don't want y'all to worry. I got this," Gotti said.

"You need a lawyer regardless…just in case," Troy said.

"I know someone," La'Shea said.

"He's not going to let anything happen to me," Gotti said.

"How sure are you about that?" Troy questioned.

"Very."

"Has he been charged?"

"Not yet."

"So how do y'all know all this?" Troy questioned.

"He knows someone that works in the prosecutor's office; they informed him that a case was being built. Based on that information, Geechi feels like someone is snitching."

"Who all knows about it?"

"A few people," Gotti said ready to end the conversation. She had already said more than Geechi would approve of. Her friends picked up on that fact and they began making jokes about her fake marriage and crime boss husband. She knew it was all in good fun and added in a couple of jokes of her own. La'Bella rejoined the party and they spent the rest of the day eating, dancing and enjoying each other's company.

●●●

Gotti was back in Texas weaving through the downtown traffic on her way to meet Geechi at his office when he called.

"Hello," she said allowing Bluetooth to pick up the call.

"When you get here, you have to act like it's real; you know that, right?" he said.

"Yes, I know," Gotti said with a smile. Geechi was always trying to coach her on how to behave as if she hadn't proven that she knew what she was doing.

"Okay. How far away are you?"

"Don't start trying to control me." Gotti laughed as she made a right on McKinney and shot the driver in the other lane the middle finger. He was dead set on not allowing her to get over which would have prevented her from making her turn, and the whole time he needed to get in her lane. "I'm five minutes away," she finally answered.

"Okay come see me when you pull up," Geechi told Gotti, and they disconnected the call.

Outside of his office building, she touched up her lipstick and fingered her 22-inch Peruvian bundles before she grabbed her green tea from Starbucks and her white Chanel purse. Her matching heels hit the ground and glistened in the sun. After much convincing, she and La'Bella had agreed to share the items. Why a sixteen-year-old needed a pair of nine-hundred-dollar heels was beyond her. Then she thought maybe La'Bella could wear them to prom. La'Bella had come out of the funk she was in last year and was having a better high school experience.

"Sister-in-law!" Tione exclaimed when Gotti walked through the door.

"Heeeyy!" Gotti said as they made their way to greet each other with a hug.

"You look nice," Tione complimented.

"Thanks," Gotti said posing in her Alexander McQueen pantsuit.

"Not the clothes, the glow. The honeymoon was good to you I see."

Gotti rolled her eyes. Tione knew they weren't really married, but Gotti wasn't surprised that she had chosen to live in a fairytale world. Tione had been trying to get them together for the past six months, and Gotti figured Tione thought this might be her chance to finally make it happen.

"Where is he?" Gotti asked.

"In the back waiting for you," Tione said buzzing her back. Gotti walked through the door on her way to Geechi's office shaking her head at Tione's ability to go from fashionista to annoying little sister.

"Hey baby." Gotti looked up to see Geechi coming from one of the back rooms.

"Hey," she said as he swept her into his arms. Geechi planted a kiss on her neck then her cheek; she looked up at him while still in his embrace anticipating a kiss on the lips, but it didn't happen.

Geechi grabbed Gotti's hand and led her into his office. She leaned against his desk and he stood in front of her still holding her hand.

"How was New York?" he inquired.

"Fun. I had a good time with my girls," she answered. He filled the spot between her legs.

"I don't want to talk too much while we're here," he whispered in her ear. "But you were careful, right?"

"Of course," Gotti replied.

"I know y'all are like sisters and you trust them. I trust people too, but some stuff I want kept between us," he said, pulling back to look in her eyes.

"I know; I do too."

"We'll talk more at home," he said with a smile. "You excited about meeting my mama?" he questioned changing the subject.

"Is she excited about meeting me?" Gotti shot back, working her neck.

"She hasn't said much," Geechi admitted and bit his bottom lip as if he was in deep thought.

"You nervous?" she asked with her eyebrow lifted. Gotti had never seen him nervous; he always gave off the impression that he was sure of whatever he was doing.

"Hell nah," he said and chuckled.

"How many women have met your mom?"

"Maannn," he said, "worry about you." He bent to kiss her cheek. "I gotta work," he let her know.

"Well, fuck you too," Gotti joked, rolling her neck. "I got shit to do too," she said, walking towards the door. He grabbed her and with his hand on her stomach, pulled her back to him. Then he kissed her cheek.

"Have a good day," he said.

"You too." She blushed and left his office. As soon as she entered the hallway, she ran into Tione.

"Damn you smiling big," Tione noted.

"Whatever."

"It's real," Tione said. Gotti thought she was referring to their marriage, but she was talking about their love.

"Girl stop living in La-La Land. What can I expect from your mother?" Gotti asked as they entered the lobby.

"Hell if she thinks you're bullshitting."

"I want to get her a gift; what should I get?"

"She likes home décor stuff."

"What kind?" Gotti liked to decorate too and felt that this was something she could get brownie points for.

"Mama likes elephants. She's remodeling her kitchen. She wants everything stainless steel and red," Tione told her trying to think of other things Gotti could buy for her. "Maybe pots," she added with a shrug.

"Have you ever met a guy's parents?"

"Yea but they're always trying to impress me," Tione said and flipped her hair.

"Come shopping with me."

"I have to work! We can go tomorrow."

"Cool. I have to get some work done for some other clients. I'm going to head to the house."

"You staying with La'Shea?"

"No, that would look weird."

"Oh you staying with your huuuusband," Tione said and laughed.

"Bye heifer," Gotti said making her way out of the building.

At Geechi's house Gotti changed into a tunic dress, black leggings and a pair of sneakers covered in rhinestones. She pulled out her Mac Notebook and set up shop at the kitchen counter. Gotti was working with a new client who had started a makeup line. They had chosen a popular influencer on social media to be the face of the company but needed help creating a marketing plan that would reach younger Millennials and Generation Z.

Gotti was so wrapped up in her work that she didn't hear the garage door slide up. She was consumed with the emails, phone calls and research that her job required.

Geechi walked into the kitchen to find her sitting at the counter. Guacamole, chips and chocolate candy covered the counter along with a bottled water. Gotti was dressed down, well in her eyes, but she still had on a face full of makeup and not one strand of her hair was out of place.

"Hey," Gotti said when she heard him drop his keys on the counter.

"You working that hard that you can't properly greet your husband," he teased.

"Whatever, we are not at work," she replied.

"You gotta be on point for Ma-dukes too. She can see through bullshit," Geechi let her know.

"And I will be."

"Dress down," he instructed. "You come over there in heels and all that makeup, she gon' think you hiding something."

"Damn, can I be me?"

"Yea, you just can't be this," Geechi said referring to her perfect image.

"This is me," Gotti shot back.

"A piece," he said, "and it's beautiful," he added turning on his charm. "Just for Ma..." his sentence trailed off, but she got what he meant. "What about your mom?"

"What about her?" Gotti wanted to know.

"You tell her? I know she has seen all the posts congratulating us on Facebook."

"Ha! We're not friends on social media; in fact, she's blocked."

"Why?"

"'Cause it's my job and she gets outta line sometimes," Gotti answered as she typed a document on her laptop.

"So no you haven't told her?"

"No."

"Are you?"

"I don't know. I don't wanna argue with her," she said.

"Well let me know what we're doing," Geechi said picking up on the fact that Gotti didn't want to talk about it.

"I wanna go buy something for ya mom; you have any suggestions?"

"That's sweet," he cheesed, "I'll pick something up."

"It has to come from me," she pouted.

"We'll put your name on it."

"Tione already said she'd go with me."

"When?"

"Tomorrow."

"You're meeting her tomorrow, though, and Tione knows Mama is going to want her at the house early to help cook and shit."

"I love southern food; what is she cooking?"

"A damn Thanksgiving feast. I told Mama she was doing too much," Geechi said, shaking his head.

"No, she isn't. I mean, I am your wife." Gotti smiled, flashing her ring.

"Now you my wife?"

"Let me call Tione to see if we need to get up and go early."

"We can go, Gotti. You can pick it out, pay for it and put your name on it."

"Okay. When?"

"Now, come on," he said, grabbing his keys.

"Let me change," Gotti said, hopping off the stool.

"Bro, you look good," he said. The dress she wore was tight at the top and flared at the waist. It was silk material and clung to her body.

"No."

"Yes. Gotti, let's go," Geechi said, walking to the door.

"Fine, let me throw this stuff away," Gotti said, rolling her eyes. Geechi headed to the car as Gotti cleaned her mess. When he was out the door, she sprinted up the stairs and into her room. The first pair of heels Gotti saw were close-toed, platform heels with a flower print. Gotti threw them in her purse and darted for the garage.

Inside the car, she waited until they were on the freeway to pull them out.

"I ought to turn around," Geechi threatened.

"I don't like being short. It's less about dressing up and more about being taller," Gotti admitted.

"I'm telling you my ma gon' think you doing too much scuffing up her new hardwood floors," he warned.

"I'm not wearing heels tomorrow."

At the mall they found some beautiful bedding that Geechi said his mother would love. They got that and two elephant statues and left the store. Gotti was happy with the gifts and was even happier that she had picked them out.

Chapter 9

"**L**et's go, bae!" **Geechi yelled from downstairs.** "Ma don't like lateness. She thinks it's disrespectful." He was about to say something else when he heard Gotti behind him. Geechi turned to face her and was taken aback by her natural beauty. The fashionista was dressed down in an orange Champions outfit. The joggers were fitted but not too tight and the long-sleeved crop top laid on the waistband and slightly fell off her shoulder. Gotti matched it with orange Nikes.

"What's this?" Geechi said, touching her hair.

"You said less is more." Gotti had taken off her wig and was rocking her own tresses. The top was pulled into a cute bun and the back was straight and resting across her shoulders. The only makeup Gotti wore was mascara, eyeliner and a touch of eye shadow. Geechi was used to the fake lashes, long weave and high heels, and he loved all that, but he was impressed with the fact that she didn't need it.

"Why you staring?" Gotti asked playfully hitting him.

"You pretty," he admitted.

"You knew that," Gotti replied. If Geechi didn't think she was pretty, why did he hit on her like he did? Even before Geechi started going hard to get her, Gotti would notice him staring at her.

"Nah I knew you was fine, could dress, and cleaned up nice. I didn't know this," he said, walking toward the garage door. Gotti blushed as she snapped the Gucci fanny pack across her shoulder. In the car, Geechi couldn't keep his hands out of her hair.

"Geechi," Gotti finally said, hitting his hand.

"Why you never look like this?" he asked at a red light.

"I always look like this," she said.

"I've known you a year and you never look like this," Geechi said as he passed through the green light.

"'Cause you see me at work," Gotti explained. His hand was wrapped around the back of her neck caressing it.

"Stop," she said.

"You might as well get into character. If you flitch when we with my mama—"

"I'm not," she assured him.

"Aiite. Aye, but you never told me exactly what you told ya homegirls," Geechi mentioned. He had intended to discuss it yesterday but with shopping and then dinner he forgot.

"Nothing."

"You told them something, mama. I know they had questions."

"I wasn't going to tell them after what you said about being paranoid and we shouldn't have told Tione, but they know me too well," she explained.

"It's cool," he assured her.

"But so anyway, I just told them we got married to protect us. You told La'Shea about the case," Gotti reminded him before she went on to tell him all that she had revealed.

"I told her what I needed to; she is one of my lawyers, so I wanted her to know what was up."

"Yea, well she was thinking why did y'all get married for something that small," Gotti went on to say.

"So you told her the charges?"

"Yea some of them...the RICO charge and fraud."

"Sheeit, those the big ones," Geechi chuckled, "They panicked?" he asked.

"Nah, just wanted to make sure I was doing the right thing."

"You feel like you did?" he wanted to know.

"Yea," Gotti answered sincerely.

"I'm not gon' let shit happen to you. I'll take every charge before I let you go down for this shit."

"I know. I told them that," she informed him.

"What they say?" Geechi said, turning on his blinker and turning right at the light, "Girl don't be stupid, niggas ain't shit," he said mimicking a girl's voice.

"Not really. La'Shea knows you're solid. They want me to have a lawyer, though. That's not a bad idea," she told him.

"Nah it ain't. They haven't brought down the charges yet though. Once I'm indicted, then it makes sense for you to lawyer up. Right now, we're not supposed to know shit is happening."

"I know."

"That's why I need you to be careful with what you say," Geechi told her.

"I am," Gotti said with a hint of attitude. She hated that he thought she was naïve.

"Even around Tione." Gotti was surprised that she knew more about what was going on than Tione because she was his righthand. "My mama don't know shit and you know Tione thinks it's a small case," Geechi said. "I'm not trying to worry people. I mean shit, it might just go away. That's why I didn't want to tell you."

"If it goes away, cool. But it's better to be safe than sorry. I needed to know in order to protect you. You can't keep secrets from your PR."

"That's why you needed to know, huh?"

"Why else?" she questioned. Geechi shrugged as they pulled into his mother's driveway.

"Don't be nervous. Remember this shit ain't even real," he told her.

"It's real today," Gotti said and hopped out of the car. Geechi popped the trunk to grab the gifts; she carried the bag that held the bedding since it was lighter than the elephant statues.

"You look so different," Tione said as soon as they walked in the house. The living area was small but elegant. A big picture window showed a view of the front porch. An off-white sofa, love seat, and tables were strategically placed around the space. Paintings, family photos and a flat screen TV decorated the walls. The living room was attached to the dining room which had a circular wooden table, matching chairs and a bench in the center of it.

"How she normally look?" Gina said coming up behind them. Gina had been on the right side of the house in her bedroom getting dressed when she heard them pull up.

"Professional," Tione answered, stepping aside so that Gina was face to face with Gotti.

"She cute," Gina said. Gina had only seen Gotti in pictures at galas or banquets with Geechi, and she always looked immaculate from head to toe. But Gina saw that as Gotti's image and was happy to see the real her. "Yea, she's real cute," Gina concluded as if she was looking at a picture of Gotti instead of face to face.

"Thank you," Gotti said. "You're beautiful," she said and hugged Gina. Gina was sixty-two and fabulous. At five-six she had a curvy yet slim frame due to her weekly workouts at the gym. Her hair was cut short and completely silver which coordinated well with her pecan skin tone.

"What's all this?" Gina asked looking down at the bags.

"I wanted to get you a gift; my mama always says not to show up at a person's house empty handed."

"Smart woman!" They laughed. "Y'all have a seat; I got something for you too," Gina said. They walked to the left through a doorway that separated the living room and dining room and then down five or six steps. Now they were in the den which was bigger with more comfortable furniture. The den led to the patio, that had been added on to the house, and the large backyard. Geechi, Tione and Gotti had a seat in the den and waited on Gina.

"Who all is coming?" Geechi asked Tione.

"Everybody," she said referring to their aunts, uncles and cousins. "Mama wanted to meet her first, so she told them to meet here at three."

Gina walked back into the room with a bag and handed it to Gotti. "You first," she said. Gotti reached into the bag and pulled out a Bible.

"Now I don't know if you're a heathen like him, but I figured you might be seeing as how you didn't think to get married in a church. I highlighted all the parts about marriage to make it easier for y'all to follow along."

"Thank you," Gotti said trying hard not to laugh.

"There's more," Gina said. Gotti reached in the bag again and pulled out the red lace lingerie. Her face contorted; she didn't know whether to laugh or to be embarrassed. "You got to have both to keep ya husband happy."

"Jesus and some lingerie!" Tione shouted, laughing hysterically.

"You can't even get a boyfriend," Gina teased.

"I don't want one," Tione shot back.

"You want a girlfriend?" Gina quizzed.

"Oh so now I'm gay?"

"Pretty girl like you, raised right with good morals and you can't find nor keep a man... you must not want one. If ya gay just say ya gay and cut out all this foolishness," Gina chastised.

"Oh my God. This is about them, remember?" Tione stated.

"Don't get smart," Gina warned.

"Can I see you in this tonight. Since it's real today?" Geechi asked in Gotti's ear.

"No," she said blushing. When Gotti looked up and saw Gina staring at them, she playfully pushed Geechi away.

"That's all right now," Gina said with a loud laugh.

"Now it's your turn," Gotti said. Gina dug in the bag containing the comforter first. Tione grabbed the end of the bag to help her pull it out.

"I love this. And I know you picked this out 'cause Geechi don't know nothing about thread count." She laughed. "Thank you."

"You're welcome."

"And what's this?" Gina said, pulling the elephants from the other bag. She unwrapped the first one, "I love it," she told Gotti.

"I'm happy you like it, Mama, 'cause she was going crazy," Geechi said. "When can we eat?"

"Everybody will be here in a minute," Gina replied.

"Come on, let's go see what Mama cooked," Geechi said, pulling Gotti up. They walked back up the steps and through the dining room to get to the kitchen.

"That was the washroom and there was a wall right there," Geechi said pointing to the left side of the kitchen. "She wanted it bigger. An island is going to go right here," he said standing in the middle of the floor.

"It's going to be nice," Gotti said. She noticed little improvements that had already been done. Geechi moved to the stove and she followed him. They opened each pot and named the food.

"Cabbage," Geechi said.

"Ooohhh dressing," Gotti said peeking through the oven window.

"Turkey," Geechi said.

"Brisket!" Gotti said and did a little dance. She straightened up when Gina walked in the kitchen.

"I'm glad you like to eat. Tione said you're from New York City; I didn't know if you were vegan or any of that other mess."

"I'm not," Gotti confirmed.

"Mac and cheese," Geechi told her.

"Red beans, broccoli rice casserole, cornbread, sweet potato pie, peach cobbler, and cheesecake," Gina said reciting the menu.

"Man, I love it here," Gotti said in amazement causing everybody to laugh.

A couple hours later everyone had arrived, eaten and now the men were outside, and the women were in the den watching old homemade movies. They all shared funny memories of Geechi, things he had done for the family that showed his character and integrity. Stories that Gotti had never heard but knew were true because of the type of man Geechi had shown her he was. Now they were laughing hysterically watching an old video of him and his friends at a talent show singing 112's *Cupid*. They were all dressed in suits that were two sizes too big singing their hearts out.

"Man turn this shit off!" Geechi fumed busting into the door. It was too late, Gotti had already saw him in second grade saying his Easter speech, she had saw him at thirteen in a school play, and videos at family functions of him being a jokester and controlling the camera interviewing other family members. Gotti had seen him win a NAACP award from the Dallas chapter for his work restoring the community center. And now she had seen Geechi perform a song at the school talent show. Something he didn't want to be a part of but did because Maleek needed background singers.

Gotti saw Geechi differently now, and he knew that by the look in her eyes.

"Don't let them make you fall in love with me," he teased.

"That could never happen," she sassed. Geechi grabbed Gotti's chin, pulled her to him and kissed her. He felt her body relax in his embrace; it was the first time she didn't pull back from their kiss first.

●●●

"You good?" Geechi asked when they walked inside his home.

"Yea," Gotti said, stumbling a little.

"I told you, you can't drink with my mama and my aunties." He laughed.

"I can drink with the best of them," she said; her speech slurred.

"Yea wine," Geechi joked, grabbing Gotti's hand and leading her to the stairs.

"You wanna watch a movie?" he asked.

Gotti shook her head no and held on to him for dear life as he led her up the stairs. All he could do was laugh. In her bedroom, Gotti slung herself on the bed.

"Man slow down, I got you," Geechi said, pulling the covers back. "I'm not going to undress you 'cause I don't want no problems in the morning," he joked.

"I'm not that drunk," she lied.

"You slept the whole ride home...snoring," he teased.

"I'm tired," she reasoned.

"Let me take your shoes off," Geechi said, bending in front of her. Gotti laughed. "What?" he asked looking back up at her.

"It's like you're proposing," she said and fell back on the bed.

"Man take your drunk ass to sleep," Geechi said, getting her situated on the bed. She grabbed his arm.

"Stay with me. I'm scared, I've never lived in a house this big. I heard something last night."

"No the hell you didn't," Geechi chortled and climbed in the bed behind her.

"You wanna get under the covers?"

"Nah, lil mama, let's just stay like this," he replied.

"Goodnight," she said before sleep overtook her.

Chapter 10

Gotti forced her eyes to open and the sunlight instantly **made her regret it.** She took a moment to gather herself before she tried again. This time Gotti was successful. She looked over at Geechi; he was not underneath the comforter with her, but his arm was comfortably draped over her body. Geechi still wore his jeans and the white tee that had been underneath his Polo shirt the day before.

"Mmmm," she growled. So much was going on with her body from the hangover that Gotti couldn't speak. Her head ached so bad she wanted to massage her temples, but her arms felt too heavy to lift. Gotti finally gained enough energy to elbow Geechi and he stirred in his sleep. She growled again.

"Fuck wrong with you?" Geechi said. His eyes were still closed as he lay on his side with his arm still over her.

"My head," Gotti answered. Speaking seemed to stir her stomach because the next thing she knew bile had crept up her throat. Gotti hopped out of bed pulling the cover with her. When the comforter dropped from her body, it caught on her foot sending Gotti to the ground. Quickly, she prevented her fall by extending her hands. When her palms hit the floor, Gotti pushed herself back up.

"Shit!" she said. Gotti darted into the bathroom, closed the door, and turned on the water in the sink before planting her head in the toilet. In the midst of vomiting all Gotti could think about was Geechi hearing her and how embarrassing this was.

Geechi laid in the bed for a moment with his forearm over his face laughing before he got up to go check on her. He turned the knob on the bathroom door, but it was locked so he knocked.

"Go away," Gotti said.

"Man open the door," Geechi said fighting hard not to laugh.

"I'm about to bathe," Gotti let him know. "Be out of my room when I come out," she demanded and then he heard the shower start. Geechi looked at his watch; he needed to shower and get his day started as well, but he also needed to take care of his wife.

Geechi made Gotti a quick breakfast of bacon, toast and eggs and carried it, the coffee and the water upstairs. He knew she would need something greasy to soak up the liquor. He set it on the desk and then left the room.

After taking her shower, Gotti peeked her head out of the door to make sure he was gone. The room was empty so Gotti hurried to the bedroom door and locked it. When she turned back around, she saw the breakfast and a smile crept up on her face. It was just what she needed. Still wrapped in the towel, Gotti sat at the desk and ate her food.

●●●

Gotti: *What do you want for dinner?* After recovering from her hangover Gotti was ready to get out of bed. She had spent the better half of the day getting caught up on TV shows and getting some much-needed rest. All day she thought about Geechi making her breakfast and how she could thank him.

Geechi: *Good morning to you too.*

Gotti: *It's clearly the evening.* She said and then looked at the time on her phone. 5:03pm.

94

Geechi: *Yea but I haven't seen or heard from you all day.*

Gotti: *You were gone when I came downstairs.*

Geechi: *You were looking for me?*

Gotti: *Nope!*

Gotti: *Dinner?*

Are you an option? Geechi typed, then deleted it. He was trying to get to know Gotti on a personal level and ignore the sexual tension that danced between them.

Geechi: *Surprise me...*

Gotti: *When will you be home?*

Geechi: *Don't try to control me.* He texted with the smiley face emoji wearing the sunglasses.

Gotti: *Okay, the food may be cold...*

Geechi: *Around 8.*

Gotti: *I'll see you then.*

Wear something sexy he typed, shook his head and deleted it.

An hour later, Gotti was dressed in ripped jeans and a big tee as she pushed the buggy through Whole Foods gathering everything she would need for dinner. Geechi wasn't lying when he said he could cook. She had taken inventory of his kitchen and saw that he had all the spices, utensils and cookware she would need to prepare the meal. The more she thought about it the more nervous she became. Gina could cook, and while all she had tasted was his breakfast, Geechi seemed to be able to cook as well. What if her food was too bland for his southern taste buds? Without further thought, Gotti picked up the phone and dialed La'Shea's number.

"I might need your help," Gotti said as soon as La'Shea answered.

"With what?"

"I'm cooking for Geechi tonight," she let her know.

"Why?" La'Shea asked trying not to sound like a judgmental mom. The truth was she and Troy were worried about Gotti. Unbeknownst to Gotti, she had a way of trying to be everything to the man in her life and sometimes that meant losing herself in the process. La'Shea had tried to discreetly learn more about Geechi's case but because he had not been indicted, there wasn't any information out there. That only multiplied La'Shea's fears; now she and Troy talked about the what ifs making the situation far worse than it was...or at least they hoped they were.

"He made me breakfast," Gotti announced.

"Ummm..."

"Ummm what?"

"This is business, right?"

"I can't cook for the man? I'm living in his house and he cooked for me," Gotti reasoned.

"I just...be careful," La'Shea said deciding it was better to leave it there.

"Can I call you when I get home if I need tips?" Gotti asked after a huff and a low sigh.

"Yes."

"Thanks."

"I love you," La'Shea said.

"I love you too," Gotti said about to hang up, but her spirit was uneasy. "La'Shea!" she yelled.

"Yea?"

"I'm not...that girl anymore. I'm not going to fuck this up or misread..."

"I don't think that you'll misread. I just know that men play games," La'Shea said. La'Shea liked Geechi and had been all for the marriage when she thought it was real. But something had changed when she learned all the facts behind the marriage, and her main objective became protecting her friend.

"I know that too," Gotti let her know.

"Okay."

"Okay," Gotti said and smiled. "Bye," she said, and they disconnected the call.

●●●

As Gotti was loading the food into the car, her cellphone began to ring. She quickly jumped in the front seat and answered it.

"Hey baby!"

"Hey Mama Gina," Gotti said recognizing her voice. It slipped off her tongue but felt natural. Gotti had a flashback of the night before when she had begun calling her Mama Gina. It had derived from a joke she made on her honeymoon with Geechi, but last night as the liquor flowed so did it.

"I got your number from Geechi; I hope that's okay."

"Of course."

"What are you doing?" Mama Gina asked. Gotti held the phone to her ear with her shoulder as she put the rest of the bags in the car and then walked the buggy to the holder.

"I just left the grocery store," Gotti said, getting in her car and closing the door.

"Well, I was thinking about what we talked about last night," Gina said.

"Okkaayy," Gotti said hesitantly as she reversed out of the parking spot. She had no idea what Gina was referring to.

"I want to start planning the reception. So both families can meet. I talked to Tione about it and we'd even be willing to have it in New York. Do you think your mom can help me find a venue?" Gotti heard the excitement in Mama Gina's voice and panic ran through Gotti's body so fast that her hands began to shake uncontrollably. Gotti didn't remember a reception being mentioned last night. And she for sure wouldn't have suggested that the families meet; that had to be Tione's idea. This was going too far; there was no way Gotti could bring her mother into this.

"I, she, we," Gotti stuttered. "She's so busy," she was finally able to get out.

"Hmm, well I can figure it out and you can help. When do you want to have it? Do you think having it in New York is the best place?"

"I... don't know. I would have to think about it." Gotti's heart was beating out of her chest. She hadn't expected this and therefore had no idea what to say or how to handle it. Unable to focus on driving; she sat in the middle of the parking garage.

"Girl, just give me your mother's number; we'll figure it out," Gina said. She was unable to understand how any mother would be too busy to plan her daughter's wedding reception.

"Hello?" Gotti said, "Mama Gina," she called even though she heard her clearly. She needed to buy time to think and strategize. "Hello?" Gotti said continuing the charade.

"Girl, can you hear me?" Gina asked right before Gotti disconnected the call. She quickly turned her phone off and sat in the parking garage for a few more moments until a car honked behind her.

"What the fuck!" Gotti said out loud. "How am I going to get myself out of this?" Five minutes into her drive, she picked up her phone and called La'Shea; when she answered, Gotti told her to hold on and called Troy.

"Mama Gina wants to plan a reception with my mother...in New York," Gotti announced.

"What?" Troy gasped.

"Oh shit!" La'Shea said. Gotti was in full panic mode; she didn't know what to do or say or think. She had missed her turn three times and was just making circles at this point. Gotti had so much explaining to do to her mom, to Geechi and to her father.

"Okay, let's calm down," La'Shea said.

"Bitch, I'm calm!" Gotti lied, hitting the steering wheel.

"We have to find a way to postpone it," Troy said.

"She was asking for my mother's number when I pretended to have poor reception and hung up."

"I'm so sorry, Gotti, but I'm walking into a meeting," Troy said cringing. "I can call you back in an hour..."

"Troy," she whined.

"I'll meet you at Geechi's; we will figure it out," La'Shea said, grabbing her briefcase and heading for her office door.

"Hurry," Gotti said and disconnected. For the remainder of the ride, her mind traveled to her mother and their piss poor relationship.

"Married?" Helen said as if it were a bad word.

"Yes," Gotti said. She was excited to tell her mother that Jeff had proposed, but as Gotti took in her mother's energy and facial expression, she was starting to sink into her chair.

"To who?" Helen asked as if Gotti hadn't been dating Jeff for the last two years.

"Jeff," Gotti answered.

"Why? Are you pregnant? We can take care of that," Helen assured her as Tabitha, Helen's assistant, handed her a cup of green tea and then left them alone on the balcony.

"No, I'm not pregnant. I...I love him."

"So what, Gotti!" Helen said as if she was repulsed. "Love doesn't pay the bills. How can you afford a wedding?"

"Mom." Gotti chuckled nervously. "You...you said there are two things you've always saved for, my degree and my wedding. I have the degree, now it's time for the wedding."

"You have got to be shitting me. He doesn't even work."

"Yes, he does."

"Where?"

"He teaches at the community college. He—"

"Oh God," Helen said, falling back into her seat as if she couldn't take anymore.

"Mama, you know that," Gotti said.

"Community—" Helen stopped and rolled her eyes. "At least he could shoot for the stars and start his career at a university. Get on the tenured track. Hell, what am I thinking? He doesn't have the education to even be on the tenured track, so what does he make $30,000 a year?"

"It's just to hold him over," Gotti said barely above a whisper. When Jeff came home and told Gotti about the job, she was so proud of him. She made him feel like the king of the world even though she knew it wasn't enough.

"What is his degree in?"

"Business. I told you that when we started dating," Gotti reminded her. At the time Helen approved of him.

"And why isn't he working in business?"

"He is trying."

"You know what they say, those who can do and those who can't teach," she said, shaking her head.

"He worked for Locke & Marks."

"As an intern and apparently couldn't seal the deal," Helen said.

So you do remember him, Gotti thought but knew better than to utter a word.

"I'm not spending my money on this shit, Gotti. Ask your father," Helen said dismissively. She loved to say that because she knew Gotti's father didn't have half the money Helen did. Helen had come from the projects and pulled herself up by the bootstraps. As a result, she had a hard time respecting anyone who couldn't do the same. That included her ex-husband who had an Engineering degree but decided to follow his heart and work in social work.

"Mom, Dad doesn't... you know he can't afford it," Gotti whispered as if she were embarrassed.

"So what? I have to do it! You always do this, expect me to save the day every damn time. You're so afraid to ask men for things because you're scared they'll leave like your weak ass father!"

"It's just, you've always said you dreamed of—"

"A lot of shit, Gotti. I have a lot of dreams that's why I am so successful.   Like you marrying someone who can support you financially so I don't have to. Do you think I'm a fuckin' bank?"

"No."

"I'll give $50,000; you'll have to ask your father for the rest. Surely he can come up with 20,000," Helen said. That was a letdown for Gotti because she knew her mother had $150,000 saved for her special day. "Ugh, I know he'll want to attend with that baby making machine he calls a wife." Helen seethed.

"Mom, what? Of course he will be there. He has to walk me down the aisle."

"At a wedding I'm paying for? Are you crazy? He always talked about me emasculating him, but he would feel comfortable parading you down an aisle he didn't pay for?" She fumed. "I can't take this; you're working my nerves. If he walks you down the aisle, I'm not paying!"

"What? See, you always do this."

"Do what?"

"Try to control me with your money. If I don't do what you say you threaten me."

"Oh I do? Fine! You know what, I won't do that ever again. Because I'm not paying for shit ever again. I have afforded you a degree from Spelman and a great job. It's time that you fend for yourself."

"I worked hard to get my job!"

"And? You're fresh out of college, do you think you got that job on your own merit? No, it was my recommendation letter that did *that for you. So you take whatever scraps your dad will throw you and you pay for your wedding. This way, we can just be mother and daughter. You won't feel like I'm holding my money over your head, and I won't feel like you're using me," Helen said nonchalantly, taking a sip of her tea.*

"Using you?" Gotti said.

"Using me," Helen confirmed.

As promised Helen didn't pay for any portion of the wedding. She did however show up in a beige dress more expensive than the twenty-thousand-dollar wedding Gotti's father was able to make happen. Helen refused to invite her colleagues because she would be too embarrassed by the cheap shot-gun wedding as she called it. Throughout the ceremony and reception, Helen could be heard critiquing everything from the décor to Jeff's suit and Gotti's dress.

● ● ●

"Good morning," Helen said when Gotti answered the phone.

"Good morning, Mama," Gotti said.

"I wanted to let you get back from your honeymoon before we discussed business," she informed her.

"What business?"

"The apartment," Helen stated.

"What apartment?" Gotti asked truly confused.

"My apartment that you and your husband live in."

"The one you gave me?"

"The one I let you borrow when I was taking care of you. Now that you're on your own and married we need to discuss payment."

"Payment? Mama I can't affor—"

"So you want me to allow a grown ass, fully capable man to live in my apartment rent free?" Helen raged. Tears welled in Gotti's eyes, but she stood stoic as they ran down her cheeks. Gotti had a good paying job for a twenty-two-year-old just out of college, but she also had expensive taste. A taste Helen had created and used to keep her in line. One that Gotti hadn't been able to stop even though her mother was no longer footing the bill. Now it was a part of her image; Gotti worked with high profile clients as a PR representative. She had to look the part. While Jeff was doing his best, he had student loans to pay back and could barely help her with the utilities.

"How much?"

"Well let's see. A two-bedroom condo in Fort Greene...I'm willing to go as low as $2800. That's more than fair, right?"

"Okay."

"On the first of the month. And the insurance on the apartment, you can pay that mid-month if you'd like."

"Thanks."

Helen didn't really want the money. She wanted an apology and for things to go back to the way they were. But if Gotti had gotten anything from her mother it was her stubbornness. So she held her ground.

By the time Gotti got back to Geechi's house and emptied the grocery bags, La'Shea was at the door. She cut through the dining room and entered the foyer then opened the front door.

"Hey girl," Gotti greeted with a big smile.

"Hey domestic woman," La'Shea joked and hugged her.

"Follow me," Gotti said and led the way. The kitchen was attached to the living room, but the kitchen had marble floors and the living room was carpeted. On the right of the kitchen was the formal dining room.

"I settled on shrimp pasta," Gotti announced. "It's what all the girls cook in the books I read." She laughed.

"That's a good choice. Simple but good," La'Shea said approvingly. She began to survey the ingredients Gotti had set out. Next, she looked through Geechi's cabinets for everything else she might need. "You should have gotten more of this," La'Shea said, waving the Tony's Cajun seasoning bottle in the air. "It's low because he likes it," La'Shea informed her.

"Damn, I didn't think of that."

"You can run and get some while I cook," La'Shea suggested.

"I want to cook it," Gotti informed her.

"Why?" La'Shea questioned, looking back at her skeptically. That had to be the first time she heard Gotti say those words. Gotti could cook well enough to make sure she didn't starve, but it wasn't her forte.

"Because you cook better than me. What if he wants me to cook again and it doesn't taste the same," Gotti explained.

"But why do you care?" La'Shea pushed. Gotti rolled her eyes. "If you like him that's fine. I just want you to be honest. Don't lie to yourself," La'Shea told her.

"I'm not lying to myself, La'Shea. He's cool; we're cool. I believe in reciprocity," she told her.

"Okay," La'Shea replied. She dropped it to avoid sounding like the mother of the crew. La'Shea wished she knew what Geechi's feelings and intentions were. If he and Gotti were on the same page, La'Shea would have nothing to worry about, but if this was business for Geechi, it could lead to heartbreak for Gotti.

"Wine?" Gotti asked, pulling out a glass for herself and then looking back at La'Shea.

"Please," La'Shea said as she washed her hands and prepared to cook.

After two glasses of wine, gossiping about La'Bella and Troy and discussing the reception, the ladies had completed the meal. They decided there was no way around the reception. It had to happen, but maybe La'Shea and Troy could be in charge of it instead of Gina. And they still had to find a way to leave Helen out of it.

La'Shea packed two to-go plates for her and La'Bella and then Gotti walked her to the door.

"Thank you," Gotti said. The two hugged and then La'Shea left. Gotti checked her phone on the way upstairs, she had about forty-five minutes before Geechi was supposed to be home. Gotti needed to take a quick shower before he arrived but didn't want him to think she had *prepared* for him. She wanted it to seem casual, like she cooked and was wrapping it up as he walked in.

Upstairs, she grabbed a comfortable tunic and undergarments and went to take a shower. Gotti was back downstairs and in her spot at the stove when Geechi walked in.

"This is what I like to see," Geechi joked. Gotti playfully rolled her eyes. He walked up on her and peered over her shoulder into the pots. His back grazed her each time he checked a pot. He smelled good...felt good. Geechi lowered his face, "Thank you," he said and kissed her cheek.

"Geechi," she fussed, pushing him back.

"You like that shit," he said, walking away.

"You want me to fix your plate?" Gotti asked.

"Yea; let me go wash my hands and shit," he said, crossing the living room and walking down the hallway to his bedroom. When he came back, the kitchen table was set. Gotti looked back at Geechi as she filled her wine glass. He was dressed in a T-shirt and Nike sweats.

Gotti removed the chilled shot glass from the freezer, filled it with two shots of D'Usse and placed it in front on Geechi. He grabbed her place setting, which was across the table, and moved it to the chair that was beside him. Gotti didn't argue; she simply took her seat.

"Thank you, mama," he said. His sexy southern drawl sent tingles up her spine. She smiled and sipped her wine. Geechi grabbed Gotti's hand and lowered his head; she did the same and he said grace.

Gotti watched Geechi taste the pasta, broccoli and garlic bread. When he nodded his head approvingly, she relaxed.

"How was work?"

"Good. I missed you," he told her.

"Whatever," Gotti said as she wrapped the noodles around her fork, picked up a piece of shrimp and then put it in her mouth.

"Did you get any work done?" he asked. Gotti rolled her eyes because he knew she had battled a hangover earlier that day.

"Yea this," she said referring to the food.

"Who helped you cook?" Geechi wanted to know.

"I can cook," Gotti shot back.

"You did this by yourself?" he asked knowingly. Geechi had a security system on the house and knew when anyone approached his porch or entered his house.

"La'Shea dropped by, but I did most of it," Gotti said in a childlike voice.

"You did good," he said nudging her flirtatiously.

"Thank you," she smirked and danced in her seat.

"Mama said she called you earlier," Geechi mentioned. Gotti could tell by the way he brought it up, sat his fork down and eyed her that he wanted answers.

"Ye-yea the phone died," she lied.

"You called her back?" he inquired.

"Not yet, I got lost. I was driving in circles for ten minutes then when I figured it out, I was slightly irritated, then La'Shea was here and I just..." Gotti rambled until she had nothing else to say. He stared at her. Gotti didn't want him to think she was trying to disrespect his mother, so she huffed and decided to tell the truth.

As if he knew she was ready to be honest, Geechi picked up his fork and resumed eating as Gotti began to speak.

"I need to talk to you... about my mom," she said and took a sip of her drink.

"What about her?" he asked, taking a sip of his. She filled her mouth with broccoli and then a little pasta as she decided where to start.

"She's...mean. To me mainly, but sometimes to others," Gotti admitted with a shrug. Her eyes filled with tears that she quickly blinked away. "So I'm just not sure about a reception because I don't know how the families will mix, and I really like Mama Gina and Tione..."

"They not gon' stop fuckin' with you because of her," Geechi let Gotti know. "Now they might talk shit," he said.

"See and I want to avoid that too...because I mean, she is my mother," Gotti said. He knew that that meant she would have to defend her, and he respected it.

"She...we had a hard time before...with my first wedding," Gotti explained. "She can be...*bourgeois*," she said and posed like royalty to make him laugh. It worked.

"Oh so you get it honestly," he said.

"Whatever," Gotti replied and then told him the story about Helen not helping with her first wedding, being rude to Jeff, even before he deserved it, and showing up to her wedding in a $25,000 dress designed by Bridgette Campbell, the person Gotti wanted to design her wedding gown.

"And I know it's not a big deal," Gotti said fearing that she sounded like a spoiled brat.

"Yes, it is. It was vindictive...she did that to hurt you," Geechi said. She smiled, happy that he understood.

"Exactly!" she said. They were quiet for a moment as they enjoyed the food. Gotti felt a sense of relief because he understood her point and didn't judge her for her feelings. Troy and La'Shea viewed her as their little spoiled sister. While they used scholarships, loans and financial aid to pay for school, her mother sent a check. Plus, Helen loved them: smart powerful women who didn't take shit. Helen viewed them as peers because they too came from nothing and did extraordinarily well for themselves. And they respected her, so sometimes when Gotti wanted to vent, they wanted to tell her why her mother was the way she was instead of just being her friends and understanding that she knew a different Helen than they did.

"Tell me about him," Geechi said. Gotti knew he was talking about Jeff.

"What about him?"

"Why didn't it work?"

"I told you...he wanted a housekeeper," she answered and then looked up at him. She knew she couldn't get out of the conversation, so she sighed and got up. "I need more wine for this," Gotti said. She filled her glass, refilled his plate and had a seat. "He wanted the divorce. He said it was because I was a bad wife," she told him. The way Jeff behaved during their divorce still hurt Gotti. "...I was never home but somebody had to pay the rent." She chuckled. "The reason why I was serious about the prenup and with making sure you knew I wouldn't try to take your money is because I know how that feels.

"He tried to sue me for my inheritance," she admitted. Gotti forced a smile but wished she hadn't when the tears fell. "He wanted alimony too because of the life I had provided for him. We stayed in Fort Greene in a condo with a balcony...he wanted that but not me." Geechi didn't know much about New York but assumed that was a good area to live in. "I didn't have money for a lawyer, but if I would have let him take Mama's stuff, she woulda..." Gotti's sentence trailed off as she shook her head. "I called my mama," she said with a shrug as if she had failed in some way. Gotti wished she could have handled it alone, and when she couldn't, Gotti felt like what Helen, and sometimes her best friends, thought about her was true.

"You were supposed to," Geechi told Gotti, grabbing her hand. "She is your mother, shit, what else was you supposed to do other than call her?"

"It's...it's just the way she makes me feel when I need her," Gotti said and lowered her head to silently sobbed. Geechi pulled her to him, and she rested her head on his shoulder. After a minute or two she sat back up and laughed. Gotti grabbed a napkin and cleaned her face. "She took care of it," Gotti let him know with a smile and a head nod. A month after the divorce was finalized, Gotti moved to a more affordable apartment in Crown Heights. She thought taking care of herself would make Helen respect her.

"But that's why I'm so nervous about another marriage...even if it's not real. I mean I didn't talk to her about it; she's gonna think I can't handle it," Gotti told him.

"We don't need her financially. All she has to do is come and have a good time. You don't need her to fix shit. You got it and I got you," he told her.

"So you still wanna have it?"

"Hell yea; my people excited. They love a good party and liquor. I think it can be fun for y'all to plan," he let her know.

"But like I told you, she kept pointing out stuff at the first wedding and—"

"You wanna ball out on the reception to shut your mother up?" Geechi replied knowing what she was trying to say.

"I know it's petty," Gotti said scrunching up her face. He pulled out his wallet and placed his credit card on the table in front of her.

"Ball out," he instructed. "The dress from Bridgette Campbell, whatever venue Tione suggests, the cake, the food; everything you wanted the first time." Bridgette Campbell was a black dress maker who had traveled and lived overseas to learn the art of dress making and material. Bridgette brought that knowledge back to America and added her creative flair to design the most breathtaking dresses.

"You sure? I mean I have money too. I'm gonna—"

"It's on me."

Gotti grabbed his face and kissed him. When she realized she was tonguing him down, Gotti stopped but was still in his embrace. Geechi smiled and bit his lip. He inched closer to her and kissed her cheek.

"My bad," she said. "I just—"

Geechi kissed Gotti this time, twirling his tongue in her mouth erased her worry. Gotti matched his vigor leaning up on her knee so that she could kiss him deeper. His hand cuffed her ass. She stopped.

"That's all I get?"

"I'm not fucking for a reception."

"What would you fuck for?" Geechi asked ready to give up any car on his showroom floor.

"Goodbye sir," she said, standing up. He stood up too blocking her in.

"I just want to know…seriously what would you give this pussy up for?" he asked, sliding his hand up her dress and running his thumb down the center of her pussy.

"Love," she said, stepping back and slapping his hand.

"You a damn lie. You on that feminist shit y'all fuck 'cause y'all want to. Yo ass scared of me," he said, walking his plate to the sink.

"Scared?" she chuckled.

"Hell yea," he said, walking out of the kitchen.

Chapter 11

"Hey Terrell! What are you doing here?" Gotti said with a big smile and hugged him. She had just walked into the lobby of Koran Motors and he was standing by Tione's desk talking to her.

"Geechi's letting me use one of his cars for prom," he said, stepping back so that Gotti could take in his ensemble.

"Okay, okay I see you looking dapper," she said. Terrell threw his hands up and did an old school one-two step. Gotti and Tione laughed at him. His jovial mood made Gotti think back to when she first met him and how his life could be on a different path right now. She smiled, proud of the influence Geechi had.

"And who is this?" Gotti asked, giving her attention to the young lady approaching them. Her hunter green, mermaid style dress matched his suit.

He beamed. "My date. Reagan, this is Geechi's wife; Gotti, this is Reagan," he said.

"Oh my god, you're so beautiful," Reagan gushed. "Terrell has told me so much about y'all."

"Thank you," Gotti said. "You look stunning!" Just then Geechi came from the back waving the keys at Terrell. Everyone laughed and cheered as Geechi led the way outside. The car had been cleaned and pulled to the front of the building for Terrell. After a few pictures and a brief reminder course on the car, Terrell and Reagan hopped inside.

Everyone watched Terrell drive off in the pearl white Bentley Continental.

"Now, Geechi, I done already told you I can't afford—" Lucindi began to fuss.

"I took him to test drive it three times," Geechi said cutting her off. "He's good." She gave him a wide grin and they hugged.

"Thank you, Geechi, for everything," she said. After saying goodbye to Lucindi and the family of Terrell's date, Geechi, Gotti and Tione headed back in the shop. Tione got busy with work at her desk while Geechi and Gotti headed to his office.

"We got plans tonight," he told her, closing his office door.

"What plans?" Gotti asked, looking at him skeptically as she leaned against his desk.

"Husband and wife plans," he said, stepping in front on her and placing his hands at her sides.

"Geechi," she said in a disciplinary tone.

"You remember Brinks, right?" Geechi asked stepping out of her personal space. Brinks and a few others owned a shopping center in South Dallas. It housed stores for clothes, hair electronics, you name it, they had it. Geechi and Gotti had gone out with him before and while Brinks was clearly the man, women still found themselves vying for Geechi's attention. They couldn't help themselves; there was something about him that made people want to be near him.

"Yea I remember."

"One of his business partners is out in LA. They own some weed spots out there," Geechi told her. "Anyway, they're coming back in town, so everyone is meeting up at Member's Only."

"Member's Only?" she asked. When Gotti started working for Geechi, she made it her business to know about all the popular spots so she could make sure he was connected to them.

"It's privileged information," he said with a smile.

"If you know, you know," she said, using the motto for Koran Motors. There were billboards along all major highways in the DFW with a picture of his grandfather's watch and the words *If you know, you know*.

"Be ready at nine," he instructed. Geechi went to sit behind his desk and opened his laptop.

"Are you throwing me out?" Gotti asked.

"As nicely as possible," the handsome young boss said with a smile.

●●●

Member's Only was a beautiful restaurant owned by Mekkhi West, a friend of Geechi's who Gotti had never met. The elegant décor and breathtaking furniture gave off a feeling of power and money. Brinks had reserved a room where only their crew gathered to welcome home his business partners, Scotti, Tommie and Nina. Scotti and Tommie were married, and Nina was Tommie's identical twin sister.

As Gotti watched Geechi move around the room it reminded her of the things she admired and respected about him. Gotti had seen him move around banquet dinners for politicians, his nonprofit events filled with kids and their parents and now a room full of self-made millionaires. And in every situation, Geechi moved around comfortably, effortlessly carrying conversations and with a swagger that demanded attention.

"Congratulations," a beautiful brown-skinned woman dressed in a form-fitting Balmain dress said, sitting next to Gotti. "Brinks is my husband," she said, extending her hand.

"Hi. It's nice to meet you," Gotti said with a big smile. The ladies shook hands. "I'm Gotti. That's beautiful," she said taking in her gigantic wedding ring.

"Thank you. I'm Chanel. This is my little pup, Justene," Chanel said, pulling a tall, slim woman to her. Justene looked like she would give any model past or present a run for their money.

"Bitch fuck you!" Justene said, pulling away from her.

"Come here, you know you're my baby," Chanel said.

"I'm Justene not her lil pup even though she is older than me. I'm sure you can tell," Justene teased as she sat beside Chanel. But both women looked young, vibrant and beautiful. Justene was dressed in a sleeveless peach dress; it pushed up her barely-there breasts and contoured her slender frame. Gotti took in the Red Bottoms on her feet and smiled approvingly.

"She's married to Chuck. Quiet dude in the back," Chanel said and pointed. Chuck was off to the side, but he didn't look left-out, more like he was taking in the atmosphere.

"Everybody in here is married?" Gotti asked.

"Yup no single bitches," Justene said. "Well Tommie," she said and made a face at Chanel. Chanel laughed and nodded her head at the girl who resembled Young MA.

"If I didn't see how lovingly you were just gazing at Geechi, I wouldn't have come over. 'Cause there are bitches in relationships that still try to get close to our men," Chanel said.

"Facts," Justene said.

"And we'll really kill a bitch," Chanel said.

"Period," Justene added.

Gotti's eyes fell on a chocolate goddess dressed in a grey Francesco Murano minidress with strappy heels. She was in a circle of men having a conversation.

"That my sister-in-law SB," Chanel told Gotti.

"She's married to Mays, dread head with his hand on her ass," Justene informed Gotti.

"Duh," Chanel said and playfully bumped Justene.

"She knows Mays?" Justene asked.

"She knows he would have to be her husband," Chanel said.

"Maybe she's having an affair. We might be those types of wives," Justene said.

"Write a book," Chanel said, and they all laughed.

"You met Scotti and Tommie, right?"

"Yes," Gotti said.

"Well," Chanel said with a shrug as they stood up, "Welcome."

"To the Gangsta Wives Club," Justene laughed.

"Goofy," Chanel said, wrapping her arm around Justene's waist as they walked off. It was at that moment that Gotti realized Chanel was saying congratulations on their marriage.

A few minutes later, Geechi sat next to Gotti.

"You good?" he asked.

"Of course," she replied with a lazy grin.

"Normally you up moving around," Geechi said.

"Normally it's work; this feels like a vibe. I like it," Gotti said.

"Yea they cool folk."

"Did you know everybody in here is married?" she said.

"Yea. All powerful men need an equally powerful woman; that's all I've been trying to tell you," Geechi said gazing into her eyes.

Gotti looked out at the room. "This is a brand," she told him.

"Man you not working, remember? Come on, let me introduce you to everybody," Geechi said pulling her up.

Chapter 12

Troy had just gone down to the front desk to pick up her meal delivered by DoorDash and to collect her mail. After walking into her 1500 square foot apartment, she locked the door and headed to the balcony. Sitting on the patio furniture, Troy opened the chicken fried rice while taking in the view. She and Dominic had had a very promising meeting with Locke & Marks about becoming their accountants. Troy was proud as she watched Dominic confidently take control of the meeting; he was knowledgeable, patient when they needed further explanation, and comfortable. The savvy CPA had moved around their conference room like it was his, making sure to keep the partners interested. Numbers could be boring, but Dominic's presentation keep them engaged.

When his name popped up on the screen, Troy smiled before answering the call.

"Mr. McCoy," she said unable to hide the joy in her voice.

"Ms. Matthews," Dominic replied. "How has your day been?" he asked.

"Stop playing and get to it...they called, huh?"

"Hell yea they called!" Dominic said, and she heard the excitement in his voice.

"See, son, I told you to follow me and I'd lead you to success," Troy joked, taking a bite of her food.

"There you go, ruining the moment," he replied.

"My fault. I'm proud of you. I knew it was ours by the way you handled the meeting. You were very comfortable," she said.

"What, you thought I would fumble...stutter...need you to jump in? I'm a grown ass man, Troy," he reminded her.

"I know," Troy said, picturing Dominic in that Brooks Brothers suit that contoured to his muscular frame better than any dress could shape hers. And Troy had a seamstress that made sure her clothes fit her toned frame like a glove. Built like Kelly Rowland, Troy worked out daily and ate right to ensure that she stayed in shape.

"Let's celebrate."

"I was hoping you'd say that," Troy replied.

"Dinner and then that Jamaican club you like?" Dominic suggested.

"I have a flight early tomorrow, maybe just dinner," she replied. The Jamaican club almost got her in trouble the last time they went.

"Nah just the club then...it opens at eight...we'll just vibe for a few hours. I'll come get you at 8:30," Dominic said and hung up before she could protest.

Troy sat back for a moment wondering if she should text Dominic and tell him she couldn't make it. The truth was the workaholic wanted to go dance, drink and enjoy Dominic's company. Troy decided not to overthink it and instead to go out, have fun and celebrate their success.

Hours later, Troy was double checking her appearance in the floor length mirror in her bedroom. She wanted to wear a dress but knew it would restrict her from dancing so instead she wore a pink cat suit with slits that exposed her side boob, hugged her fit body and gave her room to dance. Troy slid on nude heels just as there was a knock at the door. Jimmy, the doorman, had called to make sure it was okay to let Dominic up. She grabbed her clutch, pink and beige two-toned fur and headed for the door.

"Damn," Dominic said.

"You wanna come in for a drink?"

"Nah, you gotta be in early; let's go." Dominic helped Troy into her coat, she locked up the apartment and they made their way to his car.

"I like this," Troy said as Dominic whipped through the streets in his Wraith. The ride was smooth in the luxury vehicle. She drove a Bentley while in New York, and a Range Rover when she was at her place in LA so she could appreciate a luxury car.

"Thank you," he said.

"How long have you had it?"

"Few months," he answered. "I wasn't sure if I wanted it at first, but I decided to treat myself, ya know?"

"Yea, I know."

"I thought you would."

"Uh-hmm." She cleared her throat. "How is Chrissy? I heard she's back."

"She's been back for a minute now. She's good, married, pregnant with baby number two," he informed her.

"Good for them," Troy said with a genuine smile. "They are proof that it's all going to work how it's supposed to."

"Hell yea...they went through a lot, spent six years apart," Dominic said thinking about his sister's relationship. She had moved to the Dominican Republic for six years running from her love for Rambo. But it was too powerful.

"Then she was older when she got pregnant. Her pregnancy was safe, the baby is good," she said.

"Is that something you worry about?" Dominic asked. Troy hadn't meant to allude to that. She was thirty-eight and had decided she had given up the opportunity to have kids by focusing on her career. It wasn't what Troy meant to happen, but she wasn't about to live her life with regrets.

"No...I use to. Do you want kids?" she asked trying to get the heat off her.

"Maybe one. You?"

"I think I chose my career."

"Think?"

"I'm thirty-eight, I mean I could do IVF..." She shrugged and paused for a brief moment. "It's not something I think about anymore. I've accepted what is supposed to happen will," she replied.

"I have enough nieces and nephews, shit. I don't have to have kids; I spend so much time with them."

"How many you have now?"

"Five and they ain't stopping no time soon."

"But you want at least one," Troy said referring to him having kids.

"And you'll try IVF if the natural way doesn't work," Dominic said.

They looked at each other; they hadn't meant to have that conversation and yet they both knew what it meant.

"You'll find a pretty girl to give you as many babies as you want," she said; nervousness tracing her body.

"I know," he said with a confident smirk.

●●●

They were on their third Hennessy and lemonade or maybe it was the fourth. Either way they were on the dancefloor looking more like a couple in love than business partners. Troy wound her body into him, and Dominic matched every twirl of her hips with a powerful thrust of his own. He held her like she belonged to him and she completely released her inhibitions and submitted to him moving how he requested going faster or slower at his command. Dominic's hands caressed her; Troy bucked on him. Her temperature rose, her heartrate increased and as she released her second orgasm Troy wondered when they had gone from dancing to fucking.

"Shit," Troy panted. Her body went limp and she fell on his chest. He held her hips and thrust deep into her from the bottom. Dominic squeezed her ass cheeks so hard he brought her back to life. Troy threw herself up and down his thick dick until he exploded. Troy rested on his chest until their heartrates decreased. He ran his hand through her hair. It felt good: the sex, the embrace, his hands on her.

"We need to shower," Dominic said.

"You gotta go?" she asked.

"Nah. But we skipped a lot of steps because you were..." Dominic didn't finish the sentence but they both thought back to how Troy had gotten her first orgasm as they danced on the dancefloor. *Troy was grinding into him, Dominic hardened, she didn't move and neither did he. The muscular beau palmed Troy's ass as she did her thing, working her body and gyrating to the beat. Her bud blossomed and thundered with each graze of his dick. Until...*

Troy looked embarrassed when she moaned into Dominic's ear; he looked down at her knowingly. Dominic kissed her, deep and hard and Troy gave up any will she thought she had.

"I want you," Troy admitted, grabbing his hand and heading for the bathroom. Dominic had bigger plans for her, so he directed her to the front. Valet brought the car around and they sped to her place. She was insatiable, jerking him off, kissing his neck, tongue kissing him at red lights.

When Troy tried to give him head, he stopped her; now he wanted to take her up on her offer.

"I want to start from the beginning and do everything," Dominic told Troy. She looked down at him like a schoolgirl in love. He carried her to the bathroom kissing her along the way. Once inside, Troy started the shower and they climbed in. They kissed, took turns cleaning each other's backs and he gave her a few moments to thoroughly clean her important spots while he did the same.

They couldn't even make it out of the bathroom before Dominic lifted her, sat her on the counter and tongue kissed her center. Savagely, he spread her legs and sucked hard on her clit. Troy's back arched in delight as Dominic's tongue roamed all the peaks and valleys of her pussy. Lifting her left leg, Troy pulled his face deeper into her and grinded on his face. Dominic stuck his tongue in her tunnel and let her buck and twirl as he flicked against her G-spot. With his lips still sucking the life out of her pussy, he lifted Troy off the counter and sat on the ottoman to the right of the sink. Engulfed in pleasure, Troy threw her head back and rode his face until her juices smeared all over his mouth and chin.

"Oh my God," Troy panted trying to gain her bearings. Dominic lowered her to his lap. Their tongues danced as she grinded against him before seductively sinking to her knees. In one slurp Troy took Dominic's ten-inch manhood into her mouth slobbering over his length to get it sloppy wet. Troy used both hands to caress Dominic's shaft as she sucked his head with such fervor, he was climbing the walls. Watching his mentor please him with such passion turned Dominic on beyond anything he could imagine. She licked up and down his shaft to tease him and then took the head in her mouth sucking with the suction of a vacuum cleaner.

"Fuck!" Dominic groaned as his nut built. Feeling him squirm under her touch was an ego booster; Troy started sucking harder, sloppier.

"I'm 'bout ta bust," he warned, pushing her back. Troy looked up at him as she deep throated him. Mesmerized and unable to contain himself, Dominic shot his seed down her throat. She swallowed, winked and then got up to brush her teeth. When she finished, Dominic was still on the ottoman staring at her.

"Come on, baby," Troy whined as she grabbed his hand and pulled him up. "My flight is at eight," she said.

"You gotta give me a minute," he said, following her to the bedroom.

They didn't stop fucking until it was time for her to leave the house. Luckily, she didn't have to pack. Troy grabbed her laptop, cellphones and knew anything else she needed was at her apartment in LA. She hopped right off his dick and into some sweats and the T-shirt Dominic had worn under his Christian Dior collared shirt. Troy felt dirty but she would shower as soon as she got to LA.

"When you coming back?" Dominic asked when they pulled up to her gate at the airport. Troy leaned over to kiss him, her scent was on his face; she smiled and savored the taste.

"I don't know, baby. You know I live in LA too." She swirled her tongue in his mouth and lazily he matched her kiss. Blaring horns forced them to release each other.

"Call when you get there," Dominic said.

"Okay," Troy said, stealing one last kiss.

●●●

"What are you doing?" Geechi asked, startling Gotti. It was 11pm and she was in the dark kitchen with only the light from the refrigerator shining as she dug through containers of food. "Scary ass!" He teased.

"Shut up," Gotti said with her left hand still over her chest and her right halfway to her mouth. Gotti rolled her eyes and stuffed the turnip greens in her mouth.

"That chicken tetrazzini good, huh?" He chortled. Gotti hadn't been home since their kiss, so Geechi cooked and lured her home with pictures of the spread. She smiled and then dug into the container of cold chick tetrazzini again.

"I just wanted a few bites," she said, closing the containers. Geechi grabbed the fork from her and took a few bites as well.

"Yo ass can't sleep?" he asked after guzzling down half a bottle of water.

"No," Gotti said with a huff. Geechi closed the refrigerator door and the kitchen became completely dark.

"Movie night?" he suggested, grabbing Gotti's hand and leading her through the living room. She smiled thinking about how much fun they had when they met in the loft to enjoy 90s movies.

"Yea and it's my turn to pick," Gotti said. Upstairs, she stopped in her bedroom to get the big comforter and then met him in the loft. Geechi grabbed a few snacks from the bar area and had them laid out on the couch.

"What we watching?" he asked getting comfortable in his seat. Gotti sat on one side of the couch, he was on the other and the snacks were in the middle. The couple reclined their seats as Gotti pulled up *The Best Man*.

"Your real name is Geechi?" she asked. They were on the bachelor's party scene when the thought crossed her mind.

"You know that's my real name," he said and threw a Chip Ahoy! crumb at her.

She laughed. "Why is that your name?"

"My granddad's family is from the deep south...Savannah. He's Gullah," Geechi told her. "He always talked about going to visit and how big they were on African pride and spirituality. They have their own language called Geechee. My mama, pregnant and sentimental, was moved by it. She named me Geechi," he explained.

"I bet he loved that."

"Hell yea. Now why is your name Gotti?" he asked.

She shrugged. "It ain't deep like yours. My mama just wanted me to have a gangsta ass name, so people knew not to fuck with me. She pictured me walking into board meetings with the name. She thought it made a statement."

"You do walk into board meetings with that name. And that shit definitely makes a statement," he told her. They stared at one another for a moment. When she smiled, he threw a Milk Duds candy at her. Gotti ate it and then playfully swung at him; Geechi grabbed her arm, pulling her to him as he stretched out on the couch. Gotti laughed and tried to fight him.

"Chill," he said. "Ya favorite part is coming on."

Gotti attempted to sit back up. Geechi had kicked the snacks to her end of the couch and was lying back. "Lay down," Geechi said, pulling her to his chest.

"Nope!" she said.

"Look at this shit. Why you like when that man get his ass beat?" he said.

"He needed his ass beat," Gotti said, relaxing in Geechi's embrace and watching the balcony scene. She didn't lay her head on his chest, but she laid on her side beside him while he laid on his back.

"You like violence, that's why ya mama named you Gotti," he joked.

"Whatever!"

"You gon' hit her up tomorrow...about the reception?" Geechi asked, looking over at her. "I already told you I want to meet her before the reception."

"I know."

Geechi could sense her apprehension. "You want Daddy to be with you when you do it?"

"Bye," Gotti said, climbing over him and pulling her blanket with her. Geechi laughed as he watched Gotti exit the loft heading to her bedroom.

●●●

"To what do I owe the pleasure of a call from my only child?" Helen said. Tabitha had handed her the phone after announcing that it was Gotti.

"I'm married and I want you to meet my husband and come to our reception," Gotti blurted out while pacing the floor of Geechi's office. Geechi had insisted on meeting Helen before the reception so that Helen would know he wasn't someone she needed to try to bully. Geechi figured knowing that he could afford the life she envisioned for Gotti would put her at ease.

"I'm not paying for a reception," Helen said, rolling her eyes and looking up at Tabitha shaking her head.

"I don't need your money. I'm married to Geechi Koran he owns Koran Motors," Gotti said knowing Helen would look up the company.

"Listen, Gotti, I don't have time for this. You don't listen and I'm not saving you again."

"We will be in New York in two weeks so that I can start the designs for my dress."

"Bridgette?"

"Yup!" Gotti beamed.

"Hmm, we had dinner a few nights go." Helen said thoroughly impressed. Something off the rack would set Gotti back a pretty penny, so having the money to have a dress designed specifically for Gotti had Helen intrigued.

"Can we have lunch?"

"Text Tabitha the exact day and time. I'll pencil you in. He's going with you to get the dress? That's bad luck."

"We're already married, Mama. This is just the reception," Gotti said. Geechi wasn't going with her, but Gotti knew if Helen thought he was she wouldn't invite herself.

"What, did you have another shot-gun wedding?"

"Aren't shot-gun weddings when the bride is pregnant?"

"So smart in some areas but stupid in others," Helen hissed irritated that Gotti was trying to correct her. "Why did you rush to marry this one?" she asked.

"Because I love him, and he loves me and that's all that matters to us. I'm having the reception and inviting you at *his* request." Gotti tried not to, but she couldn't help but take a dig at Helen for all the digs she had taken at her.

"And you can afford this? I mean you just got your business up and running you can't be making that much money."

"He does."

"Hmm," was all Helen said.

"I'll see you Wednesday, Mama," Gotti said in an upbeat tone.

"I'll see you Wednesday," Helen said and hung up.

After the phone call, Gotti sank into the couch and sighed. She was dressed in a white pantsuit with cheetah print pumps. She wore a short, blonde wig that was cut into a stylish, layered Bob and parted to the side. When the office door opened, Gotti looked up and used her right hand to push her hair out of her face.

"How'd it go?" Geechi asked as he sat beside his wife and handed her a shot of D'Usse.

"Good," Gotti said, taking the shot and setting the cup on the table.

"Damn that was a double." He laughed.

"She stresses me," she admitted. Geechi handed her his drink and massaged her shoulders.

"Baby, if she looks you up, nothing with the case will come up, right" Gotti asked in deep thought.

"Baby?"

"What?" she asked, confusion etched on her face.

"You called me baby...it's cool, I just—"

"No, I didn't," Gotti said. She rolled her eyes and adjusted in the seat so Geechi couldn't massage her shoulders. He laughed; she was fighting him hard but losing miserably.

"No, nothing with the case will come up; why?"

"I told her your name; she'll look you up; which I want her to do, but then I thought about the case," she let him know. "Has Barry said anything else?" Gotti asked referring to his lawyer. Since she had told La'Shea about the charges, Gotti would call her periodically with questions. La'Shea originally wanted to practice criminal law but settled for corporate, so Gotti knew she looked forward to her questions and enjoyed doing research for her.

"No," he answered and then looked down at her lips. Gotti turned from him; she had been steering clear of him since the kiss in the kitchen. Last night was her first night back at his house after a couple nights at La'Shea's condo.

"I'ma see you tonight, right?" he asked.

"Yea; I was helping La'Shea with La'Bella, because she went out of town," Gotti explained. Geechi nodded and stood up. She felt like he always knew when she was lying.

"Okay," he said. "You can work in my office if you need to. I'm gone for the day. I'll see you at home."

●●●

It was late when Gotti came home with food. She found Geechi hard at work in his office. He saw her in the doorway, smiled and went to greet her, taking the bag of food from her hand. She followed Geechi to the leather sofa, he opened the to-go boxes from Olive Garden and they silently ate in his office. Afterwards, Gotti took the trash to the kitchen and came back in. Geechi was now at his desk checking a few emails.

"Who is this?" Gotti asked, looking at the old picture on Geechi's desk. She recognized his grandfather, Macc, who he and

Tione called Pops, from photos at the shop, but she didn't know the other man.

"My dad and Pops," he answered.

"Oh," Gotti said.

"What?" Geechi asked after watching her facial expression.

"Nothing I..." Gotti said then stopped. She was trying to figure out how Tione was his sister but didn't know if it was a touchy subject. Gotti knew Geechi inherited the business from his paternal grandfather, and Geechi had said their grandfather taught them the business. With that, Gotti thought Tione and Geechi had the same mother and father. Now she was seeing his father and knew he wasn't Tione's dad.

"You're wondering how they created Tione?" Geechi asked. Gotti looked at him apologetically and he laughed. Geechi knew what Gotti was thinking because the question had followed them through grade school.

"I mean I know black people come in all shades, but Tione is..." she said, sitting on the desk. He walked around the front of the desk and stood in front of her.

"She's mixed," Geechi said confirming her thoughts.

"Yea. And I thought y'all had the same father, because I know you inherited the business from your father's side, right?" she asked.

"Yea."

"So..."

"Mama ain't her biological Mama, but she raised her since she was five," Geechi told Gotti.

"Oh okay," Gotti said. She wanted to know more but couldn't tell if he wanted to divulge more information and didn't want to be pushy.

"Tione's biological mother, Corrina, and my mother were best friends. That's how my mama met my daddy. When Corrina died...well was killed by Tione's father, my mother took her in," Geechi revealed.

"I'm sorry to hear that," Gotti said. "I never even thought Mama Gina wasn't her biological mother," she said. Geechi took in her expression; she was both sad and confused.

"What Gotti?" he asked, taking a seat on the sofa.

"I still don't understand the connection," she said.

"My dad and Corrina are half brother and sister. Technically, me and Tione are cousins. Macc cheated on my grandmother with Tione's. She thought he would leave my grandmother for her, but he didn't. Even though he cheated, his loyalty lied with the woman who had always had his back. Alondra, Tione's grandmother, went back to her husband."

"Wait she was married too?" Gotti gasped. This story was better than a soap opera.

"Yea and they had kids," Geechi said and couldn't help but to chuckle.

"And she left her husband for your grandfather?"

"Maybe that's what she thought she was doing, but Pops was just having fun. Alondra went back to her family and had Corrina when he cut ties with her."

"Who is Tione's mother," Gotti interjected, making sure she was keeping up with the story.

"Yes," he answered.

"Corrina became friends with Gina, Gina was introduced to..." Gotti paused because she didn't know Geechi's father's name.

"Lorenzo," he answered.

"And where is he?" she asked.

He shrugged. "Around."

"Oh," she said and studied his face. Geechi ice-grilled her refusing to show weakness. Gotti went to him, sat on his lap and kissed his cheek. "So Lorenzo and Gina get together and have you..."

"Yup," he confirmed.

"Corrina passes. Gina adopts Tione?"

"Not officially, but yea."

"What happened with Pops?" Gotti asked. Geechi told her Pops died but never went into detail.

"He died four years ago. Lung cancer. He could never leave cigarettes alone."

"I'm sorry," Gotti said and hugged him. He held her for a moment then released her.

"You ain't the only one with a fucked-up family. Ya mom and dad still together?" he asked.

"Hell no!" She got up and walked to the window. "They met after college; he has a master's degree in engineering so I guess she thought they would make a good couple. My mom is all about business. She only wanted to get married for the gala and fundraiser appearances. She loves work, business functions, success. My dad didn't like the corporate, dog eat dog world. He wanted more kids and he wanted to fulfill his purpose."

"And moms wasn't having it," he interjected.

"At all!" Gotti walked back to his desk and sat on top of it.

"Working in Child Protective Services is an emotionally taxing job, ya know. Trying to help all those families. So when he came home, he wanted support...love, not arguing."

"He left her?"

"No, she cheated and got pregnant."

"Wait, I thought you were her only child. She got an abortion?"

"No." She paused for a moment and took a deep breath. Gotti had never shared this with anyone. She didn't even tell La'Shea and Troy, Helen did. Gotti was embarrassed...ashamed and had never talked to them about it. "She had me," Gotti said with tears in her eyes. "My dad was with her at all her doctor's appointments, the other guy...the sperm donor... was too busy. I met him once. They're a lot alike; he didn't want a kid either. I'm so happy my dad stepped up. You would think that would make her love him...she resented him though. She left him when I was six."

"Damn."

"He remarried; they have two kids," Gotti let him know. "His wife doesn't know I'm not his."

"That's real," Geechi said because her father had stepped up and protected her in more ways than one.

"I want you to meet him, but he'll be disappointed when he finds out it's not real," Gotti let him know. Geechi was great, perfect to her and for her but he wasn't hers. And although things had started to feel real, they weren't, and she didn't want to play with her father like that. Geechi walked to her.

"What if it is real; what if this is how it happened for us?" he asked, standing between her thighs.

"Stop playing," Gotti said and bumped him as she hopped off the desk.

"I feel about my mom how you feel about your dad, and I shared her with you," he said, grabbing her hand and pulling her into his arms.

"Okay," Gotti said before wiggling out of his embrace and heading to her bedroom.

Chapter 13

Geechi looked up on the security monitor and saw a familiar face roaming around the lobby. He watched the intruder for a few moments before he got out of his chair and made his way to the front. Tione was gone for the day which meant the building should have been locked up. With the way she rushed out to make it to her eyelash appointment, he wasn't surprised that she had forgotten.

On the inside Geechi's body was on fire, but he steadied his breathing and allowed his casual stroll to lead the way.

"Donny!" he greeted with his arms outstretched. Geechi knew he hated that name but so what? Donny also hated Geechi, and Geechi shared that sentiment.

"The place looks nice," Donny replied taking in the expensive décor. At the reveal party, Donny didn't really get to see the décor because of the party decorations.

"But that's not what you're here for, and let's be honest you can't afford one of my cars so..." Geechi said and paused to let his harsh words penetrated Donny's hate-filled heart. "What can I help you with?" Geechi finally asked.

"Where did you get the money?" Donny asked, figuring beating around the bush was pointless. With their history, they both knew he wasn't there for a social visit.

"Excuse me?" Geechi questioned.

"You revamped this place...totally redesigned it. The cars are impeccable..." The compliment tasted like shit coming off Donny's tongue.

"Cars aren't really your thing," Geechi replied.

"They were my grandfather's thing," Donny seethed.

"Oh really?" Geechi chuckled, "Mine too." He watched as Donny's ivory skin turned beet red. One of the things white privilege couldn't save him from.

"Your grandfather was a thief!" Donny fumed, now inches from Geechi's face.

Geechi smiled, taking in the amount of anger Donny possessed, and his inability to compose it. Geechi loosened his tie; then he wiped nonexistent wrinkles from his thousand-dollar button up only to allow his hand to run over his diamond incrusted cufflink.

"In your line of business you should really be able to control your emotions a little better. The only thing my grandfather ever stole was your grandmother," Geechi chuckled. "And he gave her back, but what thanks does he get for that?"

"He impregnated her and abandoned her," Donny accused.

"He went back home to his wife...where he belonged. You just missed Tione by the way," Geechi said.

Michael Costa, Donny's grandfather, was a helpless, hopeless drunk. He'd owned a dealership where he fixed high-end cars, but his family lived slightly above poverty because he would gamble and drink the money away before his wife or kids saw a penny. He ended up forfeiting the shop to cover a gambling debt and Macc, Geechi and Tione's grandfather, bought it. Because Macc had worked for Michael he thought Macc should just give him back the shop, but Macc loved cars. He always had and without him fixing up the cars, Michael would have never made a dime.

Michael went around bashing Macc trying to stop him from getting any business, but it didn't work. Then Michael tried to start another shop but without his handy man, it failed. Alondra had been having an affair with Macc on and off for a year before Michael lost the shop. She ended up leaving Michael and their three kids to be Macc's mistress. When she got pregnant, Alondra wanted more but Macc couldn't give it to her. As much as he liked her and their arrangement, he loved his wife, Ruby, and the life they had built together. Ruby had taught him the importance of saving, and it was equally his money and hers that allowed him to purchase the shop. Soon, Alondra went back home and even tried to pass Corrina off as Michael's, but when she was born everyone knew.

They shared custody and Macc paid child support which helped to keep Michael and his family afloat. When Corrina was sixteen, she went to live with Macc and for the most part cut off all contact with her mother and stepfather.

Geechi's mother and father had a brief romance, but he was a ladies' man who liked to party while Gina was looking for something more concrete. When Tione was five, her mother was murdered by her abusive father; Gina took in Tione which sealed the bond between Geechi and Tione making them siblings instead of cousins. Macc had a very close relationship with his grandchildren, he taught them the business and then left it to Geechi instead of his children.

"You're up to something. You're nothing but a thug just like your grandfather and father. I have the resources and the manpower to get the evidence I need. And I will. Count your days," Donny stated.

That statement shook Geechi. A clerk in the prosecutor's office had informed him that a case was presented to the District Attorney regarding his dealership. Apparently while delivering lunch to the DA and a colleague, she heard him casually mention the possibility of the case and the charges it could hold. The DA was interested in the case, but he had rejected it because the detectives didn't have enough evidence at the time. That was all the information the clerk was able to obtain. She didn't have a strong enough relationship with anyone in the prosecutor's office to ask for more information, so she didn't know which detective or even department was pursuing the case.

For a moment Geechi had begun to get comfortable thinking the trial would never happen. Now he knew it would and who was behind it.

"Give it up, Donny," Geechi said calmly. "This is getting embarrassing, don't you think? Let your drunk ass granddaddy rest in peace."

"Not until I have our shop back," Donny said.

"The door," Geechi said, pointing at the double doors. He stood confidently with his hands crossed over his lap as he watched Donny reluctantly head for the door. Geechi bit his bottom lip and waited a few moments before he went to lock the door. Before he could turn the lock, the door flew open almost hitting him in the face.

"What is it?" Gotti asked as she walked in with her computer in her hand. She had come in to show him the positive coverage they had been receiving, but the scowl, which had dissipated into a sullen look on his face, stopped her in her tracks.

"You almost took my head off," he said and turned to head to his office.

Back in his office, he sank into his couch and let out a deep sigh. He couldn't lose his grandfather's shop; it meant too much to him and all the people he loved.

"Something else is wrong," she said. Gotti set her computer on the table and joined him on the couch. "Talk to me. I need to know what's going on," Gotti said in full PR mode.

"Nothing," Geechi said, adjusting himself in his seat. He ran his hand down his mug trying to remove the look of agony that he knew decorated his face. Geechi was shook by Donny's words. He didn't even know where to start to comprehend them. Was someone snitching? Had officers been following him?

"Who was the guy that just left the shop?"

"Nobody Gotti, damn; Tione must have forgotten to lock up," he replied.

"No she didn't. I was on the phone with her. Carl was out there when she left; he said he'd do it," Gotti revealed.

"He's still here?" Geechi asked with his face scrunched up.

"I'm not sure. He was waiting on a potential client. Tione told him if he can't hit his goal, she has no choice but to fire him." Gotti let Geechi know. Geechi was usually the first to leave the office. Followed by the staff and then Tione.

"I'm off my shit. I haven't been paying close enough attention," Geechi said to himself and got up. Gotti followed him as he walked around the shop, checking offices, the conference room and the showroom to make sure they were alone.

"To what?" Gotti asked when they were back in his office.

"Huh?"

"What haven't we been paying attention to?" she asked. He heard her say *we* and it warmed his heart; she was in this with him; she had made that clear time and time again.

"Donny," he said. He returned to his seat on the couch and she followed.

"Who?"

"The guy you just saw leave. That's Tione's cousin. Macc got the shop from his grandfather, Michael," he said.

"Got it from him?" she questioned.

"Yea. Michael lost it due to a gambling debt. The guy who took possession of it sold it to Macc. Macc used to work for Michael, so he figured—"

"He'd sell it back to him."

"No." Geechi laughed. "He wanted him to give it to him on some I.O.U shit. Macc knew Michael wouldn't pay him back; shit he could barely pay his bills. Plus Macc loved cars. Michael only fixed cars; Macc started actually selling cars."

"Okay so what? Now his grandson inherited the beef?" she said with a chuckle. She never thought that could really be the case.

"Yea. He's a detective and he just hinted at the fact that he is building the case against me."

"Damn," was all she could say.

●●●

Donny punched the steering wheel as he zoomed down the street. He hated Geechi Koran with such vengeance that it kept him up at night and had started to grow ulcers in his stomach. That shop was his grandfather's and was supposed to be passed down to him. Losing it had caused a downward spiral in Donny's family from his grandfather dying from liver disease, to his mother marrying his no-good father and staying in an abusive relationship. Donny just knew that getting it back would set them on the right path for the generations of Costas to come.

Donny pulled out his phone and called his informant. They had a mutual disdain for Geechi and both relished the idea that they could end him and take what was his.

"Hello?"

"You need to meet me tonight, and you need to have some information I can use," Donny raged.

"You need to calm your ass down."

"You aren't doing your part! He is slipping away from us. Now I have the DA's ear, but he isn't going to proceed with a case he can't win. Do you have the information or not!"

"Trust me; I'll get it. I want this just as much as you. I just have to get back tight with him."

"Handle it!" Donald said before disconnecting the call.

Chapter 14

A gigantic smile covered Troy's face when she saw that Dominic was calling her. Troy had been lying at the foot of her bed with her head propped up on a pillow watching TV. She sat up in the bed and looked in the mirror. Quickly, Troy ripped the scarf off and fingered her wrap allowing it to fall across her shoulders.

"Hi, Mr. McCoy," she said. Troy was up on her elbows with the pillow snuggled against her breasts.

"Ms. Matthews." Dominic cheesed into the phone. All he saw was Troy's beautiful face, the beige camisole she wore and the thick white comforter that hid the lower part of her body. "You were supposed to call me when you made it," he reminded her.

"I know," she said with a sad face.

"And yet it's been two days."

"When I got in town I had more to do than I expected. Then I ended up sleeping the whole day and running late for my meeting the next day. I was going to call..."

"Excuses, excuses...how do you feel?" he asked, figuring something had to be going on for her to be in bed in the middle of the day.

"Sore," Troy said blushing at the thought of the sex they'd had.

Dominic licked his lips. "You'll get used to it," he said referring to the way he loved to bend and stretch her body.

"Cocky!"

"You know I'm anything but that," he said.

"Where are you?" Troy asked. She could tell he was sitting outside but couldn't make out his surroundings.

"My dad's," Dominic answered. He was on the enclosed patio with his nieces and nephews because although it was cold, they wanted to be outside. The fire pit was lit keeping them warm.

"You guys should have never moved out," she said. Dominic and his siblings were always at their father's house. Before he could reply a little boy pulled the phone down.

"This is Uno," Dominic said introducing his firstborn nephew, who was sitting on his lap.

"Hi Uno," she cooed.

"Hi," Uno said.

"That's his sister Marley," Dominic said, scanning the back porch. Marley was nearby bundled in winter clothes sitting on a blanket playing with a doll.

"You babysitting?" Troy asked Dominic.

"Always...Chrissy is cooking...Tako is helping."

"Uncle Dom...open it," a little girl in a pink coat said.

"This is Chrissy's daughter," he told Troy. "Did your mama say you can have this?" he asked the little girl. She shrugged; she was so cute that even though Dominic knew she wasn't supposed to have the juice box he opened it for her.

"Softie!" Troy joked.

"I know," he said shaking his head.

They were quiet for a few moments. "Look Troy," Dominic started off. The seriousness in his voice made her sit up in bed. "We've been knowing each other for years. We know what's important to each other and how the other moves," he told her.

"Yea," Troy agreed.

"I don't want to play games. There's no need to. I want you; I don't want to fuck with anyone else. And I don't want you to either," he said looking at her. "I want us to be locked in."

"I want that too. I wasn't playing games by not calling. I was trying to figure out what to say," she admitted.

"I miss you would have worked."

"I know for next time," she said with a big grin.

"When are you coming home?"

"As soon as I can. I have another meeting tomorrow. Then I really need to focus on this first draft...I'm hoping I can be back by Monday," she told him.

"I could help you with the draft."

"I'd rather have it done when I get there; then you can critique it."

Dominic wanted to object but he knew she was right. Plus, he had some work he wanted to have done before Troy arrived so, reluctantly, he agreed.

●●●

"Are you nervous?" Gotti asked Geechi as they sat in the back of a yellow cab on the way to meet her mother for lunch. After pining over what Donny could do and may be up to, they contemplated cancelling the trip to New York. However that would be too suspicious to Mama Gina and Tione, and Geechi was still trying to protect them. He decided it was best to keep moving like they had been. They would enjoy this time and face whatever was coming when it came. They knew they couldn't stop it; they could only be prepared for it.

Gotti had spent all yesterday at the bridal boutique with Bridgette drawing sketches of her reception dress. Ultimately, she decided on two options: one long dress for the beginning of the reception and a short one for when it was time to really party.

"Man you're scared of your mama not me," he teased.

They had gone to her dad's house for dinner last night. It was the most fun Gotti had had in a while. They played games, reminisced and ate good food. Dexter had taken her younger brother, DJ, and Geechi on a walk while Gotti stayed and talked about the reception with her stepmother, Jennifer, and her younger sister, Gabby. She assumed the walk was a chance for Dexter to get a feel for the man Geechi was; they came back laughing so she figured Geechi had passed whatever test Dexter had administered.

"Whatever. Be nice, like I am with your mama," she said, snuggling under him.

"Oh you're in character early, huh?" They shared a laugh. "As far as my mama, she's nice to you."

"My mama won't be mean to you," she let him know.

"I'm not finna tolerate her being mean to you either," Geechi said looking in her eyes. Gotti's voice got stuck in her throat. He said the sweetest things sometimes and it always seemed unintentional which made it feel more genuine.

"We're here," the cab driver announced as he stopped in front of a row of buildings. Geechi handed him the money and the couple climbed out of the car. Geechi was dressed casually in Balenciaga blue jeans with decorative rips and colorful designs that looked painted on and a white collared shirt. The design on the collar matched the colorful designs on his shorts. She wore a hot pink dress. It stopped at her knees and flared out with exaggerated ruffles. She paired it with thigh-high boots. Her makeup was beyond flawless, and her 22-inch bundles were parted down the middle and flowed in the wind as she walked. Geechi held Gotti's hand leading her into the restaurant.

Helen had watched them from the time they stepped out of the cab. She watched how Geechi stepped out first then held his hand out to help Gotti get out of the car. Helen watched as he stepped back and smiled taking in Gotti's appearance as if she were the most beautiful woman in the world. Helen watched her daughter blush and playfully hit Geechi before he took her hand, made sure she was secure in her 6-inch heels and led her; the way a man was supposed to. Helen would have preferred if he had worn a suit to meet her, then surmised that with Geechi being from the country he may not have known any better.

Helen had looked into Geechi's business and could confirm that he was doing extremely well for himself. She had brought a friend with her, Thomas, who had worked his way up from a salesperson to the VP of a chain of car dealerships. He knew everything there was to know about luxury cars and would quiz Geechi to make sure Helen's investigation hadn't missed anything.

"Hi!" Gotti said to the hostess. "Reservations for Lexington," Gotti announced.

"Ah yes, Ms. Lexington is already here. Would you like to check your coats?"

"Of course," Gotti said. After giving her their coats, the hostess gave them a slip.

"Right this way," she said with a smile as she grabbed two menus.

"Your mom kept your dad's name after the divorce?" Geechi asked as they followed the hostess.

"Hell no," Gotti laughed. "Why'd you ask that?"

"Y'all have the same last name..."

"Oh, she hyphenated my name after the divorce. She put my dad's last name first and hers last," Gotti said over her shoulder.

"Damn!"

"She's a savage."

"I see," he replied as they approached the table and saw Helen and a guest.

"Who's he?" Geechi wanted to know.

"I have no idea."

"Gotti!" Helen greeted, standing to hug her daughter. Helen had deep brown skin, dough shaped eyes and a button nose. She had the height Gotti dreamed about and because of it she carried her 187 pounds immaculately.

"Hi Mama," Gotti said and hugged her tight.

"This is my husband, Geechi," she said and stepped aside. Geechi pulled Helen to him by the small of her back and kissed her cheek. She looked shocked for a moment.

"Is that okay? I'm from Texas; we greet women differently in the south," he said with a slight chuckle.

"No, it's...it's fine." Helen stammered unaccustomed to a man taking control over her without being intimidated by her status or stature.

"Okay now," Gotti joked seeing the stars in her mother's eyes.

"Oh please, Gotti," Helen said laughing. "Oh this is Thomas," she said introducing her guest.

"Your date?" Gotti asked.

"I would only be so lucky," Thomas said, standing. Thomas extended his hand for Gotti to shake. Then turned his attention to Geechi while Gotti focused on her mother.

"Thomas and I are old friends," Helen said as they all took their seats. "He's into cars so I figured that would give Geechi something to do so we wouldn't bore him with wedding details."

"Oh," Gotti said. It all made sense; Helen wanted to make sure Geechi was who Gotti said he was. She couldn't help but to smile at her mother. Gotti and Geechi picked up their menus; from behind them they simultaneously made a face at each other. *That's yo mama*, he mouthed.

When the waiter came to their table, Geechi ordered for Gotti while Helen looked on.

"You can't order for yourself?" she asked after everyone had placed their orders and the waiter left.

"No disrespect, Ms. Lexington; she's spoiled rotten," Geechi said and looked lovingly at Gotti.

"Oh I may have played a part in that," Helen laughed.

Lunch went better than Gotti expected. Helen was smitten by Geechi's southern charm and seemed excited about the reception. Helen showed Gotti a beautiful flower arrangement on her phone. She wanted one for each table, a flower wall and flowers to decorate the entire venue. Helen said she wanted the scent of fresh flowers to remind the guests of Gotti's reception anytime they smelled them afterwards. Without Gotti asking, she wrote a 20,000-dollar check to cover the flowers and promised more.

Gotti filled Helen in on the fact that Bridgette still had to perfect the sketches for her dresses and had been sending her emails of the drawings all morning. Gotti was beyond excited. She, Tione, Mama Gina and La'Shea had a meeting to discuss location, food and dates. Troy was slacking on her best friend duties, but La'Shea had gotten her caught up on the plans and she promised to do better.

A few times during lunch Thomas leaned over to whisper in Helen's ear after he and Geechi discussed an engine or model of a car, and Helen would cheese, tap his hand and resume her conversation with Gotti. She knew he was giving Helen good reports on Geechi's knowledge.

After lunch, Helen promised to help with the preparations in any way she could.

"You went to see your father, I'm sure," Helen said, cuffing Gotti's arm as they exited the restaurant.

"Yes, Mama, of course I did."

Helen rolled her eyes. "Don't spoil my mood."

"You brought him up. He says hello." Gotti giggled, turning to face her mother.

"I bet he does," she said. Valet brought Helen her car just as Thomas hailed a taxi for Gotti and Geechi.

"I love you, Mama," Gotti said and hugged her.

"I love you too. And I like him," Helen said, tilting her head toward Geechi. Gotti gasped dramatically and clutched her heart.

"Oh here you go with your father's dramatics. Have a safe flight home, child," Helen said and kissed Gotti's cheek. She hugged Geechi and said her goodbyes before they all went their separate ways.

"Thank you for playing along," Gotti said on the cab ride back to her apartment. They were in the middle of the backseat and she was resting her head on his shoulder.

"It was my pleasure. You tired?"

"I'm always tired when I leave my mama," she admitted.

●●●

Gotti: *Y'all don't have to do everything with me*, Gotti texted to the women in the reception group chat. That included Mama Gina, Tione, La'Shea and Troy. Troy had flown into town for the sole purpose of planning the reception. But today was going to be a busy day and Gotti knew it was unfair to expect everyone to do everything.

La'Shea: *We're going everywhere.* Gotti knew she was speaking for herself and Troy.

Tione: *Same.* Tione texted speaking for her and Mama Gina.

Gotti: *I just know y'all have work...I don't want to be selfish.* Gotti replied.

Tione: *Girl chill out. Are you coming to get me and Mama?*

La'Shea: *Me and Troy are OTW.*

Gotti: *Yes Tione as soon as they get here, I will be OTW to get y'all.* Gotti said ending the conversation.

Thirty minutes later they were piled into Geechi's G-wagon, which had become Gotti's car when she was in town, driving to the hotel. The ladies were going to make sure the space was what they wanted and interview Shayla, the wedding planner that Tione had found. Tione promised she was the best for the job and that she could help Gotti pull off a flawless reception in a short timeframe.

At the hotel, the ladies tasted food, interviewed Shayla and took a tour of the reception area. They quickly agreed that Shayla was the woman for the job; she had the right connections so they knew she would get the wedding cake done properly and the decorations done professionally and on time.

Next, they went to a bridal shop to try to find dresses for Troy, La'Bella, La'Shea, and Tione. Mama Gina wanted to wear a white pantsuit but turned down the ones available at the shop. Therefore, Tione and Shayla were on the hunt for a white pantsuit. The ladies tried to make the process of finding bridesmaids dresses easy, but they were all different with different body types and opinions.

"What about Geechi's suit?" Gina asked as La'Shea tried on her sixth dress. The three women had been alternating turns.

"He knows the colors; he said he would get it," Gotti said while texting her mother. She was getting a dress made for the reception and wanted Gotti's opinion.

"And you trust him?" Gina asked skeptically.

"Yea," Gotti said with a shrug. "I mean this is important to him too..." she reasoned.

"Yea but men procrastinate," Gina told her.

"I'll stay on top of it; that way they won't argue," Tione said.

"Have y'all thought about kids?" Gina wanted to know.

"Nope!" Gotti said and then laughed.

"Y'all aren't getting any younger. Both of my kids are in their thirties and I still don't have any grandkids," Gina said almost pouting.

"Well I'm not married Mama...and that's a sin," Tione said pretending to be apologetic.

Gina laughed. "Oh shut up!"

After the bridal shop, the ladies went to look at decorations. Shayla needed to get an idea of Gotti's taste so that she could perfect the theme and begin shopping for the decorations.

By the time Gotti walked in the house, she was drained but still had to go out with her friends. They hadn't bothered to come inside; they hopped right in La'Shea's car and went to her condo to get dressed.

"You okay?" Geechi asked Gotti as she leaned against the wall peeling her heels off her aching feet.

"I had a long day," she said. He approached her and hugged her.

"What the fuck?" he said looking at her forehead confused. Gotti touched the spot he was staring at and rolled her eyes.

"My wig is lifting," she said trying to press it back down.

"Yo that muthafucka just pop up on your forehead like that?"

"Boy move," she said, trying to push him out of her way.

"For real," Geechi said, holding his place in front of her. "What if you talking to someone...it'll just pop up?"

"I was—" Gotti started to explain that she was using a bobby pin to scratch her scalp but decided against it. "I'm going to dinner with La'Shea and Troy," she told him, walking around him.

"You asking me or telling me?" he replied. Gotti looked back at him, rolled her eyes and headed for the stairs. "I thought you were tired."

"I am but Troy is leaving in the morning and we need to catch up," she told him.

"You've been with them all day," Geechi reminded her.

"I know but Mama Gina was there so we couldn't really talk. We got a lot done though. We picked the location, the menu and I hired Shayla," Gotti told him.

"So basically, you maxed my shit out," he said referring to his credit card.

"Basically." She laughed.

"You need me to wash your back?" Gotti was halfway up the stairs when she turned back to look at him. Geechi stood at the bottom of the staircase with a smirk on his face.

"Nah I got it, but thanks," she said.

"You sure?"

"Positive," Gotti said and rushed up the stairs. The women had all agreed to dress down which meant ripped jeans, a cute shirt and flats. La'Shea and Troy came to get Gotti and then made their way to the restaurant.

●●●

"Something is going on with you," Gotti said pointing her chip at Troy. The threesome was on their second round of drinks as they enjoyed chips and guacamole and waited for their food. Gotti then dipped the chip in the guacamole and waited for Troy to respond.

"I'm with Dom," Troy told them unable to contain her smile.

"With him?" La'Shea questioned.

"Yea...we—"

"Fucked?" La'Shea interjected. She knew that was what Troy was about to say based on the face she made. Troy blushed.

"You taught that young pup some tricks!" Gotti laughed.

"You remember what you said about sucking dick," Troy asked La'Shea.

"You pulled out a La'Shea trick?" Gotti screeched. "You must have already liked him, withcho lying ass!"

"Man he was fucking my soul out my body," Troy said.

"What trick?" La'Shea wanted to know.

"Staring him in his eyes while swallowing it," Troy answered.

"Two hands while you suck?" Gotti asked.

"I been on that. But I was just like fuck it I'ma go in," Troy admitted; they could tell she was feeling herself.

"You can't suck dick like a good girl. You gotta suck dick like a dirty ass hoe. That good girl shit won't work," La'Shea said.

"So now y'all are together?" Gotti said.

"Yea. He called...said he didn't wanna play games." Troy looked up bashfully and they all laughed.

"Dominic so fine. You should have been fucked him," La'Shea told her as the waiter came to deliver their food. They were quiet as he placed La'Shea's fajitas in front of her.

"Another round," Gotti said as he set her enchiladas in front of her.

"No salt on mine," Troy said, moving her saucer so that he could place her steak quesadilla on the table.

"I'll get those right out," the waiter said, walking away. The table was silent as they cut into the food.

"It's more than that, though." Troy said breaking the silence. "I think I can really be me with him. He understands my career, traveling; and he's supportive."

"That's good," La'Shea said. "I'm happy for you. Shit, for y'all," she said, lifting her nearly empty margarita glass to toast her two friends.

"Mine ain't real," Gotti reminded her.

"Keep telling yourself that," La'Shea said and rolled her eyes.

"He's on a diet," Gotti said with a smirk as she looked down. "For the reception," she said looking up at them.

"No more baller belly?" La'Shea said as if she were sad.

"And I didn't even get to rub on it," Gotti joked.

"So you want to?" Troy asked and then winked at La'Shea.

"Anyway," Gotti said changing the subject. "My dad and stepmom will be at the reception."

"Is Helen going to behave?" La'Shea wanted to know.

"We talked…she said as long as they don't say anything to her," Gotti said, shaking her head.

"Why would they?" Troy laughed, knowing Helen wanted all the smoke.

"Exactly," Gotti said, rolling her eyes.

"It'll be fine. She's actually happy for you," La'Shea said.

"You've talked to her?" Gotti asked.

"Yea; she checks in on me periodically," she said.

"Me too; she gave me the tip about Simon Cooper," Troy said referring to the new company she was going to be working with. The relationship Helen had with Gotti's friends was bittersweet; Gotti didn't always get the Helen that she gave them. Honestly, she rarely did. Gotti had no idea that for the majority of the call with her friends, Helen was talking about Gotti. How brave she was for starting her own business, how good she was at her job and how proud Helen was of her.

Chapter 15

Two Months Later

The reception hall looked like a garden filled with different types of white flowers. A beautiful arrangement of tulips in a crystal vase adorned each table. White peonies filled the flower wall with splashes of red peonies. The mothers had walked in together both looking exquisite. Helen wore a white, floor length dress with elegant beading around the neckline. Gina finally found her white pantsuit and had it tailored to fit perfectly. She wore Red Bottoms embellished with Swarovski crystal and diamond jewelry.

Next, Tione, La'Shea, La'Bella and Troy walked in with four of Geechi's good friends. The bridesmaids wore deep red, velvet, form-fitting wraparound dresses and the groomsmen wore black slacks, white button downs and red tuxedo jackets that matched the bridesmaids' dresses.

Finally, it was time to introduce the bride and groom. Geechi was standing at the door in all black with a deep red, velvet tuxedo jacket, and Louis Vuitton loafers waiting for Gotti to exit her bridal suite. Because it wasn't a real wedding her dad wasn't walking her down the aisle; she felt that was taking it too far. Gotti wanted to save that moment for the third and final marriage that she knew would be based in love. Dexter and his family were already seated inside. Geechi watched the door open and his heart rate increased. Shayla walked out first. She looked out into the hallway then smiled at Geechi.

"Come on," Shayla told Gotti.

Geechi felt his soul leave his body when Gotti seemed to float into the hallway. Gotti wore a mermaid style dress that hugged her curves. It was drizzled in Swarovski crystals and diamonds; so much so that it looked like there was no other material. The crystals were strategically placed to cover her body and the diamonds added a sophisticated bling. Gotti wore a diamond studded Goddess head piece over her body wave 24-inch bundles and as always, her makeup was impeccable.

"Damn," Geechi said as she approached him.

"Stop." Gotti laughed as he stared at her. In that moment no one was in that building except him and her; 150 people weren't on the other side of the door awaiting their entrance, and the husband and wife didn't have anywhere to be except in that hallway. Geechi wrapped Gotti in his arms, pulled her so close that she felt his heartbeat, and kissed her. His tongue made love to her mouth as his hands caressed her body. She matched every turn and flip of his tongue, her body heating up with anticipation.

"Um-hmm," they heard followed by cheers. Unbeknownst to the couple, Shayla had already signaled for the doors to be open. She had no idea they were about to have a make out session, but thought it was a beautiful moment. Embarrassed, Gotti moved away from him with her head down while Geechi beamed with pride.

"Come on man," he said and led her down the aisle. At the altar, the pastor prayed for their union and talked about the importance of marriage. He only had five minutes to talk but he had the guests ready to go to church with his powerful words. Next, the DJ played Jahiem's Never and the couple had their first dance.

"I love you, Gotti," he said to her as they danced.

"Stop," she said, pulling back. Geechi was going overboard; no one could hear them so there was no reason for him to be putting on a show. Gotti didn't play about love; he knew that. They had discussed it on one of their many movie nights when neither of them could sleep so they met in the loft and enjoyed a movie from the 90s.

Geechi held Gotti's body firm making her look up at him.

"I'm in love with you, Gotti. How could I not be? Did you really expect me to spend all this time with you and not fall in love?" he questioned. She looked down. Geechi rested his forehead on hers and they continued to dance.

"Do you love me?" he asked, "or even like me? I want this for real, do you?"

She looked up at him staring into his soul. Gotti had to be sure that this wasn't a joke before she revealed her truest feelings. She nodded.

"Yes what? I asked you like ten questions," he said.

"I love you. I want it for real too," she admitted. He smiled so big, so genuinely that her heart almost leaped out of her chest. "You already knew," Gotti told him.

"Nah, I hoped. I tried to be confident, but you had me worried," he admitted.

"Kiss me," Gotti requested humbly. Geechi stopped moving to the beat, lifted her head and kissed Gotti with the same vigor as he did in the hallway.

"Get a room!" Maleek yelled.

"Okay, okay that's enough. It's my turn," Dexter said. Geechi released Gotti so that she could dance with her father. He walked over to Helen, who was pretending not to see the loving moment between father and daughter.

"Don't be jealous," Geechi said, reaching his hand out. "Come dance with me."

Helen's face lit up as she took his hand and he led her to the dance floor.

●●●

"Are you having a good time?" Troy asked Dominic. She had just come back from taking pictures with the wedding party.

"Yea; this was beautiful," he told her as she got comfortable in her seat.

"I love weddings," Troy said smiling.

"You wanna get married," he casually asked, turning to face her. Dominic posed the question so smoothly but the depth in his eyes made Troy wonder if he was asking her to marry him. After gathering herself, she smiled and broke the powerful gaze that had her stuck.

"I don't know; do you?"

"Of course. So what, you thought you had to give that up too?" he asked.

"I guess I did," she admitted. Dominic grabbed her hand and kissed it.

"I'll marry you," he told her.

"I haven't even met your family."

"Yea you have."

"Not..."

"As my girl?" Dominic asked; Troy nodded. "You're right. We'll take care of that when we get back home." Troy smiled; Dominic did too, and he lifted her hand to his mouth and kissed it again. "Let's dance," he said leading her to the dance floor.

Before long, the reception turned into a full-fledged party. Geechi had taken off Gotti's garter and thrown it. None of the groomsmen even attempted to catch it. Then Gotti threw her bouquet and one of the guests caught it. She beamed with pride as if it truly meant she would be the next one to get married.

●●●

"Why are you looking at me like that?" Gotti asked Geechi as he drove them home after the reception.

"I can't look at my wife?" he said, lifting her hand and kissing it.

"You think you're getting some pussy, huh?" She snickered.

"I'm not ready to share my body with you," he joked.

"Whatever," Gotti said. She threw her head back and chortled.

When they got home, Geechi put on his R&B playlist and they slow danced in the living room. Gotti felt so safe in his arms. He held her tight as they swayed to Jahiem's song Ready Willing & Able. The song spoke to Gotti's heart; her body relaxed into his and she closed her eyes enjoying the feeling of serenity.

Geechi started with a kiss on Gotti's hand that led to him placing soft pecks up her arm then licking her shoulder blade before he sucked on her neck. Gotti squirmed in his arms but welcomed the affection. Geechi moved to her face and finally reached her waiting lips. The kiss made the room spin; Gotti pulled away from him when her breath got caught in her throat and she feared she'd pass out. Geechi pulled her close as his hands roamed her backside; he pressed her center into his.

All of a sudden, Gotti was irritated by the beading on the dress. It was getting in the way. As if Geechi could read her mind, he unzipped it and it fell over her left shoulder; she stepped back, tugged it over her hips and let the dress fall to the floor. Gotti stood before Geechi in nude La Perla lingerie.

"Damn," he said circling her nipple with his thumb. "What's this?" Geechi asked. Gotti wore a diamond waist bead that circled her waist; a string of diamonds attached that piece to the second piece that circled her thick thigh.

"Something sexy for you," she cooed and then twirled her tongue in his mouth making his manhood jump. Gotti slid her hand down his pants. "It's big," she moaned in his ear. Geechi scooped her in his arms; Gotti wrapped her legs around his waist, and he walked them to his bedroom.

Sitting her on the bed, they resumed their kiss as she unbuttoned his shirt. He fumbled with the lingerie trying to get it off; when he couldn't, he moved the panties to the side and caressed her pussy.

"Why you already wet?" he teased; she giggled.

"If you gon' play in it, you gotta wash your hands right quick," she told him.

"Damn!" Geechi said and ran to the bathroom. Gotti used that time to take off the nightie. When he returned, she was in the center of the bed on her knees. Geechi took in his wife's heaven-sent chocolate body and almost came in his pants. The look of hunger and anticipation peered from Gotti's eyes as she licked her lips and stared at the bulge in his slacks. Geechi took a moment to remove his pants and shirt.

He climbed on the bed and pulled her right leg to him; Gotti fell back on the bed and Geechi dove straight into her bowl of honey. He used his fingers to spread her lips as his tongue stroked her clit. Geechi swirled around her bud before pulling it into his mouth and gently sucking on it.

"Oh baby," she moaned, spreading her legs wider. He cuffed his arms around her thighs and pulled her closer to him as he devoured her sweet pussy. The taste of her essence drove him crazy. Hungrily, he slurped up her juices. Geechi massaged her round breasts and Gotti bucked on his face as he explored every inch of her.

"Like that baby," she panted. "Please don't stop." Her ran his thick tongue over her clit left to right until her back arched and she let out a moan so sensual it sounded like music to his ears.

"Turn around," he commanded after the condom was on.

"You sure you gon' be able to handle that, baby?" Doggy style was Gotti's favorite position; it was the quickest way to find her G-spot, but when her pussy started leaking and her big ass started bouncing dudes never lasted, so she settled for riding dick. That way, she always got hers; after Gotti was satisfied, she didn't mind letting her partner give her backshot as a reward for a job well done.

"Baby turn over," his husky voice made it sound more like he was begging instead of commanding. Geechi had wanted her, this, for so long. All he wanted to do was slide deep inside of her and stroke her until the sun rose.

Gotti turned over but didn't give him the perfect arch; that would have been too much. Her back was low, but Gotti didn't poke her ass out. Geechi eased in; she moaned. It was big and she needed to adjust but she didn't move. Gotti wanted to see what he had. Geechi rotated his dick inside of her, slowly, as if to stretch her walls. The wetness of her tunnel echoed through the bedroom.

"Shit," Geechi panted and paused.

Then he started to move in and out at a steady pace. Geechi was hitting her spot as if he had known where it was all along. It felt good, so good; she bounced back a little still afraid to give him too much. Geechi held her tantalizing ass in the palms of his hands and shut his eye. Seeing his dick disappear and then reappear and the jiggle of her ass, was too much. Shit, feeling her wet pussy grip his manhood, suffocating it with the plumpness of her walls, was too much, but he took it stroke by stroke.

Soon Gotti was lying flat on the bed. Geechi was still inside of her from the back, but her legs were closed as she threw her ass in a circle into him mercilessly. Gotti bounced her ass colliding with his pelvis and swallowing his dick. Soft moans escaped her lips as low grunts fell from his. Her creamy center stained his thick veined dick and he was losing his mind.

"Baby...ohmygod," Gotti said; her words running together. "I'm...I'm coming," she said as if it were a shock to her. Geechi was happy; shit, he was about to come too then she'd be riding soft dick on their reception night and that wasn't cool. Gotti's pussy pulsated, clenching so tight that it squeezed the life out of him. They came together and Geechi collapsed on Gotti's back.

"Damn Geechi," she cooed.

"I'm the man or what," he replied.

She smacked her lips and pushed him off her. "Cocky ass!"

●●●

The next morning Gotti woke up and went up to her bedroom to shower. She came downstairs in a white tee and thong panties to make breakfast for Geechi. Before Gotti could pull the food out, he was entering the kitchen.

"Good morning," Gotti said as Geechi swept her in his arms and sat her on the counter. He kissed her long and hard; his minty tongue caressing hers. When she hugged him, she smelled the freshness of his body and knew he had showered as well.

"What do you want for breakfast?" Gotti asked.

"You," Geechi said, tossing Gotti over his shoulder and palming her luscious ass as he carried her to their bedroom.

Chapter 16

Troy was petrified to walk into Dominic's family home alone, but he had to be there early, and she had just flown into town. Troy didn't want to be late, so she freshened up at the airport and put her makeup on in the cab. Troy had knocked three times and even texted and called Dominic but wasn't getting an answer. She could hear talking and laughing in the house, so she turned the knob and walked in.

From the foyer, she saw Montez, Dominic's brother. He was tall with a deep brown skin tone; his long hair was braided into two French braids. Uno, his four-year-old son, was his replica. Uno held Montez's shorts and followed him while Montez carried, Marley, the little girl Troy saw on the Facetime call with Dominic. Montez stopped and glared at her; Troy looked frightened, then his face softened.

"What's up, Troy," Montez said and came to hug her. It had been years, so she was happy he recognized her.

"Hey Montez; how have you been?"

"Good. Here, hold her," he said, handing her Marley. "I gotta take him to the bathroom. Everybody is in the kitchen and den," he said, placing his hand on Uno's head and leading him to the bathroom.

Nervously, Troy walked through the house heading for the kitchen. Standing in the doorway all eyes were on her.

"Who is she and why does she have your baby?" Leilani asked Tori. Tori's face contorted into a scowl.

"I'm Troy...is Dom here?" she asked nervously.

"Oh y'all relax," Chrissy said, coming out of the pantry with a bag of sugar. "They were about to get on your ass!" She laughed as she approached Troy. Chrissy's brown skin was radiant, and her pregnant belly looked adorable in the overalls that she wore. "I'm Chrissy," she said, shaking her hand. Troy had known Dominic for nine years, but she hadn't met Chrissy because the few times she was around the family, Chrissy was in the Dominican Republic.

"Montez gave her to me," Troy explained when Tori took Marley from her. "I was calling Dom's phone..."

"You good, girl. That's Montez's wife Tori, and this is Tako's girlfriend Leilani," Chrissy introduced. Each woman smiled and nodded their hello. "Dom is in the den, but you can come help cook." Troy almost dropped to the floor. Cook? She couldn't even boil water. But Troy wanted to bond with them.

"She don't do too much cooking," Dominic said, walking into the kitchen with a big smile on his face. Troy was happy to see him; he looked handsome in navy blue cargo pants and a hunter green and navy-blue shirt. His smile made her blush.

"Have I ever seen Dom smile?" Leilani asked the room.

"His mean ass don't smile...she might be okay," Tori said, bouncing Marley in her arms.

"I'll clean," Troy told Chrissy.

"Nah you good. Tako made the steaks, I'm just making the sides. You're a guest this time anyway...enjoy your man," Chrissy told her.

"Come on, my dad is down here," he said, reaching for her hand. Troy placed the wine she brought on the table and let him lead her down the basement stairs.

In the den, Troy met Chrissy's husband, Rambo, had a light conversation with their father, Montel, and got reacquainted with

Dominic's brothers, Tako and Demi. After a few minutes, Dominic led her back up the stairs and into the living room so they could be alone. Troy smiled up at him and he kissed her lips. She had been gone for a week and she needed him in more ways than one.

"I was calling your phone," Troy said when they finally broke the kiss.

"My bad...it's on the charger. I was coming to check it when I came in the kitchen," he told her. Dominic watched as her leg shook involuntarily. "Relax," he said caressing her thigh.

"The girls can be..."

"Mean...but they say I'm mean," he joked.

"You're super nice, baby," Troy said and kissed him again.

"You know they're going to ask you tough questions and shit. You don't have to answer anything you don't want to," Dominic let her know.

"But you'll jump in if I'm drowning, right?"

"Of course."

When the food was done, everyone piled into the kitchen. The kids' plates were made first and they sat at a small table to the side. Demi made Montel's plate, who sat at the head of the table. Chrissy was sitting down too because she had cooked, and she was pregnant. Rambo made her plate and Montez made her drink. Then it was every man for themselves.

"You're bicoastal, right?" Montez asked. The interrogation had started immediately and apparently it wasn't just going to be coming from the women.

"Yes...New York and LA," Troy answered.

"If y'all get serious—" Chrissy started.

"We're serious," Troy interjected and then looked at Dominic. He smiled and nodded to show that he agreed. Troy looked back at Chrissy so she could finish her question.

"Well since y'all are serious, where will y'all live?" Chrissy asked. The couple hadn't discussed that, so Dominic was all ears. He knew how important traveling was to Troy, and she loved the LA weather.

"Here," Troy said matter-of-factly. It wasn't even a thought in her mind. She knew when she chose Dominic that she would be giving up her apartment in LA. Troy wanted to do it, because if she wasn't working or spending time in Dallas with La'Bella, La'Shea and Gotti, she wanted to be with Dominic. "I would never even try to take him from this," Troy said referring to the closeness he shared with his family.

"I like her," Demi said. His two-year-old daughter, Camilla, was on his knee and he was sharing his food with her.

"Me too," Montez agreed.

"Kids?" Tori asked Troy. Kids were big in the McCoy family but both Troy and Dominic seemed to be married to their careers.

"God willing," Troy said.

"Marriage?" Chrissy asked.

"Eventually…we've talked about it…when the time is right," Troy answered. She was a little uncomfortable because Dominic wasn't talking. But when she looked across the table at him, Troy could tell they were on the same page.

"How will you manage your career and a baby?" Tori asked.

"Yea," Chrissy agreed. "Children take up a lot of time."

"We only want one…and I work for myself which means I make my own schedule. And I'll have Dominic and my family; it'll be fine," Troy told them. But felt like she was giving herself a pep talk because that was a concern that she had as well.

"What do you like about him…is he nice to you?" Tori asked. Troy was happy she lightened the mood.

"Yes," Troy laughed. "And he's smart and ambitious and Lord have y'all seen him in a suit," she said allowing her head to fall back like she was in total bliss. They all laughed. Soon the subject changed, and they enjoyed each other's company.

Chapter 17

In the three months since their reception, Geechi and Gotti had grown closer and were still in the honeymoon stages. After the reception, Geechi had shut down business for a week and took Gotti to a resort in The Bahamas where they drank, fucked and basked in the bliss of marriage. When they arrived home, there was a brand new, red G-wagon in the garage; she blushed when Geechi gave her the keys.

"Are you listening?" Gina said to Gotti. Gina had been having a full conversation with her as Gotti stared off with a big grin on her face.

"She don't do much listening these days. Neither does your son," Tione stated.

"I'm sorry," Gotti said with a chuckle. They were at Gina's house preparing Sunday dinner. Gotti was sitting at the counter placing the dough on the pan to make Gina's homemade biscuits.

"I'm asking you what you think about Lorenzo stopping by today," Gina said. It took Gotti a moment to place the name, but she quickly remembered it was Geechi's father.

"I, um," she stuttered for a moment. Honestly, Gotti didn't think it was a good idea, but she knew Gina had the best intentions for the reunion. So Gotti didn't want to be negative.

"Has Geechi ever said anything about him?" Tione asked Gotti.

"I asked about him and Geechi just said he's around. Y'all would know more than me, but from his vibe I'm not sure about a surprise visit," Gotti told them.

Gina huffed. She didn't want to make Geechi feel uncomfortable. A lot had transpired between Lorenzo and Geechi, and Gina recognized that Geechi still held anger in his heart over the situation. She figured a conversation with his father could help to clear things up.

"I think it's important that they speak. From there it's whatever they want to do. I didn't invite him to eat...just told him he could stop by afterwards," Gina reasoned.

"It'll be okay," Gotti said. "Geechi knows how to control himself." She smiled trying to lighten Gina's worry. "What happened between them; where they ever close?"

"Yea but after Macc left Geechi the shop things got shaky," Gina said. Tione made a face because that was how Gina remembered it, but from her perspective things had been shaky before that. Pops leaving Geechi the shop was the straw that broke the camel's back.

"Things got shaky when Pops started grooming Geechi to take over; they didn't want to take orders from him," Tione said.

"They?" Gotti questioned.

"Yea Lorenzo and Orlando," Gina answered.

"Orlando is Macc's other son," Tione told Gotti as she added more cheese to the pan of mac and cheese.

"And they worked at the shop too?" Gotti asked.

"Yea," Tione said.

"Where y'all at?" The women heard Geechi yell after the front door opened and closed. They all looked at each other knowing they needed to end the conversation.

"Follow the smell of the food," Gina said.

"Oh he was already doing that," Tione joked. Geechi walked into the kitchen and his eyes landed on Gotti as she worked on the biscuits.

"Whhhaaatt!" he teased. Gotti smiled so hard her cheeks hurt.

"Whatever. I cook," she said. Geechi walked up behind her and wrapped his arms around her waist. After kissing Gotti's cheek he realized that wasn't enough for him so he nudged her face with his, signaling for Gotti to kiss his lips. She did and they shared a couple of pecks.

"Hey now," Gina joked causing everyone to laugh.

"How long y'all got?" Geechi asked. He walked to Gina and kissed her cheek and then hugged Tione.

"Not long, gon' and turn the game on," Gina said as she exited the kitchen. Geechi headed out of the kitchen and down to the den.

"Told cha," Tione said cheesing at Gotti.

"What?"

"It's real. It always was," Tione said.

"Whatever!"

"No, tell me I was right," Tione demanded.

"Grow up, Tione." Gotti joked.

"I will dump this mac and cheese on your head so help me God," she said, lifting the glass pan and walking toward Gotti.

"Move Tione!" Gotti yelled as she laughed hysterically. "Okay," she said as Tione got closer. "You were right," Gotti admitted. Tione laughed and put the pan in the oven. Gina reentered the kitchen with her phone in her hand.

"He is almost here," Gina announced barely above a whisper.

"Oh Lord, I thought Geechi would at least be able to eat first," Tione said.

"Yea I was going to fix him a drink so he would be relaxed. How are you about to do this?"

"When he knocks, Geechi will get the door and I'm done with," Gina said and gestured like she was washing her hands.

166

"Done with it?" Tione gasped looking at her mother. Tione couldn't understand how Gina could wash her hands with a situation, she created, because it got intense.

"They are two grown men. They will figure it out," Gina reasoned.

When the ladies heard the doorbell five minutes later, they got quiet and looked around the kitchen at one another.

"I don't think he heard," Gotti said because Geechi hadn't gotten up to get the door. Lorenzo rang the bell again and then knocked; the women held their breath.

"Baby!" Gotti called right as they heard Geechi's footsteps.

"I'm about to get it. Who y'all expecting?" Geechi asked as he walked to the front door. No one answered.

After looking out the peephole, Geechi swung the door open and glared at his father. They were the same height and build; seeing that his son was a replica of him made Lorenzo smile.

"What's up?" Geechi asked through the storm door. Lorenzo took in the scowl on his son's face, which reminded Lorenzo of Macc, and shook his head.

"Can we talk?" Lorenzo asked, throwing his hands up. Geechi sucked his teeth, looked back at the unusually quiet kitchen and opened the storm door. Lorenzo went to step in but quickly realized that Geechi was coming out.

Lorenzo took a seat on the patio chair that decorated the large porch and looked out at the front yard.

"What's up?" Geechi said again, leaning against the post.

"Been a while," Lorenzo said with a nervous chuckle. He wasn't sure where to start, and Geechi's cold demeanor was making it harder.

"Yea, but what's up?"

"I miss you," Lorenzo said, looking out at the street. "I never expected all this."

"You talkin' bout when you and ya big bro tried to make me lose the shop? The one your father worked so hard for? Bought Orlando a house with, sent yo ass to school; all with the money from his shop?"

"He did those things, but we had been working in that shop since before we knew what work was. Making you lose it though, that wasn't the intent and you know that," Lorenzo said.

"How the fuck wasn't that the intent. Y'all both quit in the middle of me putting in all that money to renovate the shop. My best mechanic and my best salesman walk out that bitch without even having a conversation with me?" Geechi's temperature was rising as his nostrils flared and he sank his teeth into his bottom lip. He took a moment to calm down because the way his anger was building would leave his father in a pool of blood.

"You niggas tried to make me go broke." Lorenzo was a good mechanic; he knew a lot about cars, but his specialty was sales. He was charismatic, personable, and he knew his shit. Lorenzo had repeat customers that made the shop a lot of money, and they always brought friends with them. When Lorenzo left so did his customer base.

Orlando was a beast with fixing cars. He could refurbish any engine. He could take a car twenty years old and make it run like it was brand new. After Pops died and the will was read, the brothers stuck around thinking they could bully Geechi into going against his grandfather's wishes. If Macc had wanted them to split the shop, he would have stated that in his will; he didn't, so Geechi respected his wishes. When Lorenzo and Orlando saw that Geechi wasn't going to budge, they left him high and dry. A lot of money was tied up in the renovations and in getting more exclusive cars as Geechi worked to build the showroom he now had. Their departure caused him to look into other ways to make money and fast.

"It wasn't about you," Lorenzo stated.

"It wasn't about your son, my nigga?"

"How would you feel if you had worked for your father, helped him build his business and he skipped over you. Not to give it to your big brother but to your son?" Lorenzo asked through squinted eyes.

"Proud." Geechi answered honestly. "Cause it's *my son*, and if I got it, it would eventually be his anyway."

"I didn't see it that way at the time."

"Nah, you just followed ya brother. Didn't make your own decision based on what was best for the shop. You did that a lot," Geechi said. Lorenzo glared at Geechi knowing that he was repeating Macc's words. Lorenzo knew that Macc thought he was a follower and it hurt him that Macc had put that narrative in his son's head. They were both quiet for a minute or two.

Geechi huffed. "Look, I guess shit ain't work like you and Orlando planned," he said knowing they had tried to start their own shop. "I guess you see what's happening with me and—"

"I'm not asking for a job," Lorenzo said offended.

"Good. What do you want?"

"My son," Lorenzo answered.

"We 'bout to eat," Geechi said and shrugged. "I'll see you around," he said and went back inside and locked the door.

Geechi headed to the kitchen and looked in at the women. They stared at him but didn't speak. He shook his head and went through the den and out to the patio. He sat in the patio chair and propped his feet up on the stool.

Gotti walked out on the patio and eased in his lap.

"Who did that, baby?" he asked. Gotti didn't know Lorenzo, so he knew she didn't invite him over.

"She was just tryin—"

"Who?" he asked.

"Ya mama," she mumbled. Geechi slid her to the center of his lap with her back to his chest and her legs on top of his. Geechi kissed the back of her neck and then her cheek.

"Roll that for me," Geechi said, tilting his head toward the weed. She picked up the cigar and began breaking it down.

Chapter 18

"**G**otti!" Gotti was in Neiman Marcus trying to find something to wear to her girls' night out with Troy and La'Shea when she heard her name being called. Gotti turned and saw a woman she didn't know approaching her.

"Who's calling you?" Geechi asked, coming around the corner. Gotti shrugged and nodded her head at the woman. Ashlei had spotted Gotti coming out of Nordstrom and knew it might be her only chance to stake her claim. Ashlei didn't know Geechi was with Gotti; when she saw him, she momentarily froze in place, but it was too late to turn back. Ashlei threw her shoulders back, held her head high and approached them as Geechi stared holes in her.

"I'm Ashlei," she said, extending her hand to Gotti. The vibe felt off, the girl's and Geechi's, so Gotti didn't bother shaking her hand.

"That's cool." Ashlei said with a laugh. "You don't know me, but I know Geechi," she said then looked at him with a smile. "What's up?"

"Bitch, if you don't get yo ass on," he said.

"Don't be like that," Ashlei said.

"You wildin'," Geechi said, pulling Gotti away from her. Gotti didn't know what to do. The six months since their reception had been the best time of her life, but she'd be lying if she said that somewhere in the back of her mind, she hadn't been waiting for the other shoe to drop.

"This conversation needs to be had, Geechi, since we're sister wives," Ashlei said with a satisfied smirk.

"You got another wife?" Gotti asked him with a snicker.

"Hell nah," Geechi said laughing too.

"What you wanna tell me, lil mama. Hurry 'cause me and my husband are busy."

"Was he your husband when he was fucking me, paying my rent...eating my pussy? I was here before you and I'll be here after you. We've been doing this shit for years," Ashlei let Gotti know.

"And he hasn't upgraded you? You still just fucking for your rent money? He didn't move you in, take the stress of bills off your plate? What is your hustle; did he invest in it?"

"I don't need a upgrade, bitch! I like my carefree life. Do I look like the type of bitch to work?" she sassed.

"Then play your fucking position," Gotti spat.

"You can act tough; shit, I would do the same thing. Just know I'm fucking and sucking the nigga just like you; I go on shopping sprees just like you, bitch. I'm wifey too! He thorough," Ashlei said with a chuckle, "I didn't even know shit about you; he made sure of it. But now I know you, and you know me." Ashlei turned to walk off. "I'll see you in a few days when you calm down, daddy," she said over her shoulder to Geechi.

"She a fucking lie," Geechi told Gotti.

"What she lying about, Geechi?" Gotti spat making her way to the counter. The saleswoman had gathered their items and was waiting for them at the register. She put her items on the counter then looked at him. Geechi stepped in front of her as the cashier rung up their items.

"You believe that shit?" he turned to ask her.

"You never fucked her?" Gotti asked. "She just randomly walked up to me in the same fuckin' shoes you bought me?" she hissed. Gotti's fists clenched; she wanted to punch him in the face.

"Give me the keys," she said. Gotti couldn't control her anger and the last thing she wanted to do was fight in Neiman Marcus.

"Let me pay for this shit," Geechi told her.

"I'll get a Lyft," Gotti said, turning to walk off.

"Can you move a little faster?" he asked the clerk trying to be nice about it. Geechi knew Gotti wasn't going anywhere because he had her phone, but he wanted to hurry and get to her.

A few minutes later, he walked out the store; she was by the water fountain. A happy couple was beside her throwing coins into the fountain. When Gotti saw Geechi, she sped to him.

"Give me my phone," she demanded. In the middle of shopping Gotti had asked him to hold it.

"Come get in the car so we can talk, Gotti," Geechi said, walking toward Macy's to get to the parking garage. Gotti was heated but fought hard to relax her face in case she saw Ashlei again. Gotti didn't want her to know she had rattled her; that was Ashlei's purpose for doing what she did.

"You fucked her?" Gotti asked as soon as they were in the car. She was turned in her seat facing him.

"That shit is old."

"How old?" she asked.

"I don't even remember; Ashlei a fuckin' lie. She doing that shit 'cause I moved on," he reasoned, backing out of the parking spot.

"So y'all were in a relationship?"

"Here and there; it was never too serious, and it never lasted long," Geechi told Gotti.

"I don't know," Gotti said looking out the window as they drove out of the parking lot.

"What don't you know?"

"I don't know why this bitch would come up to me, tell me she fucked my husband, she's been fucking him and she's gonna keep fucking him," she replied.

"She a bird," Geechi stated.

"That you laid up with for years," Gotti retorted through furrowed brows. Men loved to degrade the caliber of a woman they cheated with as if they hadn't risked their livelihood for her.

"Aiite Gotti," Geechi said trying to end the conversation. He didn't want to argue with her; he couldn't win anyway. Geechi knew once a woman made her mind up on what happened it was final.

"When?" Gotti asked five minutes later.

"I told you when."

"You haven't told me shit! And chill with that cocky shit."

"You 'bout ta irritate the fuck outta me with this." He hadn't meant to say that or at least not like that. Geechi was irritated by the whole situation starting with Ashlei and the bullshit she had just pulled.

"I'm irritating you because a bitch came up to me?" Gotti fumed and swung, hitting him in the jaw. The car swerved but Geechi quickly regained control. Gotti had never hit a man before, had never even thought about it. Her love for Geechi was different; she couldn't control herself when it came to him. Gotti regretted it immediately but didn't have the words to voice it.

"Take me to La'Shea's," she told him.

"Fuck you mean take you to La'Shea's?" Geechi said, touching his lip to see if it was bleeding.

"What's confusing about it?"

"We married; you got a problem with me you can talk to me," he said.

"Obviously things are getting too heated."

"Keep your fucking hands to yourself then," Geechi shot back.

"You fucking that bitch and you know it. Shit, I know it, but you're sitting here lying! She ain't do that for nothing," Gotti said, and they rode the rest of the way home in silence.

"Give me my phone," Gotti said when they pulled into the garage. Geechi dug in his pocket and gave it to her; she hopped out the car.

Geechi grabbed their bags and carried them inside. He expected to be bombarded with questions, but Gotti was quiet...too quiet. He walked down the hall to their bedroom, and she was packing a bag.

"You not going no fucking where," he informed her.

"Who the fuck do you think you're talking to?" she seethed.

"We can talk about this shit," Geechi said. He grabbed her bag, threw it across the room and sat on the bed to talk to her.

"I'm not about to keep asking the same shit over and over. I shouldn't have to ask shit...you saw what happened...explain your relationship with her!"

"I told you we talked off and on—"

"When was the last time you fucked her!" Gotti shouted. She wasn't about to listen to him tell her any pointless information about an on and off relationship in the past.

"Gotti, a long fucking time ago. I don't remember!"

"While we were together?"

"No," he lied. Gotti walked out of the bedroom; she didn't need clothes because she could use La'Shea's. Geechi caught her at the front door and grabbed her right hand which held her keys.

"Move," she yelled and started swinging on him. He blocked a few and took a few; his main goal was to get the keys.

"You not going no fucking where," he yelled with her pinned to the wall. "You don't just leave when shit happens; that's not how marriage works."

"I need to cool off," Gotti said, trying to appear calm.

"You can go in our bedroom and cool off. You can go upstairs and watch TV and cool off. You can go sit by the pool and cool off," he said.

"Fine," she said and walked outside. Geechi saw Gotti sit by the pool and he sighed in relief. He was pissed at Ashlei. She had never pulled any petty shit like that. Even when she found out he was married. Geechi just knew she would be mad because she had rode for him for a while. They'd had a good run filled with trips, threesomes and partying so he anticipated her feeling betrayed by the news. Not because she loved him but out of fear that she'd be cut off, but Ashlei had played it cool. Because of that and the fact that he and Gotti weren't serious at the time, Geechi kept his relationship with Ashlei going. Paying her rent, that was a damn lie. She loved the night life, so he put in a good word for her at Liberty City, a strip club he frequented, and she became a bartender. Because people knew she fucked with him she got big tips and that's what paid her rent. But Geechi did slide her money here and there just because.

When Gotti proposed that they get married, Ashlei had been the furthest thing from his mind. Then she called about a week later, they met up and she seemed content with the fact that although he was married, he still made time for her. Then shit got more serious with Gotti, and he was spending less and less time with Ashlei until eventually she wasn't getting any. Geechi thought she understood; obviously she didn't.

After a few more minutes he went to check on Gotti. Geechi loved Gotti and wasn't trying to lose her or even beef with her over some bullshit he had already put an end to. When he got to the window facing the backyard, he didn't see her. His heart dropped to his stomach as he raced outside then around to the fence and saw that it was open.

"Fuck!" he screamed. The last thing he needed was La'Shea or Troy, two single women, giving his wife advice.

●●●

"Hey girl!" La'Shea sang into the phone. "You still shopping with hubby?"

"No, I'm at the Exxon around the corner from the house; can you come get me?"

La'Shea could tell something was wrong. "What happened?"

"He wouldn't give me my keys, so I had to walk. Hurry before he comes," Gotti said.

"Did he hit you?" La'Shea asked as she jumped off the couch, grabbing her car keys.

What? Troy mouthed; La'Shea shrugged her shoulders and darted out of the door.

"No, but I hit him," Gotti said with tears building in her eyes.

"I'm on my way," La'Shea said, running down the stairs and out of her building.

Gotti went inside of the store but remembered she didn't have any money. She had left the house with nothing but her phone. She wanted to cry but was fighting to hold the tears in. Gotti knew once she got with her girls, she could let her emotions show, but for right now she needed to be strong. Looking down at her phone, she saw Geechi calling. Gotti wanted to answer; hell, she would give anything for this not to be happening, but it was. She hadn't expected him to be perfect; in the beginning the marriage wasn't even real. But now it was and not because she had suggested it, but because Geechi had practically begged her on the dance floor at their reception. Gotti was so happy when he said those words; she had wanted to hear them for longer than she would ever admit. Standing there dancing with him as he professed his love for her, she felt like the luckiest girl in the world.

"Hello?" Gotti said answering the call for La'Shea.

"Are you inside?"

"Yea, here I come." She hurried out of the store and hopped in the car with La'Shea.

"Where is Troy?"

"Home...I ran out the house without telling her what happened. Shit, you were scaring me."

"Is Baby there?"

"No...she's in San Antonio for the weekend."

"Oh yea."

"What happened?"

"He cheated...I think," Gotti said with a shrug.

"We'll talk at home," La'Shea said, rubbing her knee. Gotti looked out of the window as they drove still trying to fight back her tears.

"Is that him?" La'Shea asked when Gotti's phone rang for the third time in a row. She nodded and tears fell from her eyes. "I'm so sorry," La'Shea said as her heart ached for her best friend.

Soon they pulled into La'Shea's parking spot. The ladies climbed out of the car, walked into La'Shea's building and rode the elevator up to her condo.

They walked in and Troy was on the couch looking worried. She hurried to Gotti and hugged her. Finally, they were sitting down while La'Shea prepared the wine.

"We were in the mall. I wanted something new for tonight," Gotti said. "She just came up to me, said she was fucking him before me, during me and she would continue to fuck him after me."

"Who is she?" La'Shea asked.

"Hell if I know. Her name is Ashlei...I think."

"And what is he saying?" Troy inquired.

"It's not true...well they used to fuck around, but she's lying about them still being together."

"You believe him?" Troy asked. Gotti looked up at her; and with tears in her eyes, Gotti shook her head no. If Gotti believed him, she wouldn't have left home or hit him. If she could make herself believe this woman was just jealous because Geechi was no longer with her, none of this would be necessary.

"He's not giving me any facts. I asked when was the last time; he's not answering. There is nothing for me to believe because I don't know shit," Gotti said just as he texted her.

"Give me the phone," La'Shea said but snatched it before Gotti could hand it to her.

"What did he say?" Troy asked.

"He's about to come get her," La'Shea answered and started texting back.

"What are you saying?" Gotti asked when she saw La'Shea typing a mile a minute.

"Wait," was all La'Shea said as she finished the text. "I'm not going anywhere until I'm clear on what is going on. Who was the woman at the mall? When is the last time you fucked her? If the relationship is over, why would she approach me?" La'Shea said reading the message back to Gotti.

"Yea, he gotta give up some information; this is ridiculous," Troy said. The phone went off and La'Shea stared at it while Gotti and Troy stared at her.

"What did he say?" Gotti finally asked.

"La'Shea give my wife her phone," La'Shea said, and they couldn't help but laugh.

"Just turn it off. I need to think," Gotti said and got up to pour herself more wine.

"So...if it's true do you wanna be with him?" Troy asked. Gotti didn't answer until she was back in her seat.

"If it was in the beginning...yes. Neither of us took the marriage seriously. It was business. I would be a fool to think he wasn't fucking. I didn't fuck him until our reception."

"Really?" La'Shea said with her face scrunched up.

"I told you she wasn't getting no dick." Troy snickered.

"But you were so happy."

"I love him, La'Shea," she said and shrugged.

"He better fix this shit or I'ma fuck him up!" La'Shea said. Their laughter was interrupted by a knock on the door.

"Who is that, La'Shea?" Gotti asked, "I don't feel like company."

"It's your husband," she said after looking through the peephole. Gotti adjusted herself in her seat as La'Shea opened the door.

"Hey La'Shea," Geechi said as if nothing had happened. "Is Gotti here?"

"Gotti, are you here?" La'Shea asked. Although Gotti didn't answer, La'Shea stepped to the side.

Gotti was on one end of the couch and Troy was on the other. La'Shea sat in the chair across from them. Gotti looked down at her drink; they stared at him.

"Can we talk?" Geechi asked her.

"Yea," Gotti answered. He was expecting La'Shea and Troy to leave the room or for Gotti to take him to another room but that didn't happen. He sat beside her.

"We're married, Gotti," he reminded her.

"I'm not the one confused about that," Gotti said to him.

"You can't get mad and just leave the house. Our bond is the most important now; you gotta handle our business with me not with your friends." Gotti looked at La'Shea; Geechi turned her head, so she was facing him.

"I asked you repeatedly what happened," she said.

"And I answered you repeatedly," he replied.

"No you lied repeatedly," she retorted. "That shit is old is not an answer."

"I can't go into detail if you keep hitting me," Geechi said.

Again, Gotti looked past him but this time she looked at Troy. Geechi moved over so that Gotti's eyes were on him.

"I'm sorry," Gotti said. She truly was angry with herself for behaving that way.

"Let's go home."

"You need to tell me who she is and when y'all were together," she said. La'Shea smiled.

"We can discuss that at home. This is our business," Geechi said and stood up. "It's good to see you, Troy," he said; she nodded. "Thank you for picking her up, La'Shea," he said and then reached out his hand for Gotti. She grabbed it and Geechi pulled her up.

"I'll call y'all later," she mumbled on the way out of the door.

●●●

At home Gotti and Geechi were in bed. She was sitting up against the pillows and he was lying across the bed.

"What's going on between y'all?"

"Nothing; we fucked around in the past."

"While we've been married?" Gotti asked. Geechi huffed, and she knew the answer was yes.

"In the very beginning," he admitted and then added, "The wedding was impromptu, so I didn't have time to end shit...so I...we—"

"I get it and I'm fine with that. But when was the last time? Have you fucked her since our reception?" Gotti asked. In her opinion that was when things got serious between them.

"No," he answered.

"Now is the time to tell the whole truth. I don't want shit to come back to me."

"It's not. That's the whole truth. I fucked her in the beginning."

"You should have just said that."

"Nigga, you was wildin'!"

"And I had a reason to. You were taking too damn long to answer questions. If you had told me everything when we got serious, we wouldn't have been in this predicament."

"You're right."

"Is there anything else you need to tell me?"

"No; do you have anything to tell me?" he asked.

"No."

"You sure?"

"I mean I was talking to someone when we first met, but that was before we got married."

"Oh yea?" he questioned as if he were upset.

She giggled. "Whatever. We broke up because I was spending too much time in Texas," she told him.

"We gon' fight, Gotti. We gon' have ups and downs, but I shouldn't have to come get you from your homegirl's house. That shit is childish; we gotta handle our own shit."

"Agreed," Gotti said. "I'm sorry," she said, running her hand over the barely noticeable scratch on his lip from when she hit him.

"It hurt," he lied, "kiss it."

She smiled and then leaned over to kiss him. Geechi adjusted on the bed and pulled her on top of him. As they deepened their kiss, she grinded on his manhood and he caressed her backside. He lifted her dress and pulled down her panties.

"Let me shower right quick," she said trying to get off him. He held her in place.

"I don't like how you taste straight out the shower. It be too bland. I like for you to marinate in your sauce," he said and planted a sloppy kiss on her lips as he worked her panties over her hips. "Sit on my face," Geechi told Gotti biting her bottom lip. He had said that time and time again, so she knew better than to argue. She kicked her panties off before sitting up. Gotti pulled up her grey dress and climbed on his face. He cuffed his arms around her thighs and ran his tongue over her clit, down her labia and up her vagina canal.

"Oh," she moaned as she began to rotate on his face.

"I love the sound of your moans, baby," he said then flicked his tongue over and around her clit.

"Oh shit, baby," she cooed rotating her hips.

"Mmm," he moaned as her sweetness saturated his face. Gotti pulled her dress over her head, stuck her hand inside her bra and caressed her breasts.

"Fuck baby," she said when he pressed his tongue flat against her clit and moved it at a fast speed. Geechi slowed down by puckering his lips and using his tongue to explore every inch of her. When Gotti came, she slid down and took his dick into her mouth.

"Shit Gotti," he grunted as she bobbed her head up and down his shaft. She massaged the base and slobbered on the head between slurps. Geechi reached over and grabbed a condom from the drawer. He liked head but he always wanted to come from fucking her.

"Come sit on it, baby," he groaned. Moments later, the condom was in place and she was throwing her hips in a circle as she sat perched on her tippy toes. "Fuck, Gotti," Geechi said; his eyes rolled in the back of his head.

"Oh baby," she cooed, "This dick is so good." He sat up as she bounced up and down his shaft as if he were her exercise ball. He unclasped her bra so he could massage and kiss her titties.

"Like that, baby," she coached as he sucked her left breast and she bucked on his dick, throwing her hips to the right. She could feel her climax building and her heart rate increasing. Her knees were tired but the joyous feeling his dick was giving her drowned out the pain.

"Oh my god," Gotti said. She could feel the veins in his dick stroking her walls and it gave her the strength to continue to ride. Geechi bit down on Gotti's nipple and her juices rained down on him as she came. Lazily, she continued to ride him as the orgasm shot through her body. Geechi flipped her over, pinned her legs and pounded into her until he came. She loved the experience of coming and then feeling him pound deep inside of her; it put her body on a level of satisfaction that she couldn't explain.

Chapter 19

Troy and Dominic had gone from lying in bed talking about their future to sitting in the center of the bed making out. His back was to the headboard and his legs were stretched out. She was facing him, sitting in the spot between his legs with her legs wrapped around him.

"Should we merge our businesses? I mean we do the same thing, so it's kinda like we're in competition," Dominic said, running his thumb down the lips of her vagina. Her satin panties rubbed against her clit and caused it to harden.

Troy shrugged her shoulders; she hadn't thought that far ahead. They worked together on projects; plus, he was her protégé so she never saw him as competition.

"We have a lot to bring together," she said thinking about merging their lives in marriage and having a baby together. "Maybe we just take our time. Ya know...it doesn't have to happen overnight. We know we want this for life," she said and began to rock into his thumb.

"You're right," he said, sliding his hand up her leg, gripping her thigh and then holding her hand. He held his hand up as she traced his fingers. "Marriage first," he began but she cut him off.

"Baby," she said. He looked into her eyes.

"Baby first?" Dominic questioned.

"Yea," she said and dropped her head, "because if I can't give you—"

"If we can't have a baby, I'm still going to marry you," he interjected. She smiled.

"I know but I want to do that process first. IVF can be hard," she said.

"We gonna try the old-fashioned way first though, right?"

"Yes, but I want to be realistic."

"Chrissy is thirty-eight, baby," he reminded her. Chrissy had had a healthy baby boy six months ago.

"I know but I'm not Chrissy. How long do you wanna try before we consider IVF?" she asked. Dominic paused the conversation, leaned in and kissed her neck. Troy felt her body relax before she even realized she had been rigid.

"I don't know...a year," he suggested.

"A year, Dom? I don't know if I have a year," she replied.

"I don't want you to stress about this. I want us to have fun, love each other and build all our shit from that love."

"I want that too, baby. I'm just being practical." Troy threw her arms around his neck and kissed him as she inched onto his lap.

"When do you wanna stop practicing?" he said, tracing her nipple with his tongue.

She giggled. "I mean if we're sure...we could get tested and start as soon as possible."

"We're sure; you know that. We also have to factor in birth control and how long it takes to get pregnant once you stop."

"So I'll go ahead and stop taking my birth control pills today."

"Cool, then I can take the condom off," he said.

"After we get the results," she said, pulling back to look at him.

"Of course," he smiled.

"I still have to talk to my OBGYN to make sure everything is good," Troy informed Dominic.

"I'll go with you, if you want," he said.

"I want that," she said and kissed him.

Hours later they were in the kitchen putting their takeout food on a plate.

"Have you been to see your grandmother?" Dominic asked. Troy had been raised by her grandma, who now suffered from dementia and had to be put in a nursing home. Troy had tried to take care of her at home and failed. She worked hard to be able to afford the home, that was ran more like an expensive retirement village, for her grandma.

"Of course; we wouldn't be having this conversation if she hadn't approved." Troy laughed. "She just smiled," she said grinning. "When I talk to her about work, she doesn't react, but when I told her I was going to get married and have a baby she cheesed so big," Troy said. Dominic saw the tears well in her eyes; she loved Grandma Clemmie and had always worked hard to make her proud. If she had known a husband and a child would put that smile on her face, Troy would have saved a ton in student loans.

Dominic eased behind Troy and hugged her tight. "I want to go with you to see her," he said.

"Okay," she replied smiling up at him. Dominic bent to kiss her and then they resumed making their plates.

Chapter 20

Geechi had just come home from work and was walking around the house looking for his wife. She had been in New York working with other clients for the past three days and he had missed her. The look on Gotti's face when he entered their bedroom made Geechi stop in his tracks.

"What's wrong with you?" he asked from the doorway. She rolled her eyes, put her phone in her pocket and hopped off the bed.

"Gotti!" he called, grabbing her arm when she pushed past him.

"Every two weeks I'ma have to hear some more shit, Geechi?" Gotti fumed. He stepped back and ran his hand down his face. He had no idea what she was talking about and he didn't feel like finding out. Geechi wanted to come home, fuck his wife and take her to dinner. "You said you haven't fucked her since the reception," she said. He frowned, *more shit about Ashlei* he thought while shaking his head.

"I haven't," Geechi said, following Gotti down the hallway.

"She said you have," Gotti countered over her shoulder.

"She a fuckin' lie...and why the fuck you still talking to her?" he questioned.

"She messaged me on IG," Gotti said. She turned to face him and worked her neck as she spoke. His nostrils flared and he took a deep breath to calm down.

"I'm not fuckin' with her; I don't know what else to tell you," he said, nonchalantly. This shit was old news to him, and he wasn't interested in continuing to give it life.

"So you don't care?" she said, looking at him like the wrong answer would result in a bloody lip.

"I don't care about arguing over the same shit every day; no, I don't," he said, walking by her.

"I'm not going to look for shit," Gotti pointed out.

"When she came at you with the shit you should have shut it down."

"Who said I didn't?" she fumed now back in his face.

"Why you coming at me with it?"

"Because the shit was brought to me!" she screamed. Geechi didn't reply; Gotti took his actions as proof that it was true and that he didn't care.

"Fuck it, I'm leaving!" she seethed. That was the only thing she knew to do.

"Here you go with this shit," he fumed.

"Obviously you don't give a fuck. If a man was coming to you with shit about me, you wouldn't even bring it up to me?" Gotti questioned.

"Not if we had already discussed the shit," he said.

"You a fuckin' lie," she spat. Gotti marched away and grabbed her keys off the holder. He grabbed her and spun her around to face him.

"Get off me," she screamed and swung on him. He moved out of her reach and glared at her.

"What I tell you about that shit?" Geechi said, walking up on her.

"Stop fuckin' grabbing me!"

"Didn't we discuss this childish ass 'I'm leaving' shit? It's not nobody's business what goes on between us. Did I tell Tione that you have a problem keeping your hands to yourself?"

"Is that supposed to scare me," Gotti said, pushing past him.

"I'm trying to have a conversation with you," Geechi said, blocking her from exiting the house.

"If you can't tell me why this bitch won't leave me the fuck alone, don't say shit to me."

"She can't move on because she wants what I gave you. This shit ain't rocket science."

"Obviously you made her feel like she could have it," Gotti shot back. "Move!" she said and pushed him.

"You not going no fucking where...calm yo ass down and chill the fuck out. You always on this insecure ass shit," he fussed.

"Insecure?" she questioned.

"You heard what the fuck I said," Geechi said, walking off.

"Was I insecure before the bitch approached me?" Gotti screamed, charging at him. She muffed him from behind. Geechi's head flew to the front and he spun around, grabbed her arms and pushed her into the wall.

"Stop putting your muthafuckin' hands on me!" Geechi raged. He stood over her as she cowered in the corner. Gotti had never seen him so mad and she was sorry for what she had done. Still, he seemed unable to understand or care where she was coming from.

"You know what, Geechi," Gotti said through a shaky voice. "Fuck you and fuck this!"

"If you leave don't bring yo ass back," Geechi said, leaving the living room and heading for their bedroom.

Gotti grabbed her keys with tears in her eyes and darted out the door. She drove around for a while because she didn't want to go to La'Shea's...didn't want to get La'Shea involved. Geechi was right, they had to be able to handle their own differences. It was hard because Gotti was so close with her girls and they had gotten her through some tough times. After thirty minutes, Geechi hadn't called like he did the first time she left. Gotti felt like she had no choice but to go to La'Shea's.

"Hey!" La'Shea greeted, swinging her front door open. When she saw the look in Gotti's eyes worry covered her face. "What—"

"I don't want to talk about it. Can I have the guestroom?" Gotti said already walking toward it.

"Of course," La'Shea said and closed and locked the door.

A few hours later, La'Shea entered the bedroom with junk food and wine. Instead of talking they watched reruns of *Living Single* until they heard the doorbell.

"I'm sure that's your husband," La'Shea said, getting up to answer the door. When Gotti heard his voice, she slid on her shoes and walked to the living room. La'Shea had a shocked expression on her face when she turned to face Gotti. Gotti looked around for Geechi but he wasn't there.

"He...he brought you some clothes," La'Shea said, holding the handle of the small suitcase. Gotti felt sick. That act hurt her worse than Ashlei sending the messages. Tears rushed to the brim of her eyes. "Got—" La'Shea's words were silenced when Gotti threw her hand up.

"Just give me some alone time," she said and went into the guestroom. She turned off the TV, climbed in bed and pulled the covers over her head.

●●●

Two days later, Gotti had to be at Koran Motors for a meeting; otherwise, she wouldn't have been anywhere near Geechi. She was dressed in a red, fitted, calf length skirt and a white wraparound shirt, standing in the breakroom making herself a cup of coffee.

She felt his presence but decided to ignore it. Then she felt him on her.

"Move," Gotti said slightly elbowing him. Geechi ignored her request, wrapped his arms around her and pulled her back to his chest.

"I miss you," Geechi said and kissed Gotti's cheek before snuggling his face in the nape of her neck.

"Whatever Geechi; move," she said. Gotti tried to wiggle out of his embrace, but he wouldn't let her go. It felt good, he felt good and she fought hard not to melt in his arms.

"Come home," he said.

"If you wanted me at *your* house, you wouldn't have brought my clothes to La'Shea's."

"I brought a few outfits since you insisted on leaving," Geechi said. She turned to face him.

"You did that to be petty."

"You needed to know how it feels to be dismissed like that, Gotti."

"And do you need to know how it feels for someone to come up to you and tell you they fucked me and are going to continue to fuck me?" she questioned through furrowed brows.

"We handled that problem," Geechi told her. Gotti turned up her nose; he still wasn't getting it and that was about to make her spaz.

"Obviously we didn't if the problem is in my inbox," she pointed out. Geechi sighed deeply; he could tell Gotti was getting pissed and didn't want that. He missed her and just wanted her to come home.

"I was frustrated because I already told you what happened...therefore nobody else should have been able to tell you shit about it. You should believe what I say." He explained his true feelings.

"Why?" Gotti questioned. That made no sense to her, and she didn't feel like Geechi would take his own advice if the roles were reversed.

"Because I never gave you a reason to doubt me. I told you when that shit happened...that's it," he said. Geechi felt that their bond should be so solid that when he told her what happened in a situation, it should end all communication with anyone else. But he didn't factor in that they hadn't had time to build the bond he had envisioned in his head.

"I don't care if I need you to explain that shit 100 times," she said raising her voice.

"I should explain it 100 times," he agreed, throwing his hands up in surrender. Geechi had been so focused on his point that he hadn't considered hers. Gotti rolled her eyes, turned her back to him and stirred her coffee.

"I handled it wrong," he admitted. "I love you; this shit...having to explain myself is new to me. I'ma fuck up sometimes," Geechi said, "but I gotta be able to trust that I can fuck up in front of my wife without her running to tell her friends."

"You can," she said, facing him and leaning on the counter. "I didn't tell her nothing. And you have to understand I'm an only child. I don't handle confrontation head on. I never had to. Sometimes I'ma need to walk away."

"Understood," he said with a smile. She smiled too. Geechi leaned in; Gotti met him halfway and they kissed.

"Come to my office," he said, grabbing her hand.

"I'm not giving you pussy every time you piss me off," Gotti said, pulling her hand back. The truth was it was time for the meeting to start and they didn't have time.

"You giving me pussy cause we made up," he told her.

"No we haven't," Gotti said, picking up her coffee.

"The fuck we just do?"

"Talk about it...I'm still at La'Shea's 'til you come get me," Gotti said and walked off. Geechi watched the sway of her hips for a moment.

"Gotti!"

"Come on, so we can get this meeting started," she said heading for the conference room.

Chapter 21

Gotti had been back at home for over a week and things were going well, but she still had a nagging feeling that Geechi wasn't telling her everything. A part of her wanted to let it go, to start from right then and continue to build their relationship. But another part of her nagged and nagged for her to find the information. It told her she could forgive him and move on but only after she knew the entire truth.

Maybe he had fucked Ashlei after their reception, would that be unforgiveable? No. Especially not with the unconventional way their relationship came about. Wouldn't him fucking Ashlei after they became serious be the equivalent of her boyfriend cheating within the first couple of months of them being together? Or would it be worse? Geechi knew what she had been through, knew she was apprehensive, claimed he loved her and had realized that months before the reception; therefore, he should have put an end to outside relationships before the reception, right?

She had searched his office for clues and came up empty. She searched their bedroom, his closet, even the garage and didn't find one receipt, earring, nothing that would give her the answers she needed. *Maybe he wasn't doing shit* Gotti reasoned as she sank to the floor in the bathroom. Maybe he had stopped talking to Ashlei like he claimed, and she became upset and tried to ruin their relationship like he said.

Gotti was happy with that outcome, happy that she hadn't found anything. Then she crawled up on her knees and dug through a drawer in the bathroom. His drawer. Where he kept his razors, floss and hygiene products. In the very back, inside of a case that was supposed to be for his glasses sat a phone.

Gotti's heart was racing a mile a minute. She wanted to put it back but couldn't. Prayed it had a code she couldn't crack, but it didn't. After 45 minutes of searching every app, she had found more than she had bargained for. Pictures, videos, text messages. Most of the numbers weren't saved but the messages were clear.

214-875-9585: *Are you pulling up tonight?*

Geechi: *Yea.*

The communication between Geechi and Ashlei had died down over the last several months but he had talked to her, fucked her and given her money since the reception. Text messages from Lark confirmed that he had fucked her in the past and still flirted as recent as a month ago. Gotti's stomach hurt; her head was spinning. She sank to the floor, but tears wouldn't fall. She was numb.

Geechi had gone to Las Vegas on a business trip; Gotti didn't want to confront him over the phone; she wanted to do it in person. Gotti wanted to see his face when she handed him the phone. He would be back first thing in the morning for work and she would meet him at the office.

With the phone still in her hand, she sluggishly walked upstairs, poured herself two more shots and turned on some music.

The sound of K Michelle's Giving Up On Love blared through the speaker as Gotti watched the video of her and Geechi celebrating their nuptials at V-Live one year earlier. Gotti was on the couch in the loft drowning her tears with D'Usse as images of happier times flashed across the screen. Maleek had recorded them that whole night saying he had never seen his homeboy so happy. Maleek sent it to them as a wedding gift and they had it saved to a flash drive so that they would always have it. What was once the happiest time of her life was now the biggest mistake she had ever made.

Unable to contain her anger, she threw the bottle of D'Usse at the 80in flat screen TV. It cracked, rocked, and fell...just like her marriage.

Gotti pulled out the phone and reread every text message. She watched the videos of him in the club, women all around his section. In one video he could be seen caressing a woman's breasts. In another a stripper was dancing on him as he palmed her ass; Ashlei was there. Gotti read the group texts with his friends rating women, discussing ones they had fucked, reminiscing about women Geechi had fucked. Geechi wasn't replying but that didn't do anything to ease the pain. They were clowns and he was a clown for being associated with them.

At some point, after crying her heart out, she fell asleep on the couch. The sun woke her up and reminded her of the heartbreak that sleep had rescued her from for a few hours.

Gotti got dressed in a black latex skirt that stopped above her knees and a button up crop top shirt that stopped where the high waist skirt began. She paired the ensemble with open toed Louis Vuitton heels and a matching mini clutch. Gotti looked like a model when she exited the house through the garage and hopped in Geechi's Bugatti.

●●●

"Damn, I been calling ya damn phone all morning," Geechi said as Gotti entered his office. He zoned out as he watched her sashay to him. His wife's thick frame filled out the skirt perfectly making his dick twitch and rock up.

"Maybe you were calling the wrong one," she said. Gotti's icy voice wiped the lustful glare off Geechi's face, and when she handed him the iPhone 7 that he knew could ruin their marriage, all the color drained from his face. Geechi was too shook to even take the phone from her. Gotti smacked him in the face and the color rushed back to his caramel skin.

Geechi couldn't speak; a million thoughts were running through his mind, but he couldn't formulate a sentence. He knew his life was over, he knew that no matter how much he loved Gotti, wanted her, was changing for her, he couldn't dispute what was in that phone.

"Wh-why you going through my shit, Gotti?" *WHACK*! Gotti landed an open-handed slap right upside his head.

"Wrong fucking answer!" she fumed.

"We can't do this here," Geechi said, grabbing her arm trying to pull her to the door. He knew they needed to go home to resolve this dispute.

"We gon' do this shit right here," Gotti said, snatching her arm back.

"You're mad at me about some old shit in an old phone," he said. Old wasn't the right word. Geechi should have said irrelevant because it didn't mean shit to him, it couldn't hurt or jeopardize shit...unless she let it. He wasn't going to leave her or embarrass her; he was entertaining his friends. On some dumb shit, no doubt, but it didn't *mean* shit.

"Old?" she said with a devious chuckle.

"Yea that shit is old," he continued. "Old as in it didn't mean shit," he tried to explain. He had lost all his cool, nothing he was saying was making sense, although he thought it did in his head. Geechi couldn't explain why he had done what he did, but it didn't mean shit, and he was hoping against hope that Gotti could somehow understand that.

"That's not what old means," she informed him.

"You get what I'm saying though...that was the old me," he said.

"A bitch asking you to pull up a month ago! Lark texting you some shit about a cucumber challenge! Fuck you mean old?" Gotti seethed. Geechi's facial expression ignited fire in her belly; she became so heated she momentarily blacked and threw the phone at him. It crashed into his face and made his lip leak.

"Go fire that bitch!" Gotti demanded as the phone dropped to the floor.

"What?" he said, catching the blood in his hand.

"You heard what the fuck I said. Don't make me say the shit again," she fumed. He grabbed a tissue from his desk and held it to his mouth.

"I can't," Geechi said.

"You can't?" she raged.

"Will you listen to me for one second," he begged in a low voice. "How can I fire her for no reason...she can claim sexual harassment, baby, and with the other case—"

"What other case? What the fuck is going on with that?" Gotti questioned.

He stepped back, appalled by the accusation. "You think I'm lying about that shit?"

"When is the shit going to be over because I want a divorce," she told him.

"Divorce?" That wasn't an option for him.

"You couldn't delete the shit, Geechi? Even after Ashlei came up to me? ...You didn't care enough to delete the evidence? You didn't care if I found out the truth?" she questioned.

"If you went through the phone you know I haven't been fuckin' with her," he said, removing the tissue from his lip and dropping it in the trash.

"But you did after the reception, and you providing this bitch's lifestyle?" Gotti boomed. "Lark, Geechi?"

"Baby, me and Lark haven't fucked since before you started working here," he explained. That was the truth, but Geechi knew she wouldn't believe him.

"But you flirting with the bitch...why? And you got me in here working with her?" Gotti screamed ready to swing on him again. "Do you know how stupid I look?"

199

"If anything that bitch is envious," he said thinking about the little comments Lark sometime made regarding Gotti.

"Envious? Why would she be, knowing she can fuck my husband whenever the fuck she wants to!"

"No the fuck she can't. Do you know how many times she has thrown pussy at me?" Geechi said figuring he should get credit for the pussy he dodged. Her facial expression told him that wasn't going to happen.

"No tell me?" Gotti said, walking up on him.

"It doesn't matter. I curved it every time."

"I *hate* you," Gotti said with so much pain in her voice his heart dropped. "I don't want shit to do with you. I don't want to work here. You are *disgusting*," she told him. Geechi reached for her.

"Don't fucking touch me!" Gotti said, hitting his hand. "In six months I want a divorce whether the trial has started or not." She slid her dark shades over her eyes and exited his office and then the building. Gotti hopped in his Bugatti and drove to the airport to catch her flight back home to New York.

●●●

Three days had passed and while Geechi wanted to give Gotti all the time she needed to heal, he missed her and wanted to explain things to her.

"What's up?" La'Shea said with a confused expression. She was surprised to see Geechi when she opened her front door.

"Can you tell Gotti to come to the door?" he asked.

"Gotti?" she said, wrinkling her face. "Gotti isn't here," La'Shea let him know.

"Look La'Shea, I know she's pissed and she has every reason to be—"

"Geechi!" she said cutting him off. "Gotti isn't here. I haven't seen her," she said. La'Shea was now thinking back to when she saw Gotti last. They had texted a couple days ago and Gotti was very short with her replies. She said she was swamped with work, so it didn't alert La'Shea that they hadn't talked.

"What happened?" La'Shea asked worried. Geechi could tell she was truly confused.

"Nothing," he said, backing away. "We got into an argument. I thought she came here. My bad," he said and left before she could say anything else. La'Shea immediately grabbed her phone and called Gotti. Gotti didn't answer so she called Troy; Troy hadn't spoken to Gotti either. Thirty minutes later, she still wasn't able to get in contact with Gotti, so she called Geechi.

"Yea," he said answering her call. She could tell a lot was on his mind.

"I have tried to call her 10 times in the last thirty minutes, and I can't get in touch with her. Troy hasn't talked to her either...what the fuck happened?" La'Shea demanded to know.

"Look, we got into an argument."

"About what?"

"Our business. I shouldn't have gotten you involved."

"But now my friend is missing and I'm worr—" she paused to look at her phone. "This is her," La'Shea said. Before she clicked over, she heard him yell, "Tell her to call me."

"Hello?" she said.

"Hey; why you blowing me up?" Gotti asked. She had been in bed under the covers since she arrived in New York. She only came out to pee and eat. Gotti was more upset at herself than Geechi; angry that she had fallen so hard for him. She knew she had feelings for him before she ever suggested getting married, but Gotti thought she could keep her feelings in check. She had failed; she believed that they could be together and happy forever. The fact that she had played herself hurt to the core.

"Your husband came here looking for you," La'Shea said.

"Oh."

"What happened?"

"We're getting a divorce. He won't stop cheating," Gotti said. She knew she would have to have this conversation with her friends eventually, but she wanted to postpone it for as long as possible. Gotti had assured them that she knew what to do with Geechi, that she could handle it. She didn't even want to think about what she would say to her mother. Had she not fallen for him, or at least admitted it, and allowed herself to be happy, telling Helen would be easy. But now Gotti couldn't even pretend she didn't care.

"The stuff with ol' girl was true?" La'Shea said.

"Amongst other things," Gotti replied.

"Damn," was all La'Shea could say.

"I don't really want to talk about it. I'll be back in Texas tomorrow to get my things. Will you call and tell him? Tell him I'll do it while he's at work."

"Okay. Are you coming by here?"

"I need to leave my stuff there until I can get it back to New York."

"That's fine; you can just bring it and I'll send it to you."

"Thank you," Gotti said.

"I love you," La'Shea said.

"I love you too. Tell Troy I'm fine; I just need a few days."

"Okay," La'Shea said and Gotti ended the call. La'Shea sat for a few minutes before she dialed Geechi's number.

"Yea," Geechi said.

"She's gonna get her stuff tomorrow while you're at work so y'all don't have to see each other."

"I don't want her to leave. Can you tell her that; she's not answering my calls," Geechi said.

"Well she doesn't want to be there; can you respect that?" La'Shea shot back. Geechi was talking to her as if she were on his side. True, she had been rooting for them. La'Shea wanted her friend to be happy, and for a moment it seemed like he could handle that. Now it was clear that he couldn't.

He was silent; La'Shea hung up.

●●●

The next day, Gotti flew into DFW Airport and drove to Geechi's house in his car. She had planned to let him know the car was there so that he could go get it. As pissed as she was, she didn't trust leaving it at the airport and risking something happening to it. But contacting him proved to be harder than she thought. Gotti felt drained; she wanted all of this to be over. She would go to his house, get her things, take them to La'Shea's and then leave his car there for him to pick up. Gotti had no plans of telling him she was going back to New York on a red eye.

"La'Shea didn't call you?" Gotti asked when she walked in the house and Geechi was sitting at the kitchen counter.

"We need to talk," he said, hopping off the stool.

"I just wanna get my things, Geechi," Gotti said, turning in the opposite direction to go to the bedroom.

"We not doing that," Geechi said, pulling her back to him.

"No," she said, yanking her body out of his embrace, "we're not doing this. I'm leaving, I'm done. Just let me get my shit. All the information I need was in your phone," she spat and rolled her eyes.

"Gotti, you went in that phone with a motive, so whatever you saw you made fit what you thought," he said. Yes, there was dirt in the phone, but he also recognized some things that were innocent that Gotti could have misconstrued by not having the back story.

"That 'are you pulling up' shit was TiTi; she is the hostess at Liberty City. She was asking if I was coming so she could get my section ready," he told her.

"Okay Geechi," Gotti said exhaustedly.

"As far as Lark," Geechi continued.

"I don't give a fuck!"

"I'm going to fire her; you're right I was foul, and I should have been honest from the beginning. You shouldn't have to see her or worry about me being around her."

"I won't see her, and I won't worry," Gotti assured him.

"Gotti, I love you," Geechi professed.

"You really gon' make this hard for me? After all the shit you know I saw, you're going to continue with this shit? Instead of just letting me go?"

"I'm not trying to hurt you. I just want to fix shit. We started off on a shaky foundation..."

"Here we go with this," she said, throwing her hand up. "It started for me the same way it started for you, and yet nobody has come to you about me," she pointed out.

"I figure I can take the guestroom and you can stay in our bedroom as we build the trust back," Geechi said disregarding her statement. He wasn't trying to hear anything about divorce, leaving or clothes being packed. Geechi had finally settled in the fact that they were married, and it would only be her for the rest of his life. Oddly, he found solace in that. Maybe he was a little late, but he was there now. She only needed to give him a fair chance.

Gotti rolled her eyes and charged for the bedroom, but he blocked her path.

"Move!" she yelled and hit him across the face. His glasses flew off his face and hit the ground. His face hardened as if he wanted to swing back, but he took a deep breath instead.

"Move," she gritted and charged him again. Geechi lifted her off her feet and pressed her against the wall.

"Calm the fuck down," he demanded.

"Let me go!" Gotti said still swinging. Finally, she broke out of his clutches. She was out of breath and over the entire situation.

"Where you going?" he asked as she walked to the door. She snatched it open and slammed it behind her.

Gotti stormed down the sidewalk, hopped in the car and drove up the street to the store. Once she was there, she called Gina.

"Hello?" Gina said.

"Hey, Mama Gina, are you busy?" Gotti asked fighting back tears.

"No; what's wrong?" Gina asked muting her TV; she could tell Gotti was crying.

"I'm-I'm sorry to call but Geechi and I broke up, and I'm trying to get my clothes from his house, and he won't let me," Gotti said, embarrassed by the childishness of their relationship.

"Broke up? Why?"

"I'll let him tell you what he's been doing throughout our relationship, but can you...will you call him?" Gotti asked.

"Meet me over there. I'm putting my shoes on now," she said, sitting up in her recliner.

"Thank you," Gotti said, wiping her tears. After Gotti's phone call with Gina, she called La'Shea because she realized she would need boxes.

● ● ●

When Geechi heard someone at the door, he prayed it was Gotti coming back. Looking out the peephole, he saw that it was his mother, so he swung the door open. Gina walked in with a scowl on her face and Gotti came in behind her.

"You called my mama?" Geechi said looking at her like she had committed the ultimate betrayal. Gotti didn't speak. She was too angry and too hurt; he had turned into someone she didn't know.

"Let her get her things," Gina said glaring at him.

"Man, I already told you," he said looking at Gotti. Gina stood between them.

"You can't make her stay here. Let her get her stuff," Gina said making him look her in the eyes.

"You childish as fuck," Geechi said to Gotti as she headed for the bedroom. When Gotti heard a knock at the door she turned and waited.

"Who is that?" Geechi asked her. He could tell that she was expecting someone.

"La'Shea."

"Why?"

"I need help," she told him.

"Just go have a seat, Geechi," Gina hissed. Reluctantly, he walked to the sofa, but he talked shit the whole way.

"Leave my cars here. You had my shit for three days doing God knows what. Because I know your ass wasn't at La'Shea's."

"I never said I was," she shot back.

"Where the fuck where you at?"

"Geechi!" Gina screeched.

Underneath his anger he was hurt. Geechi loved Gotti and wanted her to stay but felt rejected every time she left him. He had fucked up, that was clear, but he never dreamed his relationship with her would blossom the way it had. Geechi met Gotti and wanted to fuck. As he got to know her better, he thought she was beautiful and respected her hustle which made him want to actually fuck with her. Not in the way of a committed relationship, but he wanted to spend time with her, get to know her, multiply her hustle; things like that.

Even when they got married it was strictly business for him with the hopes of some pleasure. Geechi thought it would be beneficial to the both of them and he had planned to give her a lump sum of money when it was all over. But somewhere between her moving in, the movie nights and sharing secrets he had fallen in love. Even before he knew it himself, and just like that, she was ready to throw in the towel. Gotti felt his vibe, she knew how he felt about her and because of that Geechi felt that she should try to work through it.

He understood that from Gotti's perspective it seemed like a lot of shit was happening, but it wasn't. This was the same situation being stretched out.

"Right this way," Gina said to La'Shea, who walked in with three big boxes. Geechi was seething.

Gotti packed all the things she knew she would need: papers, personal documents, her electronics and then whatever clothes and shoes would fit. The most important thing to her was getting away from him for good.

"Yo childish ass was never ready for marriage. You deserve to be with your friends," Geechi said. He sat on the kitchen counter facing the living room while eating dry cereal as they pushed the boxes down the hallway to the foyer.

Gotti was hurt beyond words. As if his previous actions hadn't embarrassed her enough. Now Geechi was taunting her and blaming her for the demise of their relationship. When she got to La'Shea's apartment, she left the boxes in the car. "We can get them later," she said.

La'Shea watched her friend walk as if the weight of the world was on her shoulders and it broke her heart.

"Auntie!" La'Bella cheered when Gotti walked in. She had no clue what Gotti was going through.

"Hey Baby," Gotti said giving her a tight hug.

"What's wrong?" La'Bella asked.

"Just tired," Gotti said with a forced smile.

●●●

Later that night, La'Shea went to take Gotti some food.

"You wanna talk about it?" La'Shea asked as she set the cheeseburger and fries on the bed.

"I don't know what to say," Gotti said with a shrug. "I thought it could work. I believed in the fairytale," she said and broke down crying. "La'Shea, why he work so hard to get me if he didn't give a fuck about keeping me," Gotti sobbed as La'Shea held her. Her heart was shattered; especially with the way he behaved today. Who was he, and why had he switched up on her as if she had wronged him?

"I'm so sorry, baby. I don't know why he did this. I think...maybe he didn't know keeping you would be so hard for him...but I...I think he loves you he just; he," she stopped because she couldn't put it into words. Geechi had always been a standup guy so La'Shea didn't believe he had pulled Gotti in just to hurt her. She just thought maybe it happened too fast, and Geechi wasn't as ready as he thought he was.

"I just want it to be over. I don't want to see him again. I just want to leave Texas and be done," Gotti cried.

"Don't worry about your things, I will have them sent to you, okay? And I'll handle everything involving Geechi going forward."

Gotti pulled back from her. "Can you...I want a divorce...can you..."

"Yes," she said, pulling Gotti to her and hugging her tight. "I'll draw up the papers and I'll make sure he signs them."

Chapter 22

La'Shea had the papers drawn up and sent to Geechi a week ago but she hadn't heard a response from him or his attorney. After three days, she had begun to call him on his cellphone and his office phone, but he never answered. La'Shea wanted to handle this for Gotti as quickly and painlessly as possible, so she decided to pull up on him at his office. Her six-inch heels click clacked against the marble floor as she entered the building.

"Hi Tione," La'Shea greeted with a big smile. "I'm here to see Geechi," she said.

"Hey La'Shea," Tione said looking at his calendar. "Did y'all have an appointment today? He's in a meeting right now."

"I'm a part of it," she lied. Tione trusted the relationship between Geechi and La'Shea; plus, she had no idea what was going on with Geechi and Gotti, so she let her go back.

La'Shea stormed into the conference room interrupting the sales meeting and slammed the folder on the desk. "Sign the fucking papers," she hissed.

"Give us a minute," Geechi said coolly, to the room. The employees gathered their things and left.

"I don't want a divorce," he said, pushing the folder across the table to La'Shea.

"What? After the shit you pulled? You're gonna take her through a nasty divorce like the last nigga?" she seethed.

"It's not about that. I'm not that nigga; I don't want her money. I want her. I understand she's mad—"

"Mad?" La'Shea screeched. "She's broken. She loved you, trusted you and you did this bullshit. Knowing what the fuck she had been through, you decided to play with her emotions!"

"I wanna give her more time," Geechi said trying to remain calm.

"This is not about you and what you want. She wants a divorce; if you ever loved her sign the fucking papers and stop dragging this out. I wouldn't be here if she hadn't begged me to handle this for her. It's over for her, Geechi. This shit that you're doing, fighting for her," she said with air quotes. "Is just turning the knife in her back. If you love her, let her go," La'Shea pleaded.

He pulled the folder to him, flipped it open and with a lump in his throat he signed the papers. Geechi slid the folder back to La'Shea. She took one document out and placed it on the table in front of him.

"My resignation," she said and put the folder with the divorce papers in her briefcase. As she marched for the door, she was stopped in her tracks. Through the glass walls of the conference room, La'Shea saw that Tione was being followed in the room by police officers and detectives.

"The fuck is going on?" La'Shea asked Geechi, who had yet to turn around.

"The police are here and detectives...they gave me this search warrant," Tione said when she entered the office. Geechi spun in his seat and jumped up. Tione's eyes were as big as saucers as they begged La'Shea for answers.

"Let me see it," La'Shea said.

"No, you quit, remember? I got it," Geechi said, taking it from Tione. "Call Barry and don't worry," he told Tione. "Don't tell Mama anything; I will talk to her when I get out."

"Get out?" Tione screeched. She was the only one in the room that didn't know what came after a police raid.

"Geechi Koran," Donny said entering the room. Tione looked up at him with a glare so deadly it was miraculous he didn't instantly die of a heart attack.

"You jealous mutha—" Tione's sentence was quickly cut off.

"Tione!" Geechi yelled. All that emotion was what Donny wanted and Geechi was too smart to give it to him. Now La'Shea was confused; it was obvious they knew this detective and had a bad history, but who was he?

Donny stepped past his first cousin with a smirk on his face and stood face to face with Geechi. "Turn around and put your hands behind your back? We have a search warrant for the premises and an arrest warrant for you."

"For what?" La'Shea questioned.

"I got it," Geechi told her. He did as he was told. Geechi was dressed in blue slacks and a cream, button up with a burgundy sweater over it. Too suave for jail, but he knew this day could come.

"Call a staff meeting. Finish whatever deals are close to closing but put a halt on everything else. Shut shit down. When I get out, I'll have more answers for everyone," Geechi said continuing to give Tione instructions.

"Where is Gotti; what do I tell her?"

"Nothing...we're getting a divorce," he revealed.

"What!" Tione gasped. "But Geechi, what...what," she stammered looking at the officers search through his things "What is—"

"Tione, I got you. Do you got me?"

"I got you," she assured him.

"Do what I asked, okay?"

"Okay," Tione said sounding more like the little sister. She looked like she wanted to cry.

"Geechi Koran, you have the right to remain silent..." Donny said reading him his Miranda Rights. They walked Geechi out of the building as his employees watched with shocked expressions.

"Shit," La'Shea said under her breath knowing she would have more bad news to deliver to Gotti.

Chapter 23

Gotti had gotten out of bed, showered and was now going through her boxes. She half listened to Wendy Williams discuss all the latest hot topics in the background. Gotti pulled out a pair of heels Geechi had surprised her with after seeing her looking them up online. She still missed him, or maybe it was the lie he presented that she missed. Either way, Gotti understood that her life with him was over, and she was trying to find peace in the healing process.

She was surprised to hear the buzz on the intercom indicating that she had a visitor, but Gotti was happy when she heard Troy's voice over the intercom. Gotti buzzed her in and then went to the front door to wait for Troy. She looked stylish in a red Cavalli dress and heels.

"Walk sis!" Gotti said cheering her on. Troy was happy to see Gotti in good spirits but sad at the same time. La'Shea had called and told her about Geechi's arrest so part of the reason Troy popped up was to be there when Gotti got the news.

"I do what I can," Troy said when she reached Gotti. The two embraced and then walked inside the apartment.

"You brought food?" Gotti said, rubbing her hands together.

"Chicken wings, fries and chocolate cake!" Troy said; she too was ready to dig in. After fixing their plates, they sat in front of the TV with a glass of wine.

"Thank you for watching my place while I was in Texas," Gotti said, taking a bite out of her wing. When she and Geechi agreed to truly give their marriage a try, Gotti decided to give up her apartment in New York, but at the last minute she ended up keeping it. Gotti wasn't quite ready to trust him that fully. Her apartment was her security; Gotti's instincts were right. Troy would come to the apartment every few weeks and make sure everything was intact.

"No problem girl!" Troy said, waving her off.

"So what's up with you and Dominic?" Gotti asked cheesing. She wanted to hear good news about a couple doing well. Troy was apprehensive about answering Gotti's question. She and Dominic were doing good. Really good. He had gone with her to her OBGYN appointment and Dr. Gabel said everything looked good. She was producing eggs, not at the rate of a younger woman, but the doctor didn't see any reason why Troy couldn't get pregnant the natural way.

They had also taken their STD tests at Dr. Gabel's office and everything came back negative so now they were fucking like rabbits trying to create life. But Troy didn't feel comfortable telling her friend that because Gotti was going through so much and had no idea that more was coming.

"Good," Troy said with a smile.

"That's all you have to say?" Gotti asked. She and her friends didn't typically keep secrets; they told each other everything about their relationships, so Gotti was thrown off by Troy's secrecy. "You've known him so long...I think you can trust him," Gotti said.

"I do trust him," Troy said.

"Do you love him? Do y'all say it?" Gotti probed.

"I love him," Troy confirmed, "we say it."

"Who said it first?"

"He did."

"He's always loved you though," Gotti said with tears pooling in her eyes.

"Gotti," Troy said, dropping her wing and scooting towards Gotti.

"No," she said. "It's...they're tears of joy. I'm so happy for you, and I'm so happy that real love exists," Gotti said as Troy's phone rang. Because it was sitting face up on the table, Gotti saw it first.

"La'Shea is Facetiming you. Let's make her jealous," Gotti said. She picked up a wing and her wine glass and posed as Troy answered.

"Oooh so that's how y'all do me?" La'Shea laughed, pretending to be upset that they were hanging out.

"Heeeyyyyy girl," Troy sang to further taunt her.

"Wings and wine, huh?" La'Shea said. Gotti could see the sadness behind La'Shea's big smile.

"What happened?" Gotti asked. She could tell by Troy's sigh that she knew what was going on.

"Y'all planned this?" Gotti asked, looking at Troy and then back at La'Shea on the phone.

"I was already coming over," Troy told her. That was true; Troy planned to come chill with Gotti this week, but she chose today because of the news La'Shea had.

"And I felt that that was perfect because I had to call and give you some news. I thought it would be good that someone was there with you," La'Shea explained.

"What?" Gotti said preparing herself for more of Geechi's antics. "You saw him with someone?"

"No baby. I had him served, but the carrier said he threw the divorce papers right in the trash. So I sent them directly to him, but he nor his lawyer responded. Earlier today, I went to his office and demanded that he sign them."

"And he did," Gotti said cutting off La'Shea's story. Neither Troy nor La'Shea missed the twinge of hope in her voice. Hope that he fought for her.

"He did," La'Shea said. "I told him if he ever loved you, he would. And finally he did."

"Well good," Gotti said looking down and organizing magazines on her table.

"But as I was leaving," La'Shea said. Gotti looked back up. "Detectives came in with a team of police officers. He has been indicted and they arrested him."

"What?" Gotti gasped. She had convinced herself that Geechi's contact in the prosecutor's office had been wrong about him being investigated. "So he's in jail...right now?" she said.

"Yes. Tione was there; he gave her instructions to shut down the shop."

"His mother..." Gotti said knowing that Gina would have a panic attack when she learned about Geechi's arrest. And if Gina heard the charges before he could explain, she would have a full-blown heart attack.

"He told Tione not to tell her anything, that he would talk to her when he gets outs," La'Shea said.

"And when will that be?" Gotti wanted to know.

"He'll have to see a judge then they will set bail. It could happen today or maybe tomorrow," La'Shea told her.

"He...his mom will panic. She speaks to her kids every day; if he doesn't answer and then if Tione is acting sketchy..."

As if on cue Gotti's phone rang and it was Gina.

"It's her...it's his mom. What do I say?" Gotti said wide-eyed.

"Maybe she doesn't know. Maybe she is just checking on you," Troy reasoned.

"Yea," Gotti said, nodding her head. "You're probably right," she cleared her throat, sat up straight and answered the call. "Hello?"

"Hey Gotti," Gina said into the phone.

"Hi Mama Gina," Gotti said; she could tell by Gina's tone that she knew.

"Are you...have you... heard?"

"Heard what?" Gotti said, her heart beating out of her chest.

"Geechi...it's on the news. He isn't answering his phone, and neither is Tione," Gina said as she tried to understand what she had just heard on the news. They had to have the wrong person; this had to be a mistake, but Gina didn't know where to start to resolve it.

"The news?" Gotti questioned, looking at La'Shea on Troy's phone. La'Shea jumped up and turned on the television to see what Gina was referring to.

"Yes, racketeering or some shit...fraud; something about a RICO charge. Geechi don't sell drugs," Gina assured Gotti.

"I know, Mama; we're gonna figure it out," Gotti told her. She was unsure of what to tell her; Gotti and Geechi had never talked about what she would tell his family. Geechi was always sure that he would be able to handle that.

La'Shea turned her phone to face the TV. A picture of Geechi in a club standing on the couch with champagne in his hand appeared on the screen. *Why would they choose that picture? That isn't a true depiction of who he is,* Gotti thought. She could already see how the media and the police force were trying to spin this story.

"Rapper Geechi Koran has been arrested in affiliation with a string of charges including Racketeering for shipping illegal merchandise to China and other places around the world," she reported.

"Rapper?" Gotti screeched.

"And why are they trying to make it sound like drugs..." Troy said just as pissed as Gotti.

"Did you see it?" Gina asked. Gotti's heart broke. Gina loved her kids and seemed so lost, so confused by what was going on.

"Yea I saw it. It's not drugs and I'm not sure why they are trying to make it sound that way, but I'm on my way to you. It'll take a few hours, but I will be there," Gotti assured Gina.

"Okay, I'll try Tione again," Gina said before they hung up.

Gotti immediately looked for a flight to Dallas. Her foot tapped impatiently as she waited for the information to load. Troy and La'Shea didn't speak; they knew Gotti needed to call the shots.

"La'Shea," Gotti called.

"Yea?"

"Don't file those papers," Gotti said, choosing the next flight out and entering her card information.

"Of course not," La'Shea said.

"Can you keep checking to see his exact charges, bail, all of that," Gotti said to her.

"I'm on it."

"I need to pack a quick bag, and then can you take me to the airport?" she asked Troy.

"Of course," Troy replied.

Gotti got up from the couch still working on her phone and went to her bedroom. La'Shea and Troy looked at each other neither knew what to say or how Gotti felt. All they knew was to be there for their friend.

"Will you be able to get her from the airport?" Troy asked La'Shea.

"Yes. Tell her to text me her landing time and the terminal information. I'm going to see what I can find out about his charges."

"Okay, talk to you later," Troy said, and they hung up.

●●●

It was eight o'clock at night when Gotti pulled up to Gina's house in the Camry she had rented from Enterprise at the airport. Gotti had called and told Gina she was on the way, so she wasn't surprised that the door was unlocked.

"I don't know, Mama. Geechi said he would handle it and he will. He said it's not bad," Tione tried explaining to Gina for the 100th time. Gina wanted answers that Tione didn't have. She was scared for her brother and wanted to provide assurance to her mother, but she couldn't.

"Not bad?" Gina screamed. "He's in jail...I looked up his charges. That shit holds twenty, thirty years!"

"But he didn't do anything. They have to have something wrong...they're calling him a rapper and shit. They, they, Mama, they have this all wrong," Tione tried to convince her as she herself was losing her mind.

"Gotti!" Gina called out when she saw Gotti entering the den. "What have you found out?" Gina asked as she rushed to her. She just knew Gotti had more information than Tione; she had to; she was sharing a bed with the man for God's sake.

"He wasn't able to see the judge. He was questioned by the detectives and my friend La'Shea, she's Geechi's lawyer—"

"She quit!" Tione raged. Now that Gotti was there she too wanted answers. Tione was just as lost as her mother. Shit, there was nothing Tione could say to calm Gina because she didn't know anything.

"She quit, Gotti? Why?" Gina asked.

"It's," Gotti paused and took a deep breath, "a misunderstanding," she said trying to sound confident. As a brand strategist Gotti knew the importance of getting in front of a problem and making it work for the greater good of the client. Geechi was her client; it was Gotti's job to calm down his mother.

"The case?" Gina asked. Gotti could see her eyes as they filled with hope.

"I...no...well kinda. La'Shea didn't quit...she's helping. He will see the judge tomorrow and I will pay the bail so he can get out. La'Shea is working with Channel 4 News; they reported false information and we can sue them for slander and defamation. She's gonna make them recant," Gotti explained. Gotti wasn't 100 percent sure about anything she had just said but she had to make them believe she was.

"But as far as the charges..." Tione said.

"I'm gonna meet with Barry—"

"Barry?" Gina asked.

"Yes. Geechi's lawyer. We're gonna figure it out. Geechi wouldn't want you stressing, Mama. Please try to relax yourself. Maybe take a hot bath and get some rest. We will figure this out," Gotti assured her.

"Come on, Mama, let me run your bath water," Tione said trying to steer her to the doorway.

"I can run bath water, Tione," Gina snapped; she hadn't meant to, but she was worried. Gina kissed both of them and left the room.

"What the fuck?" Tione said looking at Gotti confused. She needed the truth not the bullshit Gotti had just given Gina.

"It's a lot, I know," Gotti said, rubbing her temples.

"And a divorce? I thought the point of the marriage was to protect him from the case." Tione felt that there should be no talk about divorce because love wasn't the purpose of the marriage. Protection was. So whatever they were going through needed to take a backseat to her brother's freedom.

"Other things happened; the plans changed," Gotti said offended by Tione's attitude.

"But that shit shouldn't matter if the purpose of the marriage was—"

"Your brother will be fine, Tione," Gotti said, cutting her off.

"I...I'm not tryin' to sound insensitive. I don't know what happened between y'all. He just told me that you guys are getting a divorce today...like you said it's a lot," Tione said. "I just...he's my little brother; I need him to be okay," Tione tried to explain.

"Geechi will always make sure Geechi is okay. And if he can't, he has women around him that will. I'm gonna stay in the guestroom," Gotti said. She had already discussed it with Gina; she was just letting Tione know that their conversation was over.

"I have to go home. I'll be back first thing in the morning," Tione said. Gotti nodded and kept walking to the back.

●●●

The next morning Gina was making breakfast. Gotti was on the phone with La'Shea discussing their strategy and Tione was on her computer tying up loose ends for Koran Motors. The two sat side by side on the couch but didn't speak. Tione's inability to pretend to care about what Gotti may have been going through made Gotti think it was all fake. That Tione never cared about her and that she knew what her brother had been up to all along.

"Geechi!" They heard Gina scream from the kitchen right before something dropped. In Gina's excitement, she had dropped the bowl of pancake mix. Tione jumped up and ran for the living room but Gotti stayed seated. She heard them laughing and hugging and it warmed her heart. Gotti grabbed her phone and headed for the guestroom. When she walked out of the den Geechi stood frozen. He hadn't expected her to be there; he missed her, and he wanted her, and he was happy to see her. Gotti kept walking to the guestroom ignoring the magnetic pull of his energy.

"She came last night; Tione wouldn't tell me anything. I was panicking so I called her," Gina explained.

"I didn't have anything to tell you, Mama; I'm in the dark too."

"Meet me in the den, we'll talk. Let me thank her for coming," Geechi told them and headed for the back. When he got to the guestroom, he leaned on the doorframe and watched her gather her things.

"You leaving?" he asked.

"Yea. We need to meet up though...to discuss things," she said, putting her charger in her bag.

"I'm not contesting anything in the divorce," he told her.

"Not about that...about the case," she replied.

"You don't have to worry about any of this, Gotti. I trust Barry to handle it. I signed the papers," he told her.

"I don't think it's smart to get a divorce right now. I think we should stick with the original plan. What are you going to tell them?" Gotti asked referring to his family. Geechi entered the bedroom, closed the door and sat on the bed. His hands covered his face as he allowed his true emotions to show. While he knew this could happen, he had gotten comfortable in the fact that it hadn't. He thought that the investigation had been stopped because of a lack of evidence.

"Did you fire her?" Gotti asked. Her back was to him as she stuffed her things into her duffle bag that sat on the dresser.

"Not yet, I—"

"Don't. You were right...it's not smart. Your mom thinks it's drugs...explain that it isn't and tell her not to watch the news. La'Shea is working on having them to retrack the story. They're trying to make it sound like drugs. They called you a rapper," Gotti told him.

"I'll get Barry on it."

"We need La'Shea. They can work together. What are you telling them so that I know," she said getting back to the topic of Tione and Gina.

"That I shipped cars overseas, not drugs. That it's not as bad as the news is making it sound. That I will handle it," Geechi said.

"When you get settled, call La'Shea so we can meet you and Barry," she said, zipping her bag.

"I can't call you, Gotti?" he asked looking up at her. She stared at him through the mirror. She shook her head no, grabbed her bag and headed for the door. He blocked her path.

"I love you. I'm sorry. I signed the papers cause that's what *you* want," he let her know.

"Okay."

"Okay Gotti?" Geechi questioned figuring she could have said more than that. Did she still love him; did she truly want the divorce?

"All y'all care about is this case, Geechi. I'm gonna do my part," she hissed.

"Y'all?" he asked completely confused as to who else she was talking about.

"Move."

"What happened?"

"Call La'Shea to set up the meeting," Gotti said with a deep sigh. Geechi could tell she was frustrated so he stepped out of her way. She headed up the hallway and a few seconds later, he followed her.

"You not gon' eat?" Gina asked, coming out of the kitchen.

"No," Gotti said with a fake smile. "I gotta go," she said and kissed her cheek.

"You not gon' stay with me?" Gina asked. "I'll cook for you," she offered, "everyday. And Geechi's ass ain't gon' be here."

"Damn Mama," Geechi said pretending to be hurt.

"I'll be back to see you," Gotti promised and then left. Geechi noticed that she didn't say anything to Tione. He looked at Tione and she had a guilty expression on her face.

"Come on, Mama, so we can talk," he said.

"Let me fix your plate," she said, going back into the kitchen.

"It's not drugs," Geechi said after they were all sitting at the table. "It's cars."

"Cars? You can't ship cars; you own a dealership?" Gina questioned.

"I know, Mama, it's bullshit. They are making it worse than it is. There was no point in putting it on the news," Geechi said, forking his eggs and then putting them in his mouth.

"So what's with the racketeering charge?" Tione asked; her breakfast was untouched. She couldn't eat when she was stressed.

"Yea and the RICO charge," Gina added.

"It's the same charge," Geechi told them. "They are trying to say I had a criminal enterprise," he explained.

"Oh Lord," Gina said.

"They are trumped up charges; they're trying to make this shit stick. I could tell by the questions that they were asking that they don't know shit," Geechi said, drizzling syrup on his pancakes.

"What's to know?" Gina asked, chewing her sausage.

"I mean they don't have shit, Mama," he corrected himself. She nodded.

"I don't want y'all to worry. I have a strong team...we're gonna get this shit handled."

"I prayed last night and gave it to God. I knew you wasn't doing all the shit they were claiming," Gina said, drinking her orange juice. "As far as Gotti—"

"She don't wanna be married, Mama. Like you said, I can't force her. What happened with y'all?" he asked Tione.

"I," she said and stirred in her seat. "I offended her. I was scared. I didn't want to hear about a divorce, I wanted her to do what she said she would...protect you," Tione said knowing she had crossed a line with Gotti.

"You can't keep a man that don't want to be kept," Gina said looking at Geechi. She had no idea about the original reasons for Geechi and Gotti's nuptials, so she didn't understand what Tione meant by protection. Still, Geechi felt like a child getting chastised. Gina picked up her half-eaten plate and went to the kitchen. The entire situation had ruined her appetite.

"She found out about Lark," Geechi confessed to Tione.

"That shit is so old," Tione said.

"We texted sometimes...it didn't mean shit, but it wasn't always business. I never doubled back though."

"Why Geechi? Damn, that girl loves you; why would you play her like that?" Tione said raising her voice.

"Whose side are you on? I love her, you know that shit. She left; not me," Geechi said looking at her sideways.

"She left because you acting like a lil ass boy. But what did she do when you needed her the most?" Tione questioned and then answered for him. "She put her shit to the side to be right here fixing shit for you. We," she said referring to black women, "always have to put our pain to the side to make sure everything keeps running smoothly. You were supposed to protect her as she protected you, and you didn't do that! Period. Stop tryna make it seem like she betrayed you by choosing herself.

"Part of this is on me and Mama...we put you on a pedestal, made you king without you doing shit to deserve it, and now you think that's what women owe you."

"I never said she owed me shit, and I never asked her to protect me; the marriage was her idea. And stop talking to me like I'm some bum ass nigga. I handle my muthafuckin' business. I deserve every ounce of respect I get!"

"So because it was her idea that gives you the right to not honor it?"

Geechi shrugged. He didn't want to talk about it anymore; he knew he had messed up with his wife. That he had hurt her; he didn't need everybody reminding him ever chance they got.

"I know you love her. Why won't you fight for her?" she asked, not knowing that Geechi had been trying to get back right with Gotti.

"If you have to tell him to go get her, he doesn't deserve her," Gina said reentering the dining room.

"I agree," Geechi said out of spite.

"We ruined you; we made you right when you were dead ass wrong. We encouraged your playboy ways; we enabled you and now you expect your wife to do the same." Tione went to the kitchen and emptied her plate in the trash, then came back through the dining room. "I see through all that tough guy shit, Geechi. You're playing yourself," Tione said, grabbing her purse and walking toward the door. When it slammed, Gina took a seat.

"What aren't you saying?" Gina asked. Geechi sat for a minute as the anger in him dissolved into hurt.

"I love her, I want her, but I don't know how to get her," he admitted.

"First you need to understand what you did and why you did it."

"I cheated, Mama. It ain't rocket science," Geechi replied. He expected Gina to come with some world-class advice but if that was all she had, she was losing her touch.

"Why? Why did you cheat on a woman you worked so hard to get? A woman that you say you love. Why did you fuck it up?"

A woman that put her freedom on the line for you, he thought.

Geechi didn't speak because he didn't know. He hadn't looked at it that way. Geechi had been thinking of all the things he should have done to avoid getting caught up, but he hadn't asked himself why he did it in the first place.

"Figure that out, fix it and then *try* to get her back. But for now, back off and let her give what she has to give. You don't have the right to ask for more," Gina schooled him and then walked away.

● ● ●

Tione hopped in her car and sped off. She was happy Geechi was out. Happy that he seemed confident about the case; she trusted him and believed that if he was going to prison, he would prepare them for it. But Tione was mad at how she handled Gotti on his behalf. She didn't come at Gotti disrespectfully, but the implication was there. Tione picked up her phone and Facetimed Gotti.

"I'm sorry," Tione said as soon as Gotti answered.

"It's fine. I'm sure Geechi told you to—" Gotti started. She figured Geechi had told Tione to call and apologize to make sure Gotti stayed on board.

"Geechi didn't tell me shit. I didn't know shit," Tione said referring to the cheating; she needed Gotti to know that. "But I'm sorry for making you feel like you owed loyalty to a muthafucka who wasn't loyal to you," she said.

Tears fell from both of their eyes. "Even if the muthafucka is your brother?" Gotti laughed.

"Even if," Tione said.

Chapter 24

Two days after his arrest, Geechi and Barry met La'Shea and Gotti at La'Shea's office. The strategy was to get the heavy charges thrown out and fight the lesser charges in court. This was something La'Shea and Gotti knew would need to be done even before Geechi's arrest because they had discussed the possibilities at length. They didn't know the exact charges or what evidence the police had, so the women worked with hypotheticals based on what the clerk had told Geechi.

Geechi took the advice his mother had given him and respected Gotti's wishes; he didn't stare at her too long and he didn't ask to talk after the meeting like he wanted to. He didn't hug or kiss her. Geechi sat in the meeting, gave his opinion, listened to their suggestions and helped to formulate the plan. After the meeting everyone went their separate ways.

When La'Shea made it home that evening, the front desk clerk waved her over.

"The police were here," she told La'Shea in hushed tones.

"What! Why?"

"They were looking for you," she revealed.

"Me?" La'Shea gasped.

"Yes, they had a warrant for Gotti Koran," she said with a shrug. "Said she's your friend and had been spotted here and that we should call if she comes back."

"Did they leave a card? She's my client, but I'm unaware of any arrest warrants."

"Yea, here it is," she said and slipped La'Shea Detective Costa's information.

La'Shea walked in her apartment and dropped her briefcase on the chair. She was heading for the bar when she heard La'Bella come out of her bedroom.

"Hey Mama," La'Bella greeted with a smile.

"Hey baby," she said and stopped to hug and kiss her.

"You mind if I go to San Antonio this weekend? Dad said he'd meet you halfway," she said referring to Kyle.

"Umm," La'Shea said, rubbing her head. So many thoughts were rushing in her head, so she wasn't paying much attention to La'Bella. La'Shea searched her mind to recall what La'Bella had said.

"Yes, baby, that's fine...when?" she asked, pulling a shot glass from the bar. And then reaching for the tequila.

"When can you meet him? He said today but you look tired," La'Bella said.

"I'm okay, baby, but it's Wednesday." La'Shea reminded her.

"We have a short week at school, remember? And I want to spend time with Kelsie," La'Bella whined.

"Okay...fine," La'Shea said with a smile. She welcomed the drive; it would help to clear her mind. La'Bella could drive there, and she would drive back.

"I told him that since I have my car—"

"You're not driving all the way to San Antonio alone, La'Bella," La'Shea said knowing exactly where she was going with this. "Is he leaving after work?" La'Shea asked as she filled her glass. La'Bella was now seventeen and trying to get more freedom, which La'Shea understood. But taking a four-hour road trip alone was out of the question.

"Yea, let me call him," La'Bella replied.

"Okay. I need to make an important call in my room. I'll be out in a minute," she let her know.

"Okay Mama," La'Bella said going into her bedroom.

La'Shea downed her drink, paced for a moment and then dialed Detective Costa's phone number. He answered on the second ring.

"Detective Costa," he said.

"Hi Detective, this is La'Shea Yarborough. I am the legal counsel for Gotti Koran, you're looking for her?" she said.

"We sure are," he said arrogantly.

"For what?"

"In connection with the Geechi Koran case. We believe she played a major role in helping to facilitate the transportation of vehicles overseas," Costa said.

"What evidence do you have? My client had nothing to do with Mr. Koran's charges," La'Shea replied.

"Then why are you her counsel?" Costa questioned as if he had solved the case.

"She's going through a divorce," she retorted. Donny had heard Geechi tell Tione that he and Gotti were getting a divorce. As a cop he paid close attention to signs. He could tell by Tione's expression that she was blindsided by the information. With that and the look of despair in Geechi's eyes, Donny knew he didn't want the divorce. But Donny had it backwards; he assumed that Geechi was divorcing Gotti to protect her from the case.

He had a lot of circumstantial evidence which led to the judge finally signing off on the search warrant, but they needed something concrete; and he was certain Geechi's love for Gotti would give them what they needed.

"I heard," he said, and La'Shea could tell he was smiling. "Gotti Koran has until tomorrow at 5pm to turn herself in. If we find that she has no involvement, we will let her go. It's as simple as that, but she better be willing to tell us what we need to know. Any more questions," he said, cockily.

"I have all I need," La'Shea said and hung up.

She walked out of the bedroom in search of another shot. "What did your dad say?" she asked La'Bella.

"He's on the way. He will meet you in Killeen. He said you drive so fast he has to get a head start." They both laughed. "Maybe you can come to San Antonio to get me. You could see grandma and maybe we could have family time before Kelsie goes back to college," La'Bella suggested.

"I like that idea," La'Shea said with a smile. La'Bella smiled too. La'Shea decided to let Gotti get a good night's sleep. She would meet up with Gotti first thing in the morning to discuss the situation, but she needed the rest of the night to come up with a plan.

●●●

Donny sat in his car, threw his head back and howled a laugh so loud it echoed through the car. Everything he'd planned was happening exactly how he'd planned it, and Donny couldn't be happier. He had infiltrated Geechi's clique and gathered enough circumstantial evidence to justify a search warrant and Geechi's arrest. But Donny knew he needed more. Jamison, the prosecutor, was on him to get the hard facts so the evidence would stick. Donny knew Geechi had a ring of people that assisted him with illegally exporting cars to China. While he hadn't been able to get to that circle of people, Donny had gotten to the circle just outside of it. Donny was confident that the informants would be able to infiltrate the inner circle. With Geechi's hands tied with his legal matters, he would need someone to keep that business going.

What Donny hadn't seen in the beginning was Geechi's wife. He'd heard that Geechi was married; shit, it was plastered all over the news. But the look in Geechi's eyes when he told Tione they were getting a divorce, told Donny that Geechi wanted to protect Gotti. That made the detective look further into the time the couple meet and when they got married; the timing was very suspicious. Donny figured the divorce was to distance Gotti from Geechi's illegal activity since she had a PR firm that was very successful. Donny wanted to indict her to ensure that she couldn't provide the money Geechi would need to fight his case.

"We need to meet," Donny said when the informant answered the phone.

"It's hot right now," the informant stated. Donny's skin crawled at the cocky way he spoke as if he had a say in the matter.

"And who do you think made it hot? I can make it hotter," Donny replied.

"You threatening me like we're not on the same team." Truthfully, they weren't, but Donny needed to reel in his attitude because he still needed the snitch.

"It's not a threat and it's not directed at you. I'm talking about *him*."

"Cool. I'll be in touch," the caller said and hung up. Donny looked at the phone in disbelief. The detective couldn't wait to show his snitch who was boss.

"Disrespectful moolie." Donny gritted.

●●●

"Vodka and soda," Donny said, sliding into the seat at the bar. The club was packed so it had taken a minute for him to make his way to the bar. Then Donny had to stand around until a seat became available.

"Detective," she said with a flirtatious grin. The bartender licked her lips and set a drink in front of another patron. After making a few more drinks, she made Donny's and placed it in front of him. Donny grabbed her hand seductively and placed a fifty-dollar-bill in it.

"Can we talk?" he asked.

"As long as you're drinking," she said, twirling her tongue over her luscious lips. The sexy siren wore a crop top shirt with Liberty City across it and a pair of shorts with her ass spilling out. Her caramel complexion reminded him of Werther's Original candy. The short blond Bob she sported along with her makeup and nails made Donny's dick jump. He loved a hood chick with attitude and spunk. Just to play with though. Never for anything serious. Or maybe it was the fact that Geechi had dated her for so long that made Donny curious about the treasure between her thighs.

"You single?" he asked.

"You know that," she said with a wink. He had asked that before; she figured he was trying to work up the courage to ask her on a date. She would respectfully decline but flirt anyway to keep the tips coming.

"What happened with Geechi?" Donny asked. She stopped in her tracks and looked at him. "Another," he said, pushing his empty glass to her with two one-hundred-dollar bills under it.

As she made his drink, she tried to figure the detective out. He had been coming into the club for the last two months. Donny, who she knew as Costa, always tipped heavily and flirted. It wasn't abnormal for a police officer to frequent a strip club or to try to get pussy from the girls, so that was never a red flag. But why was he bringing up her ex? The bartender went back to Donny and served him the drink. Everything was about a transaction for her, if Donny had money to spend, she had time to give.

● ● ●

"Hey," Gotti said, opening the door to the hotel room for La'Shea. Gotti didn't want to stay with La'Shea or Gina because she didn't want to pretend to be happy. If she had a bad day, Gotti wanted to be able to cry her eyes out without wondering if they heard. Gotti didn't want to be coddled; she wanted to go through the pain of this divorce and come out of it. Plus, she didn't want La'Bella to see her so weak.

"Hey!" La'Shea said passing Gotti a coffee from Starbucks. They took a seat in the living room and Gotti sipped her drink.

"Is there liquor in here?" she asked.

"Yea, I added some…I have bad news," La'Shea told her.

"Oh Lord," Gotti said, putting the drink down.

"Drink," La'Shea said with a smile as she drank the liquor infused coffee.

They looked at each other and took a few more drinks before La'Shea began to speak.

"The police came to my building," she said.

"What…why?"

"Looking for you," La'Shea said.

"For me!" Gotti questioned on the edge of the seat with her eyes bucked.

"You have to turn yourself in by 5pm."

"I…for what…wha…what?" she stammered. Gotti thought about the meeting she had attended with Geechi and wondered if the police somehow knew about it. She pondered if La'Shea knew. Gotti concluded she was being paranoid. If La'Shea would have even suspected it, she would have mentioned it by now.

"They think you know something, so they want to question you."

"And I could go to jail?" she asked, incredulously.

"You would be turning yourself in. You would be fingerprinted and photographed," La'Shea explained.

"A mugshot? My mother will kill me!" Gotti jumped off the sofa and began to pace the floor. What if her other clients found out about this? *What will this do to my business*, she thought. The strategist immediately began to develop a plan on how to spin this in her best benefit. *The brand strategist willing to go to jail for her clients. That could work*, Gotti thought. One of the perks of her career was being able to scrub the internet of any unflattering information involving her clients. As soon as this was over, she'd do just that for herself.

"Gotti!" La'Shea called because she had zoned out.

"Yea?" Gotti said.

"If you talk..." La'Shea said. Gotti glared at her.

"I don't have shit to say. The fuck!" she raged. They were silent for a moment; Gotti sat back down. "La'Shea, what am I supposed to do?"

"Am I talking to my friend or Geechi's wife?"

"I'm not telling on him," Gotti said with a shrug. In that moment Gotti realized that Geechi had given her everything she needed to take him down. *Why*, she wondered. Did he trust her that much?

"Then I'll have your bail money ready," La'Shea said. She wasn't judging Gotti; whatever she wanted to do, La'Shea was going to back her up. "I don't want you to have to spend the night. Maybe if we go early..."

"Let me get dressed," Gotti said, getting up and heading to the bedroom.

"I'll call Geechi," La'Shea said, pulling out her phone.

"No," Gotti said. "Let's see what happens first."

In the bedroom Gotti's eyes welled up with tears but she didn't let them fall. This was what she had signed up for, even if she didn't think it would get this far, deep down Gotti knew it could. She could do a night in jail because Gotti knew Geechi wouldn't let it last any longer. Telling him now would only make him panic and maybe there was no reason to, not yet anyway.

As she searched her bag for clothes, Gotti figured that jail was cold like hospitals, so she put on black jeans and a white V-neck with a pair of sneakers.

"Do I need anything?" Gotti asked, walking out of the room.

"No," La'Shea said, standing up.

"Are you crying?" Gotti gasped because while La'Shea loved hard she was always stoic in the face of adversary.

"No, just worried; this is a big deal."

"I'm just going with my gut. I know you think I should tell Geechi, but I have to turn myself in regardless so what's the point?"

"I'm following your lead, but you need to be prepared to spend the night," La'Shea said and they walked out of the door.

●●●

During the interview Gotti stayed engaged enough to try to learn what information the detectives had, but La'Shea did most of the talking. Regardless of them being detectives they were human beings so Gotti knew they could slip up and reveal too much information.

When Gotti was booked and taken to the holding cell, she felt a sense of relief because the police didn't have anything...photos, recordings, nothing. If they did, they would have presented it in an effort to get her to talk. The detectives were guessing at everything and while they were good guesses, Gotti felt confident that it wasn't enough. They could only make this stick if someone folded. She especially watched Costa; she recognized him as the guy that had visited the shop. He tried to appear confident and poised but Gotti could see his desperation to find any little thing that he could use against Geechi. This was personal to him; Gotti figured that was something they could use.

Even though she turned herself in early, Gotti still missed the judge and had to stay the night in the cold holding cell with no clock. A few times throughout the night she had fallen asleep only to wake up with no idea how much time had passed. Gotti didn't eat so by the time she went to see the judge, the blueberry muffin La'Shea slipped her tasted like heaven. Her bail was set at 25,000 dollars of which 2,500 had to be paid; La'Shea took care of it and within two hours Gotti was a free woman... for the time being.

"You didn't tell Baby did you?" Gotti asked when she got in La'Shea's car.

"Of course not. She's in San Antonio with Kyle and Kelsie anyway," La'Shea informed her.

"Good. Can I see your phone?" La'Shea passed it to her and Gotti called Tione.

"Hello?" Tione said.

"Hey, it's Gotti. Where is your brother?"

"Hold on," Tione said. They were at Gina's house; Tione was in the kitchen and Geechi was in the den watching SportsCenter.

"No! Just tell him to meet us at La'Shea's in two hours," Gotti said.

"Okay," Tione said and Gotti hung up.

"I need to go by my room to get clothes."

"Why don't you come stay with me?" La'Shea offered.

"I've gotten used to having my own space again," she said with a smile.

After handling her hygiene, they went to get food and then went to La'Shea's to wait for Barry and Geechi.

"You do all the talking," Gotti said when Barry and Geechi knocked on the door. "I will jump in when I need to," she let La'Shea know.

"Okay."

Once everyone was seated and La'Shea had offered the men a drink, she got down to business.

"Gotti just got out of jail," she informed them.

"What!" Geechi shouted and looked at Gotti for answers. She kept her focus on La'Shea.

"They came here looking for her, but she wasn't here. So I was able to talk to Detective Costa and we orchestrated a time for her to turn herself in," La'Shea said.

"That muthafucka!" Geechi gritted.

"He questioned her," La'Shea said. "He seemed thrilled when I called him. Like this shit is personal for him."

"It is," Gotti told her.

"Can y'all fill me in on who the fuck he is," La'Shea said.

"Long story less long. Geechi's granddad took over Costa's granddad's shop, made it better, got rich. Fucked Costa's grandma, got her pregnant, gave her back and lived happily ever after with his wife. They blame him for their demise and think the shop rightfully belongs to them," Gotti said.

"Man call that nigga Donny; that Costa shit just makes him feel important," Geechi said.

"The fuck!" La'Shea said still processing Gotti's rundown of their history. Barry was processing it too.

"This works in our favor," Barry said.

"My thoughts exactly, but I want to save that," Gotti said.

"Save what?" Geechi asked her. She looked at La'Shea.

"We may be able to get the case thrown out," La'Shea told Geechi.

"But I want to hold on to that. Getting it thrown out just means they can retry it. I want this shit done with," Gotti said.

"Why didn't you tell me they had a warrant for your arrest?" Geechi asked Gotti. "This shit is going too far, man; I'll just cop a plea," he said through furrowed brows.

"She doesn't want to do that," La'Shea told him. The whole 'Gotti not talking to him' thing was agitating Geechi.

"She doesn't have a choice," Geechi said looking at Gotti.

"They don't have shit," Gotti finally spoke to him.

"They have enough for search warrants and arrest warrants," he shouted.

"If we stay solid, I don't think anyone will have to do time. They want me because they think I'm..." she said and paused trying to find the right words.

"In on it," Geechi said trying to finish her sentence.

"No...your weakness. They think you'll confess for me." Gotti was good at reading people; she had taken persuasion and debate classes in college. Gotti knew when someone was bluffing, and she knew how to read below the surface.

"You are!" Geechi said shocked that she seemed oblivious to that fact.

"I think we should stay solid," she said, sitting back.

"Once they see that Gotti doesn't know anything, the department may drop the charges," Barry said.

"I'm not getting that impression," La'Shea interjected. "The police want a conviction and I don't think they care how they get it."

"They are using fear to divide us, to scare us into solving their case for them. The police don't have videos, pictures, nothing that incriminates us. The detectives would have showed me yesterday."

"Gotti, Donny has something; maybe he isn't laying out all his cards yet."

"The police have your bank statements and proof that you sold one car overseas, but they can't prove racketeering, they can't prove you are the boss of a criminal operation. At best you're a straw buyer," Gotti told him.

"They not stupid, Gotti, they know I wasn't doing that shit alone," Geechi said. She glared at him; there were certain things Gotti hadn't told La'Shea and things she knew Geechi hadn't told Barry. Gotti hated that Geechi was allowing his emotions to cause him to over speak.

"You know I'm right," Gotti said to La'Shea. "You looked into the case...you told me they didn't have shit." Since Geechi's arrest his case had been all La'Shea worked on because she knew Gotti still loved him; plus, Gotti was tied to the case as well. La'Shea felt like saving him meant saving her. Now she regretted giving Gotti so much information because Gotti was using it to put herself in the line of fire. When the best friends were doing all their research, they didn't anticipate that Gotti would be charged as Geechi's co-conspirator, but that didn't change much lawfully...it only played with their emotions.

"Put your feelings for me aside...if he was your client, what would you tell him?" Gotti said to La'Shea.

"She's right," La'Shea said.

"I thought corporate law was your thing," Geechi said.

"Criminal law was my first love."

"You sure you wanna keep going with this?" he asked Gotti. She nodded.

"Okay, we have a plan," Barry said. "I was in the middle of drawing up the motion to dismiss the RICO and fraud charges. I will send it to you so you can go over it when I'm done," he told La'Shea, standing up.

"Sounds like a plan," she said, standing up as well. They shook hands and then he dapped up Geechi, and La'Shea walked Barry out. Gotti picked up her phone and pretended to be doing something important so she wouldn't have to talk to Geechi.

"Gotti," he called in desperation.

"All they can prove is that you did it *once*. They can't touch your crew because they don't know shit about it. Let's not let our emotions fuck this up. People worked with you off your word and your granddad's reputation—"

"I'm solid as fuck don't play with me," he gritted, thinking she was suggesting that he might snitch. Geechi would never give up his partners, but he also wouldn't let Gotti do time. He'd just take his time and rebuild when he got out.

"Then we're good," Gotti said and turned her attention back to her phone.

"Thank you, Gotti," Geechi said. She looked up at him just as he was looking at her. Gotti smiled as La'Shea walked back in.

"Y'all need a minute?" La'Shea asked.

"No," Geechi said, standing up. "I wanted to talk to you," he told La'Shea.

"About what?"

"You think I should fire Barry; I mean what is he really doing?"

"What I need him to...filing the motions, handling the court dates...plus, he has connections that we may need. I'm not in criminal law so I don't have the relationships he has," she explained.

"Aiite cool. I just wanted to make sure," he said. "Later Gotti," Geechi said over his shoulder.

"Bye," she mumbled as La'Shea led him out.

Chapter 25

When Gotti got word that she would be charged alongside Geechi, she didn't know what to feel. Their trial would take place together, but they would have separate juries to decide their fate. Both Troy and La'Shea had advised her to do what Geechi had asked multiple times, which was to let him fight the case alone. Gotti didn't see how that was possible since she was already being charged.

She had overheard La'Shea telling Geechi that Gotti could plead out, blame him and get off scot-free, so she wasn't surprised when Geechi came to her as if it were his idea. Gotti was at his mother's house having dinner with Tione and Gina when he walked in as if he were shocked to see her and then asked to talk to her in the back room. Gotti looked around the table at Gina and Tione. *We didn't tell him*, Tione mouthed. She could tell by their facial expressions that they were just as surprised to see him as she was.

"I have a plan," Gotti told Geechi after he tried to encourage her to plead out.

"And what is that?" he asked, sitting on the bed.

"We blame each other," Gotti revealed.

"Gotti!" he said as if that were the dumbest plan in the world.

"Just trust me," she said with a slight attitude.

"It's not about trusting you."

"It's about protection, right? That was the whole point of this, so why are you changing up now?" she questioned.

"It's different now, Gotti. Once we go on trial, I have no control over what they give you," he expressed.

"This whole case is circumstantial both La'Shea and Barry said that," Gotti reminded him.

"People have been convicted off circumstantial evidence," Geechi informed her.

"All that they can prove is that you sold a car...they can't prove you had the knowledge to know it was illegal. All we have to prove is reasonable doubt. If we point the finger at each other that creates reasonable doubt," Gotti explained.

"Or they could convict both of our asses."

"I'll make a deal with you," she said.

"What's that, Gotti?"

"If they throw out the RICO charge, we do it my way. Because that was my idea and that would mean I know what I'm talking about," she said.

"You're not a lawyer, Gotti...Barry and La'Shea would have thought of that shit. You said it first, but I'm sure it was on their minds."

"Deal or no deal. If not, this whole shit was for nothing," Gotti said. His mind went to their marriage, his cheating and the pain she suffered because of it.

"Or maybe it was for us to get together, get married and live happily ever after," Geechi suggested.

"Well...we know that's not true."

"I love you, Gotti," he said to her. Gotti broke eye contact; she wasn't trying to hear that shit. It would do nothing for her, the same way it did nothing for him.

"Then stick with the plan...making a deal doesn't guarantee my freedom. They could give me time for knowing about the shit. I didn't sign up for that, Geechi. I signed up for this. To fight," she explained. Geechi thought about their marriage; they should be fighting for that. As if she read his mind, Gotti rolled her eyes and looked toward the door.

"I'ma go eat, Geechi," Gotti said barely above a whisper. "Do we have a deal?"

"We have a deal," he replied. She nodded and headed for the door.

"Gotti?" he called. She looked back at him.

"Can I take you out sometime. Maybe dinner..."

"I'm going back to New York tomorrow until the trial starts. After that I'ma be in New York for good," Gotti said and exited the bedroom. In the hallway she took a deep breath and walked to the dining room.

"You okay?" Tione asked when she returned to the table.

"Yea."

"What he say?"

"Just stuff about the trial," Gotti told Tione.

"You hungry?" Gina asked when Geechi came up the hallway.

"Nah," Geechi said and kissed his mother's cheek. "I just needed to talk to her about court," he let her know.

"Later Tione," Geechi said. Their relationship was still rocky because Tione didn't like the way Geechi did Gotti, and he didn't like that Tione took Gotti's side instead of being neutral.

"Bye Geechi," Tione said.

● ● ●

Later that night Gotti was back at the hotel packing for her morning flight. She was excited to get back to New York and dive into work.

While Geechi had taken up the majority of her time, he was not her only client. In fact, over the last few months she had hired one of the interns that had been working for her. Now, including herself, she had a crew of five. Gotti was considering finding a small office space but decided she should wait until after the trial. Gotti hadn't told her mother or her employees anything about her legal or marital woes, and she had no plans to.

All Helen had to do was Google Geechi and everything involving his legal troubles would come up. But because Helen was happy with their relationship, she didn't pry. Helen wasn't much of a prier unless Gotti brought her new information that she wanted to confirm or if Gotti got too quiet. Therefore, Gotti made sure to put in weekly calls to her mother to keep her satisfied.

"Hey girl!" La'Shea said answering Gotti's call.

"I know you love me and want the best for me, La'Shea," Gotti started off.

"Okay..." La'Shea said. She could tell by Gotti's tone that a 'but' was coming.

"But please stop trying to go through Geechi to make me change my mind."

"I just—"

"I know, but I've made my decision, and I'm tired of explaining it over and over again. You say you're following my lead, but then you go behind my back and undermine me."

"That was not my intention," La'Shea said appalled by the accusation.

"We're going to trial," Gotti told her.

"Okay."

"You said all we have to do is prove reasonable doubt."

"I said we have to prove reasonable doubt...you added the word *all* to make it sound easy. It's not," La'Shea told her.

"We should imply that it was each other," Gotti said.

"An implication may not be enough. And I don't like the idea of blaming each other," La'Shea told Gotti, flopping down on her bed.

"Why?"

"Because y'all are married...the jury will assume if one of you knew, then the both of you did it," La'Shea explained.

"Well what do you suggest?" Gotti asked.

"I don't know. Let me think on it."

"You didn't send me a bill. I'm not asking you to do this for free," Gotti said.

"Ha! And I'm not. Geechi paid me."

"Oh," Gotti said.

"Oh," La'Shea mimicked.

"I love you. My flight is at 10am but I will call you when I land," Gotti said.

"I love you too."

Chapter 26

Gotti was at home in her cold bed twisting and turning. It had been a month since she last visited Texas and, in another month, she would be back to face her charges. Gotti trusted her gut which was telling her to keep pushing and that everything would work out. Yet tonight for some reason sleep wouldn't come to her. No matter how she fluffed her pillow or changed her position, she couldn't get comfortable.

Gotti laid on her back staring at the ceiling going over the case. Geechi was sure there was a snitch especially after new evidence had been entered about a storage unit used to house cars before Geechi shipped them overseas. The police knew that a Bentley truck had been on the showroom floor and then it disappeared with no paperwork. Only someone on the inside could provide that information.

Gotti's mind raced with possibilities but she tried not to let her emotions get involved. If they did, she would go through the numerous woman Geechi had probably been with and the information they could have found out. Geechi wasn't that sloppy though. It had to be someone close.

"Lark?" she said and sat up in bed. Lark was close in proximity because she worked for him... "Oh shit," Gotti said when the light bulb went off in her head. "Carl!" Carl was Lark's husband and he had been staying late supposedly trying to get more sales. "How could you be so damn stupid!" Gotti said as thoughts of Geechi's recklessness raced through her mind. Geechi had fucked Lark and was stupid enough to text and flirt with her. Gotti reasoned that Carl had found out and played it cool. Now he was working with Donny to take Geechi down. "Ugh!"

Gotti grabbed her phone and paced the floor as she called him. It was one in the morning in New York which meant it was 12am in Texas; she knew Geechi was up.

"Hello," he said breathlessly, finally answering her call. Gotti hated that the first thing she wondered was why he was out of breath. She wanted to curse him out. To call him all types of idiots and make him feel low, but what would that help? Gotti took a moment to gather herself. "Gotti?" Geechi said into the phone. His voice was almost panicked like he was worried about her. Gotti's eyes filled with tears; she was supposed to be with him figuring this out, but she was miles and miles away. He sounded like he wanted her, needed her there with him. Her hurt turned into anger.

"Carl," she said.

"Huh?" he replied. For a moment Geechi thought she called him the wrong name, but he knew she couldn't possibly have a death wish. "What?" he said with an attitude.

"Carl; you dumb ass. Did you really think you could fuck that man's wife right under his nose, and he wouldn't pay you back? Think about it. He stays late. The day Donny showed up at the shop Carl was there. He told Tione he would lock up. Carl thought everyone was gone and he was giving Donny free rein. You fucking idiot! You're about to lose your granddaddy's shop over some pussy," she seethed.

"Gotti!" Geechi yelled into the phone. She was being beyond disrespectful. Before he could say anything else, she hung up. Geechi sank down into his seat. He had been doing a late-night workout when she called. Typically he would be in the club or with a woman to blow off steam, but he couldn't do anything else that could further jeopardize their relationship. Everything in him said if he handled his business like a man, he would get his wife back. And Geechi believed that with his whole heart.

"Hello?" Tione said, rolling over in bed to answer her phone.

"We shutting down shop," Geechi told her. After he got out of jail, they took a few days off, then it was business as usual. Tione figured that would continue at least until the trial began.

"What?"

"Send an email. Be there tomorrow and turn them around at the door. If someone has to go into their office to get their personal belongings let them do that only. I'm sending Maleek up there too incase shit gets out of hand," Geechi said. He put their call on speaker and sent Maleek a text letting him know he needed him or one of his employees at the shop at 8am tomorrow.

"What's going on?" Tione asked.

"Tell them we're closing indefinitely."

"Indefinitely?" she questioned.

"Yea Tione. After the trial we'll rehire those that we want. If anyone needs a letter of recommendation, tell them we'll provide one. You have access to everyone's computer, right?" They had bought a software program that allowed them to track the things employees were doing on company computers. That included any internet searches, emails or documents they had typed.

"Yea," Tione said. His big sister was still trying to process what was going on as she sat up in her bed in the dark.

"I need to know what Carl and Lark have been up to."

"I'm on it," Tione said, throwing her covers back.

"Get some sleep. We'll handle it in the morning."

"Sleep? Hell no! I'm on this shit right now. I'll let you know if I find anything." Geechi couldn't help but smile; Tione loved being a detective.

● ● ●

"What's this, Costa?" Ashlei asked looking around the hotel room at the other people in attendance. She was dressed in powder pink leather shorts and a cute pink bubble jacket that stopped at her belly button. Ashlei's hair was pulled back in a long, weave ponytail and she wore open toed clear heels. Donny had asked her to meet him at the hotel, and while she wasn't going to fuck him, Ashlei figured she may be able to string him along and get some real money out of him. She had Bernie, a member of the security team at the club, in the lobby waiting for her to call if shit got out of hand.

"Have a seat," Donny told her.

"Who they?" she asked, pointing at the two men. One was seated at the desk and the other was on the bed.

"Your partners," Donny said with a smirk.

"Uh-uh, bye," she said, charging toward the door.

"You told me about the storage unit, that was helpful," Donny said making Ashlei stop in her tracks. "Now you just need to tell it on a stand."

"A stand? Hell no!"

"Or go down for prostitution," he said.

"Muthafucka, I didn't fuck you, and I had no intentions of doing so," she told him, and anyone else that may be listening in.

"I have text messages where we talked sex and money," Donny reminded her.

"You was talking sex; I was talking money," Ashlei said with her hand on her hip.

"Officers are on the way up here as we speak," Donny informed her. That made the other two men nervous. They too had been lured there under false pretenses. Neither had agreed to testify, only to help bring Geechi down.

Ashlei pulled out her phone to text Bernie. Just as she clicked his name a text came in from him. Bernie said four officers had just walked through the lobby and that he was about to leave. She had five minutes to get to the car before he pulled off.

"Uh-uh," Ashlei said again. "I'm leaving," she announced, walking to the door. Donny stepped in front of her.

"Fuck you mean the police? I never told you I was testifying to shit, then you got these other muthafuckas here."

"Orlando, have a seat. You've been thinking you were running shit for a while. You haven't been. I have our conversations recorded. You'll just need to confirm the facts on the stand. You too, Carl," Donny said to the guy sitting on the bed.

"Look, I never told you shit about a storage unit," Ashlei said. "I never offered you sex for money. You can bring whoever in here and I'll tell them that to their face. I don't know what type of snitch shit y'all on, but I wants no parts of it."

Donny smiled when they heard the knock on the door. He opened it and in walked four police officers. Ashlei could have pissed on herself; she had allowed greed to get her in a predicament she would have a hard time getting out of.

"Ashlei, Carl, Orlando, these officers would like to have a conversation with you. We can do this the easy way or the hard way; your choice," Donny said.

Chapter 27

N ovember rolled around and it was finally time for the trial to begin. The defense could have kept pushing it back, but Gotti wanted to get things over with, so she told La'Shea to accept the first available court date. Gotti, Geechi, Barry and La'Shea walked into the courtroom together. Troy, Tione and Gina were already seated on the front row. Gotti wore an ankle length black skirt, a cream blouse and black and cream heels. November finally brought a cold front to Texas, so she also wore a red peacoat over her ensemble. Geechi was dressed in a black Armani suit with black Louis Vuitton loafers with red bottoms.

Gotti gave a quick smile to Gina who looked more worried than she expressed. Gina was trying to trust her son. When Geechi said everything would be fine, Gina tried to live her life that way, but today her worry showed on her face. Jury selection had already taken place so while Geechi and Gotti sat at the same table, Gotti's jurors were placed on the right side of the courtroom and Geechi's were on the left.

"I would like to enter a motion to dismiss the charge for RICO Act," Barry said once the proceedings began. He walked to the bench and provided the documentation to the judge.

"On what grounds?" she said, flipping through the information.

"The prosecution has no evidence of repeated acts of crime. Nor do they have evidence of a criminal organization perpetuating the acts," Barry explained.

"Mr. Koran has illegally exported cars numerous times," Jamison, the prosecutor, said jumping up. He was a round white man with a receding hairline.

"Where is the proof?" Barry asked looking at Judge Henderson.

"That will be revealed during the trial," Jamison answered, also looking at the judge.

"Is the State withholding key evidence?" Barry asked Jamison through furrowed brows. "All evidence must be made available to both sides," Barry schooled him. "If not that's grounds for dismissal."

Jamison looked flushed. Barry redirected his attention to Judge Henderson. "My team and I have gone through what little evidence is available numerous times. Jamison is simply dragging out a case that he can't prove and wasting taxpayers' money. The whole case should be thrown out," Barry told the judge. She looked at Jamison for a rebuttal, but he had none.

"The RICO charge is dismissed," the judge had no choice but to say. Gotti released a sigh of relief.

"We would like to enter a motion to have the charges against Gotti Koran dropped," La'Shea said as Barry headed to the table, and La'Shea made her way to the bench. She was dressed in a midnight blue skirt suit with matching heels as she approached the bench.

"Objection!" Jamison yelled. He was clearly still upset about the RICO charge being thrown out. La'Shea had already told Gotti that this was a long shot. The prosecution wanted a conviction; so without Gotti helping them, they would want her head on a silver platter. Still, La'Shea would present the motion because all the judge could say was no.

"Gotti Koran is married to Geechi Koran and no evidence of illegal exportation was found until she entered his life. If anything, she may very well be the mastermind," Jamison stated.

"Mrs. Koran worked strictly as the publicist for Koran Motors; she had no authority over the finances or tax information," La'Shea said getting back to her argument.

"Not as the publicist, no," Jamison agreed. "But as his wife she is involved," he added.

"The motion to dismiss the charges against Gotti Koran is denied," Judge Henderson said hitting the gavel.

Gotti was unbothered but worked hard not to smirk; she knew the jury was watching and she needed to play her part. Geechi glanced at her; she gave him a weak smile to assure him that she was okay. After the motions, court ended for the day and would resume the next day.

●●●

The trial lasted for four days. On the second day, the prosecution revealed that Geechi was already under investigation for tax fraud when detectives found out that he was selling cars overseas without an export contract. The defense argued that it was simply an oversight and refocused the attention to the facts of the case which were the prosecution could only prove that Geechi had done it once. La'Shea and Barry went back and forth breaking down the circumstantial evidence of the case. When it came to the fraud charge, they pointed out how the couple, although married, filed their taxes separately so Gotti didn't know all that Geechi had going on. This also helped Geechi. He wasn't given the chance to report the income earned from the Bentley before being charged with the crime.

On the third day, witnesses started to testify. While Geechi knew his uncle was one of the witnesses, it still tugged at his heart that Orlando would testify against him. When Lorenzo found out that his brother was a part of Geechi's takedown, he did all he could to contact Geechi. Lorenzo settled for a letter that he left on Gina's porch telling her that he had nothing to do with it. He said that

Orlando had urged him to reconnect with Geechi, and now he saw that his reason behind that was to try to gain information. Gina relayed the message to Geechi but he didn't believe a word of it.

Because the recordings were illegally created, Barry had them thrown out. Still, Orlando was subpoenaed and had to testify. Although Orlando had his grudge against Geechi, he didn't like how Costa tried to play him, so he acted as if he didn't recall any of the conversations.

Next, Carl was called to the stand and he sung like a bird. In the hotel room, he pretended like testifying wasn't an option because Ashlei and Orlando were so against it. Once he was alone in the interrogation room, he agreed to tell all that he knew. Carl talked about the Bentley truck and Geechi's suspicious behavior after he was indicted. He also testified about a conversation he overheard between Geechi and Gotti where they spoke about the ways to get away with illegally exporting the cars.

In his redirect, Barry brought up Geechi's affair with Lark. Tione had found emails on Carl's computer where he and Lark argued when he accused her of flirting with Geechi in staff meetings. Carl threatened to take Geechi down since she loved him so much. Barry wanted to call Lark to the stand and make her admit to the affair, but Geechi felt like that would be too much on Gotti.

Ashlei entered the courtroom dressed in black slacks, and a white crop top that showed parts of her belly as she made her way to the stand. Gotti couldn't help but to roll her eyes. Geechi looked over at Gotti apologetically, he knew she was pissed that Ashlei was involved. The prosecution asked Ashlei about the storage unit which she denied ever having knowledge of.

Donny sat in the courtroom pissed. He felt like the case was falling apart at the seams. All of his precious evidence had either been thrown out or his witnesses, who he had spent time and money coercing, had turned on him. Not to mention, his captain wasn't pleased with the way Donny had handled the investigation.

●●●

They were on the final day of court and awaiting the verdict when Gotti stepped away to get some air. She walked outside for a moment then walked upstairs to go to the bathroom. This was the last day she would see Geechi because La'Shea was handling the divorce so Gotti could let go and move on. She had to admit it was taking a toll on her. Still, Gotti was excited about putting this whole debacle behind her.

Geechi noticed Gotti had been a little different today, more distant than she normally was with him, and he wanted to make sure his wife was okay, so he went looking for her.

When Gotti saw the hand stop the elevator door from closing, she moved to the far-left corner to make room. Gotti wasn't expecting it to be Geechi. Her eyes dropped to the floor when he entered.

"I just wanted to check on you," he told her as the elevator doors closed and they headed back downstairs.

"I'm fine. Ready for it to be over," she said politely.

"The trial, right?" Geechi questioned.

"All of it," Gotti confirmed. Geechi had a lot to say to her; he knew now wasn't the time, but he didn't know if the time would ever come. Gotti wanted to walk away, and Geechi knew he couldn't make her stay but that didn't mean he couldn't try.

"I'm sorry I hurt you," Geechi said. "I left a lot of loose ends," he shrugged trying to explain his actions, "on some immature shit really. I guess I didn't want to have those conversations. Didn't wanna tell my homeboys I was on some new shit. Just figured they'd see it, them and the women, and move on and that was foul. I didn't handle my shit like the man that I am.

"I wasn't fucking with her when she came up to you, Gotti, but I did fuck with her after the reception. I could tell you it didn't mean shit because honestly it didn't...the sex, the interaction; it didn't mean shit. But my betrayal meant ending our marriage and that crushed me, so I guess what I'm tryna say is it meant something in the end," Geechi said rambling. He had planned this conversation in his head, but it wasn't flowing out of him like he anticipated it would. Like it would if his heart wasn't really feeling the pain of his wife's absence. But Geechi prayed that Gotti understood what he meant. He moved closer to her. "I'm sorry for how I treated you when you came to get your shit; I just...I didn't want to lose you. As far as the other shit, the texts, videos; a lot of that shit was old. I should have gotten rid of that phone and put that life behind me and I'm so sorry I didn't."

"It's fine, Geechi. Right now we gotta focus on this," Gotti said referring to the trial.

"And after the trial?" Geechi asked wanting to know if they could work on their relationship.

Gotti shook her head no.

"I love you, Gotti," Geechi said, now standing over her. Gotti was in the corner and he had both hands on either side of her holding on to the rail. "I want us, Gotti. I have taken time to really see the role I played in this bullshit and I won't do the shit again," Geechi pleaded. "Look at me," he begged, but Gotti wouldn't look up at him. She couldn't.

"Look me in the eyes and tell me you want a divorce," he challenged. The elevator dinged and Gotti finally looked up.

"I want a divorce." Their family was standing in front of the elevator when it opened so they saw Geechi on Gotti, saw her push him back and saw the look of sadness and disappointment in his eyes as he watched her exit the elevator.

"You good?" La'Shea asked, rushing to her.

"Yea," she said, smoothing out her plaid slacks and black button up shirt.

"Let's go in, it's time for the verdicts," La'Shea told her. That was the reason everyone was standing there waiting for them.

"Two hours...is that good?" Gotti asked trying not to panic.

"We're about to see," La'Shea answered.

Everyone piled back into the courtroom and took their seats and soon it was time to read the verdicts. The judge instructed Gotti to stand up.

"Madam foreman," Judge Henderson said preparing to reveal Gotti's verdict first. "On the charge of tax fraud, how do you find Gotti Koran?"

"Not guilty," the foreman said.

"On the charge of conspiracy to commit a criminal act, how do you find Gotti Koran?" Judge Henderson asked.

"Not guilty," the foreman said.

Gotti dropped her head and smiled. Geechi stood up and hugged her tight. Once the courtroom had settled down, Geechi was told to stand as his foreman prepared to deliver his verdict.

"Sir foreman, on the charge of tax fraud, how do you find Geechi Koran?" Judge Henderson asked.

"Not guilty," he answered.

"On the charge on straw buying how do you find Geechi Koran?"

"Guilty," the foreman answered. Geechi expected that and knew that being convicted of this crime meant probation and forfeiting the money he was paid for the car.

"You okay?" Gotti asked, standing up after court was adjourned.

"Yea," he said and the two embraced. She walked away from him, he grabbed her hand; without looking back, she wiggled it out of his grip and kept walking. He stood there for a moment before Tione and Gina ran up to hug him.

●●●

"I think you're being too aggressive," Tione told Geechi when they were in the car leaving the courthouse.

"How am I being aggressive?" he inquired.

"Maybe the way you had her pinned in the elevator," Gina said.

"I didn't have her...I didn't mean to pin her. I was just..." Geechi's sentence trailed off because he didn't know what he was doing other than trying to get Gotti back. Nothing was working, and he didn't know what else to try. Gotti wouldn't talk to him so how could they ever reach a breakthrough?

"Being aggressive," Tione said.

"How much time am I supposed to give her?" he questioned; truly wanting to know the answer. They didn't reply. "She tryna divorce me," he said.

"As much time as she needs," Gina finally said.

"Write her a letter," Tione said as a joke, but the idea resonated with Geechi. With a letter he could organize his thoughts and express exactly how he felt without getting tongue tied.

●●●

"You don't want wine?" La'Shea asked Troy. They were at La'Shea's apartment celebrating with homemade tacos and wine.

"I *can't* have wine," she said, spinning around and leaning on the counter.

"Why?" Gotti asked with her face scrunched up as she bit into her taco. The smirk on Troy's face revealed the reason. Gotti's eyes bucked; she jumped off the countertop and ran to Troy. The three women hugged and cheered in the kitchen.

"That was fast!" La'Shea said.

"I know, we've been trying for three months. My doctor said the birth control could take up to a year to get out of my system, but..." Troy smiled.

"Oh my god! I'm so happy for you!" Gotti said and hugged her again.

"What did he say?" La'Shea wanted to know.

"I haven't told him," Troy admitted and dipped her chip in the salsa.

"Why?" La'Shea asked.

"It's early and I'm...nervous. I've taken three tests, but I want to see my doctor first."

"And I'm sure he wants to go with you," Gotti said.

"I know but if it's a false alarm—"

"You took three tests; it's not a false alarm," La'Shea assured her.

"But...if, I don't know...if something happens because...with my age," Troy said, and they knew exactly where she was going with this conversation.

"Giiiirrllll, we are about to have a fun pregnancy not a stressful one!" Gotti said.

"Nothing is going to happen. You need to tell him when you get home; don't make him miss the doctor's appointment," La'Shea said.

"You're right," Troy agreed. She and Gotti would be catching a flight back home tomorrow, and she would order dinner for Dominic and tell him the good news.

"I fucked Kyle," La'Shea rushed to say.

"Biiittcchh! What? Why won't you let that man have peace," Gotti said.

"What does that mean?" La'Shea replied.

"You don't want him, La'Shea," Troy said trying to be gentle with her comment.

"He doesn't want me; he said no strings attached," La'Shea told them.

"Yea 'cause he knew that would get your fast ass," Gotti said.

"He has a girlfriend," La'Shea revealed; she still wasn't sure how she felt about that.

"You broke your rule?" Troy gasped.

"He didn't tell me til after."

"I bet you were pissed," Gotti said.

"I was at first, but it was a one-time thing so I'm good," she said with a shrug.

Troy and Gotti looked at each other and rolled their eyes before they got back to their girls' night.

●●●

"Oooh!" Dominic said when he walked into Troy's candlelit apartment. She had created an area for them on the floor surrounded by pillows and more candles. Troy was dressed in a black, satin robe with nothing under it...he presumed.

"Ooh," she mocked him and then they kissed.

"Are you ovulating again tonight?" he asked, taking off his shoes and loosening his tie.

"I don't want us to only be romantic when I'm ovulating," she said.

"I mean me either...I'm just asking," Dominic replied as Troy grabbed his hand and led him to the pallet on the floor.

"What did you order?" he wanted to know.

"I had Tako to make something special," she told him.

"Really? What?"

"Steak and lobster," Troy answered.

"Damn baby; thank you," he said ready to dig in. He'd had a long day at work and because of it he had only eaten gum and pretzels.

She watched and even laughed as he demolished his plate filled with steak, lobster, mashed potatoes and Cajun corn.

"You got dessert too?" he asked.

"Yea; let me get it," she said and went to the kitchen. Troy came back holding a silver platter covered with a lid.

"Damn baby, you went all out. What is that red velvet cheesecake?" Troy sat down and Dominic lifted the lid. He was confused at first; maybe even irritated because he wanted that red velvet cheesecake. His eyes zeroed in on the white stick. He snatched it up and brought it to his face to examine the results; she sat back and smiled.

"Really baby?" he said.

"Really baby," she replied, sitting on his lap. They shared a passionate kiss as he gripped her butt.

"I took four tests so I'm pretty sure, but I made an appointment with Dr. Gabel." She let him know.

"When?"

"Friday morning since you don't normally go in on Fridays; is that cool?" she asked.

"Hell yea," he said.

Dominic kissed her cheek; Troy kissed his lips. He twirled his tongue in her mouth and she let out a gasp as his hands ran up her robe caressing her naked ass. Before long he was sucking her tittie as she fidgeted with his pants finally exposing his dick. She eased down on it while they stared in each other's eyes.

"Mmmm," she moaned, rotating her hips as she took in more and more of his manhood.

Chapter 28

G otti rushed into her building in an effort to shield herself from the harsh December weather that New York provided. One thing she could say she missed about Texas was the winter weather. Gotti debated if she wanted to check the mail or not. Ultimately, she decided to check it, because she had yet to get a post office box for her business. Therefore, important contracts still came to her home address.

Inside of her apartment, Gotti removed her coat, gloves and scarf and began sifting through the mail. A letter for Geechi sent her heart into overdrive. It had been a few weeks since the trial; Geechi had been sentenced to probation like they expected, and he had to pay restitution. Gotti wondered what the letter could be about; she was sure the divorce had been handled by now; maybe it was in regard to that. The anticipation was killing her, so Gotti ripped the letter open and with bucked eyes she read all four pages.

Geechi was exposing himself in a way she had never witnessed; it wasn't about being cool or tough it was about Gotti understanding that Geechi knew he fucked up, how he fucked up and what he wanted to do to fix it. After reading it the first time, she read it a second time as if it was the first. Gotti reread her favorite parts and stopped to analyze them.

It took conversations with my mom and Tione to see this shit clearly. She was happy they weren't pacifying him. She loved his family and they said they loved her, so knowing the women were holding him accountable made Gotti's heart smile. *This shit is on* me; it's all on me. Timeframes, pettiness, payback none of that shit would have mattered if I had handled my business as a husband. During their arguments he kept trying to tell her it was old information as if that made it hurt less. In her opinion if it was old, he should have thrown it out with the trash. *I shouldn't have put myself in that situation. I should have told her what was up and then prepared you in case she tried some shit like that. I didn't, and for that I'm sorry.*

I know I didn't always see my errors in the situation. To me it was old shit coming back up, but I didn't consider how I hadn't protected you. The shit was old to me, but I was still taking part in it, making it relevant. Gotti remembered how he made her feel for leaving, like it was her fault, like she had done something wrong; it was good to see that he was seeing the situation clearer now. *I thought Ashlei was foul for the shit she did. I figured she was being malicious all because I wasn't fucking with her like she wanted me to. That shit was betrayal to me, but I didn't consider how putting her in the position to do that, was betrayal to you.* That sentence made her flop down on the couch.

I thought you would know I loved you, but how could you if my actions didn't show it? I was moving like I didn't have anything to lose and I fucked around and lost everything. But if you let me, I'll rebuild it all.

Tears stained Gotti's face because she had needed that apology more than she knew. The letter also mentioned a flight to Saint Lucia. He would be there for three days and wanted her to come...if she wanted to. It was his way of getting some much-needed relaxation after everything that happened with the case. Gotti looked at the ticket, then reread the dates. She could go and not see him, since they were flying from different airports and he had gotten her a separate room. Geechi let her know that if she came, he would not try to force her to talk to him or to spend time with him. He wanted her to have a good time after all he had put her through. Gotti bit the side of her mouth. She had never been to Saint Lucia; she loved the beach and it was all expense paid. Gotti knew she wanted to go...she knew she would go; she just wasn't sure how she would act around Geechi or if she even wanted to see him.

Gotti felt stupid for going so she told Troy and La'Shea that she needed a few days to herself so they wouldn't be alarmed when they didn't hear from her. Gotti didn't want to take the chance of them calling, or Troy showing up at her apartment, and having to explain where she was. Gotti knew if she told them not to, they wouldn't ask questions; they would even pretend not to judge. But her best friends would be judging, and Gotti didn't need or want that. She needed some dick though, and she wasn't ready to share her body with anyone else no matter how dumb being with Geechi made her feel.

●●●

Saint Lucia was a beautiful island in the Caribbean. The eighty-four-degree weather was a nice contrast to the thirty-degree weather Gotti had left in New York. The beaches were beautiful, the people were welcoming and the resort Geechi booked gave Gotti every reason not to leave the premises.

After checking into her room, Gotti showered and changed into a swimsuit with a colorful coverall that looked more like a form fitting sundress. She went to the bar outdoors by the pool and ordered food and a drink as she allowed the sun to kiss her skin. Gotti wasn't sure when Geechi would be getting there; she hadn't talked to him at all, not even to let him know she'd be there.

She was enjoying the St. Lucian Crab Back when she looked through the lobby and saw him enter. Gotti dipped her meat in the lemon garlic butter and continued to eat as if she hadn't seen him.

●●●

Geechi hadn't heard from Gotti since the last day of court. He knew she had been in contact with Tione, because Tione casually mentioned it, but she didn't say anything about a letter. He knew that if Gotti told her about the letter, Tione would jump at the chance to throw it in his face. She hadn't, which left Geechi wondering if Gotti had received it at all. He fought the urge to call her; he was trying to fall back. He had sent the letter and booked the vacation, there was nothing else he could do but to allow her to come to him.

"Reservation for Geechi Koran," Geechi told the clerk. She began typing information on the computer and eventually gave him the keycard to his room. "Can you tell me if Gotti Koran has checked in?" he asked her.

"Let me look that up for you," she said and punched a few more keys. "Yes...a couple of hours ago," she confirmed. Geechi nodded, trying to keep his cool, but on the inside he was a kid on Christmas. On his way to the elevator, Geechi looked through the tinted glass doors and saw Gotti. She was sitting at the bar by the pool. She wore a colorful dress, a big hat and sunglasses. The waiter took her empty glass and replaced it with a new one.

Geechi had planned to take a nap in his room because he hadn't gotten much sleep. Now he was going to freshen up and randomly be at the bar; Geechi just prayed she didn't leave before he made it back down.

Thirty minutes later, Geechi entered the pool area. He saw her sitting at the edge of the pool with her feet in the water. Gotti had removed the dress she wore and was now in a two-piece swimsuit with slits and peekaboo parts all over it. His dick jumped at the sight of her curvaceous body. Geechi hadn't had sex since her; he thought about it numerous times, but then he'd think of Gotti finding out and he couldn't risk that.

Geechi pretended not to see his wife as he walked her way while fictitiously typing something on his phone. Gotti played right along sipping her drink and swaying her feet in the water. He went to the bar instead of approaching her and ordered a drink for himself and one for her. When the bartender served her, he pointed in Geechi's direction, but Gotti didn't look back; she took the drink and nodded her head.

"Can I join you?" he finally had the courage to ask. She looked up at him and squinted although the Chanel shades protected her eyes from the sun. "I mean if you wanna be alone—"

"I would have stayed home," she said. He smiled and took a seat.

"You look good," Geechi complimented.

"You too," Gotti said. He was keeping off the weight he had lost in his stomach area for their reception.

"I missed—"

"I don't want to do that." She stopped him. "I don't want to talk about divorce, trials, infidelity. I'm just a girl in a bikini in Saint Lucia, and you're just an attractive guy who bought me a drink. It'll be like role playing," Gotti said with a smile.

"How many drinks have you had?" he asked because she was hitting on him. Geechi understood not wanting to talk about their problems, he was all for that, but he hadn't expected her to be so receptive to him.

"A few but it's not that."

"What is it?"

"This is a beautiful island; I just wanna have fun."

"Me too," he said smiling at her.

"My room is amazing. It has a plunge pool and everything," Gotti told him.

"I wanted to get us a cottage, but I didn't know if..."

"The room is perfect. The terrace overlooks the beach... it's beautiful; thank you."

"Anything for you," he said. *Except fidelity,* she thought. Geechi saw the change in Gotti's face and knew it had to do with his cheating. "Even that Gotti," he said looking out past the infinite pool at the ocean. "We started off on the wrong foot; I didn't tighten up as soon as I should have. But I promise I can even give you that," he assured her.

"They have a lounge...maybe we can go tonight," she suggested. Gotti had already been thinking about going, then seeing him after, but she brought it up to change the subject.

"I would love to."

"Okay...well I'm gonna go rest. I'll meet you in the lobby at eight?" she said, standing up. He stood up too.

"Yea, eight is fine," he said. Geechi watched Gotti walk to her chair and scoop up the dress. She threw it over her body, slid the sandals on her feet and left. He ordered food and sat at the bar to eat before he went to his room.

●●●

The lounge had a live band playing Caribbean music. There was something about the sexy beat that granted Gotti the freedom to sway her hips and bounce her ass without a care in the world. When they first got there, Geechi didn't want to dance, so she found someone on the dancefloor and danced with him. Before long, Geechi was on his feet dancing with her. They shared drinks and light conversation but mainly they danced and laughed. There was an older white couple on the dancefloor trying hard to catch the beat and hold on to it, but somehow it continuously escaped them.

In the elevator on the way upstairs, Geechi was leaned against the wall and Gotti was in front of him kissing him so sensually it put a spell on Geechi. His mind was gone as she darted her tongue in and out of his mouth with her body pressed against his.

"Did you bring condoms?" she asked breaking their kiss. It took him a moment to register what she had said and why the majestic feeling of her body intertwined with his ceased.

"Nah... I mean I didn't want to assume," he explained, "but I haven't been with nobody," he wanted her to know. "I know you may not believe me," Geechi continued to ramble. They had always used condoms, but he was hoping they could make an exception in Saint Lucia.

"It's cool. I brought some; we'll go to my room," Gotti said and leaned back in to finish the kiss. Geechi let her tongue explore his mouth for a moment, but his mind hadn't left the fact that she had condoms.

"You have some?" Geechi asked as if he hadn't heard her the first time.

"A single woman can't have condoms?" She laughed. Gotti could tell he didn't like the thought of her walking around with condoms, but she didn't feel that it was worthy of an argument or even a conversation. Why was it controversial for a woman to protect herself? And if Geechi had a problem with it because he viewed her as his woman, well, he was sadly mistaken.

"You're not single yet," he said. She wondered if that meant the divorce hadn't gone through but didn't ask. Gotti didn't want to talk or think about those things; she wanted to fuck him for three days and then go back to her life in New York. She resumed the kiss until the elevator reached their floor. Then she tugged on the black, barely there bodycon dress she wore and strutted down the hallway in her seven-inch stripper heels.

In the room, she began to peel off the dress as Geechi watched from the bar where he was fixing himself another drink. "You gon' leave those on for me, baby?" he asked when Gotti bent down to unclasp her heels. His eyes low, his voice husky as if the sexual tension had given him some sort of high. She felt it too...had felt it since he sat by her at the pool. Her body was craving him, begging her to indulge even before the trip, at court, in the elevator; while Gotti's mind was trying to move on, her body wanted to stay put. She knew her pussy was wet because she had thought of nothing but him fucking her for the past 5 hours; Gotti wanted to get straight to him pounding her but what fun would that be? The anticipation was the best part.

She stood back up in a pair of thong panties she had picked up at the stripper store along with her red leather heels. The thongs had a very low V cut and most of her freshly shaven mound was visible. Geechi's mouth watered; his dick hurt from being pressed against the fabric of his jeans. He pulled his shirt and undershirt over his head, then took off his pants releasing his monster. Although it was still confined by his boxer briefs, she saw the bulge and licked her lips. Geechi took it out and stroked it. The sight of him and his tool caused her nipples to stiffen. Gotti made her way to him, dropped to her knees and took him deep inside her warm mouth. She held his dick at the base, jerking him off as the majority of his dick plunged in and out of her mouth. Gotti loved the feel of his thick rod lodged in her throat; the gagging that it caused made her pussy wetter with each slurp.

"Fuck Gotti," Geechi gasped feeling like he was about to have a heart attack. Gotti was swallowing his dick in a way she never had. She wasn't big on sucking dick because her pussy was so good. Shit, he didn't mind skipping head to push up in her, but this... "Fuck," he groaned. This he had to have from here on out.

Her cheeks tightened; his toes curled. Salvia ran from her mouth coating his dick; precum oozed out and she slurped it up like it was her favorite snack. It wasn't just the way she was sucking his dick; it was everything: her posture, she was sitting on her shins with her feet crossed at the ankles almost bowing before him. It was the red thong that rode her hips and disappeared in her ass.

He pulled himself out of her mouth. Gotti dropped her hands and looked up at Geechi; her gaze mesmerized him. With her eyes still on him, she brought her head to the tip of his dick and pulled him back into her mouth. Without using her hands, she bobbed up and down his shaft; her gaze deepened as she tongue-kissed the head. Seeing Gotti twirl her tongue around the head of his penis was almost more arousing than feeling it...almost. Geechi pulled out again; he wasn't trying to bust down her throat and have to take a break before enjoying her fat, wet pussy.

"Stand up," he commanded; she did so. He ran two of his fingers down the seat of her panties; her wetness had soaked them. Geechi pulled them off and backed her onto the bed. He ran his tongue up her lips tasting the wetness that had seeped for her pussy. Parting her lips, he dove deeper inside of her allowing his thick tongue to work her over. Using the tip of his tongue, he circled her clit until it hardened and then pressed his tongue against it making wave motions.

"Oh shit" Gotti panted, spreading her legs wider and cuffing his head. Geechi didn't need her guidance, but she needed something to hold on to. He French-kissed her center until she moaned out. Roaming down to her love tunnel, he stuck his tongue inside and caressed her walls by moving his tongue in a circular motion. Gotti bucked on it chasing the nut that was building inside of her. She looked down at him; his tongue disappearing inside of her, being coated with her creamy filling, it drove her crazy. She threw her head back and fucked his face until it was covered in her juices.

"Condoms are in the drawer," she said and pointed. "Fuck me on the terrace, baby," she said. Gotti's energy was gone but her need for pleasure wasn't. Geechi grabbed the condom and then scooped her up and went to the balcony. He hoisted her in the corner. Her back was against the rails, each leg spread wide and pressed against the railing on each side of him. Gotti's head fell back over the side of the balcony as he plunged deep inside of her. He kissed up her legs as he grinded inside of her until she started matching his every stroke. Gotti wrapped her heeled feet around Geechi's neck, and he lifted her off the rail. It was as if she was swinging into him. Geechi's dick entered her and hit the bottom each time caressing her G-stop. Her wetness, her moans, his grunts and the smacking of their bodies filled the silence.

"It's so good baby," Gotti cooed. "Fuck me," she begged. With her body pressed against the rails again, Geechi dug deeper inside of her hitting every wall. She felt the orgasm building, but it was unlike one she'd had before. It was more intense; Gotti wanted to scream out but had to remind herself that they were outside. Gotti rotated her hips into him, her breathing was labored, and she felt like all the energy was being sucked out of her but that only fueled her more. Gotti knew she was on the cusp of something great.

"Shit," she panted. It was as if fireworks went off inside of her leaving her momentarily deaf. Gotti's body quivered but her pussy wouldn't stop coming; she had no control over it. Geechi kept smacking into her even as she squirted all over his lower half. It wasn't as messy as the videos, but it was unmistakable.

"You good?" he asked with a smirk after he came.

"I...yes," she said. Geechi put Gotti down and her legs were so weak that she almost fell. He caught her.

● ● ●

"That was your first time?" he asked in the shower. She nodded and then washed his shoulders with the towel.

"Now I know where your button is; I'ma hit that hoe every time," he joked. Gotti leaned her head back and he kissed her.

Over the next two days they went on an adventurous excursion in the tropical rain forest, spent time at the beach and fucked until it was time to check out and go to the airport. Geechi's flight left after hers, but he still went to the airport when Gotti did. They had a good time on their trip: laughing, joking, flirting, kissing and fucking. Geechi felt like he had his wife back, so he was confused as to why in the two days they had been back in the States, she hadn't answered his calls or texts.

Geechi didn't want to call Tione and ask if she had spoken to his wife, he didn't want advice from his mother, and he didn't want to have to go to La'Shea. He wanted to pick up the phone, call his wife and figure shit out between the two of them.

He sat at the foot of his bed trying to come up with what to say, then he reasoned that she may not answer the phone. What would make today any different from yesterday when he had called?

Geechi: *Do you love me Gotti. Even a little? If not, I will stop texting you. But if you do, I wanna keep fighting for us.* Five minutes after the text he threw the phone down in frustration. Geechi replayed the events in Saint Lucia: they fucked like rabbits; she was completely comfort with him; he knew how to read her so he would have been able to tell if she wasn't. Gotti had initiated sex, came up with activities, kissed him long and hard at the airport.

"What the fuck is the problem?" Geechi asked himself. He thought about what his mom had told him and added a new text.

Geechi: *My mother said I shouldn't come after you until I understand why I did what I did. I do. And I won't hurt you again.*

Gotti: *Why?*

He was surprised when she texted back so quickly. It confirmed that she had been receiving his messages and that she simply didn't want to talk. Geechi took a moment to think of how to express himself properly. He felt it could be taken the wrong way if he didn't explain it well, and he didn't want anything to drive a bigger wedge between them.

Geechi: *I was scared. I wanted you and our marriage, but it was a lot. Marriage is something I've been taught to fear by old heads who don't know shit. I felt inadequate...overwhelmed. Because forever is a long time and I was scared of having to be perfect forever. I guess I thought I could ease myself into it. I was uncomfortable being vulnerable with you and sharing my fears with you.*

Gotti: *Thank you for being honest.* Gotti was on her couch as they texted back and forth. What Geechi said was deep; she felt like it was his truth, but she didn't know what to do with it. Gotti didn't know if he had changed or if he just wanted to.

Geechi: *Your turn...*

Gotti: *???*

Geechi: *To be honest. Do you love me?*

His heart beat out of his chest for thirty minutes until he realized she wasn't going to answer. Throughout the night each time his phone went off he hoped it was her, but it wasn't. The next morning before he got out of bed or handled any of his hygiene, he texted her again.

Geechi: *I'll take that as a yes. You love saying no so if there was a chance that you didn't love me you would have said it.*

Gotti woke up to the text from Geechi and although she didn't want to, she smiled and felt a level of peace. Gotti threw the covers back and got up to prepare for brunch with her girls.

●●●

"What are your plans for Christmas?" Gotti asked Troy and La'Shea as she spread cream cheese over her bagel. Originally, she was satisfied with her chicken and waffles, but the way Troy demolished that bagel made her pick one up.

"I'm gonna be with Dominic and his family," Troy said.

"I'm going to San Antonio," La'Shea answered.

"Don't y'all normally got to New Mexico?" Troy asked, picking up one of Gotti's chicken strips and dipping it in the honey mustard.

"Um-hmm. I'm...gonna be with Kyle," La'Shea rushed to say and then gulped down her Mimosa.

"What!" Gotti gasped. She knew they had had sex, but she also knew their history. It had been hard to separate because of the kids, so Gotti never figured La'Shea would put herself or the girls in that type of situation again.

"I thought he had a girlfriend," Troy pointed out. She too knew the history and she knew La'Shea needed to move with caution.

"They broke up," La'Shea said with a shrug. The girls stared at her as she forked her fruit and put a strawberry in her mouth. La'Shea knew this would be a big deal to them; they had held her while she cried over their divorce. La'Shea understood that the marriage had to end but she felt selfish for taking the only father La'Bella had known from her. They had built a family with Kyle and Kelsie but when she got the job in Dallas, she did what was best for her and moved four hours away against the advice of her mother and Kyle.

"So he could be with you?"

274

"No! I mean, how would it work with him in San Antonio and me in Dallas?"

"True," Gotti said and nodded.

"Of course most of his work is done from home, and his job has offices in Dallas but—"

"La'Shea!" Troy shouted.

"What?"

"Do you want that, truly?" Troy asked staring into her eyes.

"It came out of nowhere...like all of a sudden you're scared to be alone," Gotti mentioned.

"I'm not scared to be alone," La'Shea said with a chuckle. She had been enjoying single life with the exception of her most recent sex drought. Things with Kyle were just happening; she wasn't making them happen and she wasn't trying to stop them. "I don't know, I don't know," she said.

"You should know before you drag him to Dallas," Troy fussed.

"He...he's not the same Kyle. He's not going to drop everything and come to me," La'Shea told them reciting what Kyle had told her.

"Good," Troy said.

"He says I can be emotionless," La'Shea said with her lip upturned. Gotti and Troy made a face and then focused on their food.

"What does that mean?" La'Shea questioned, dropping her fork and glaring at them.

"You're not a lawyer for nothing, La'Shea. You definitely know how to..." Gotti started.

"Disassociate," Troy interjected.

"So I'm a heartless bitch?" she questioned dramatically.

"When you need to be," Troy told her.

"And sometimes you're a savior," Gotti told her and grabbed her hand lovingly. She thought about how La'Shea came in and helped her with Geechi's trial and the divorce.

"Something about him feels right," La'Shea admitted.

"Maybe it just feels familiar," Troy reasoned.

"What about you?" La'Shea said to Gotti. "What are you doing for Christmas?" she inquired in an effort to change the subject.

"I don't know. Geechi's mom wants me to come to Texas, but I'm not sure if I want to do that. Mama likes to go to Hawaii, but I can't go because she'll ask about Geechi."

"You haven't told her everything?" Troy asked.

"Or...nothing," Gotti admitted.

"Have you talked to him?" Troy asked.

"He's been texting," she said.

"And have you been replying?" La'Shea wanted to know.

"Maybe..." she answered with a smirk on her face.

"You have the right to work it out with your husband, Gotti. If he's showing you that he changed, why not?" La'Shea said.

"Husband...the divorce isn't final?" she asked. Gotti figured without him contesting the divorce it should have been done already.

"You told me not to file the papers," La'Shea reminded her.

"Until after the trial..." Gotti said.

"You never said anything else about it. I was giving you time."

"I didn't think I had to...you said you'd handle it. We already signed..."

"Do you still want that? Have y'all talked about it?" Troy wanted to know.

"I saw him," Gotti said. Since La'Shea was bearing her soul, she decided she would too.

"When?" La'Shea sked.

"In Saint Lucia."

"Saint Lucia?" Troy and La'Shea said in unison.

"He sent me a letter and—"

"A letter," Troy gushed.

"Shut your pregnant mushy ass up. What did it say?" La'Shea said.

"All the things he did wrong; things he has done to change," she answered.

"So you decided to go on a trip," Troy said.

"He had already booked it. He sent me my ticket...told me he wanted it to be a relaxing trip for us and that if I came, I didn't have to see him. I chose to see him."

"So you want to work it out?" La'Shea questioned.

"I don't know what I want so I'm doing whatever I feel. If I want to be with him, I spend time with him; if I need space, I take it," she told them.

"As you should," Troy said.

"And then it's like this marriage was built on a lie; I don't want it. If I decide that I want to work it out, we need to do it right," Gotti said.

"So get divorced and get remarried?" Troy asked.

"Hell no!" La'Shea said. "That's too much paperwork; save the damn trees. The foundation was shaky, yes. But everything has been knocked down and y'all are fixing the foundation now. Then, if you decide, y'all will rebuild on a solid foundation."

"I like that; it's not like y'all are continuing to build on top of bullshit," Troy said.

"Yea, y'all are at ground zero starting completely over. At the most, have a vow renewal," La'Shea said, eating some of her pancakes.

"Change the subject," Gotti said getting back to her bagel as she fought tears. That was a good idea, but she wasn't sure if she wanted the marriage at all, let alone having to rebuild from the ground up.

"Dominic wants to get married before the baby comes," Troy said.

"Do you want to?" La'Shea asked.

"Yea. It's just Grandma Clemmie. If we do a destination wedding, she won't be able to come."

"What about something small at the nursing home. Y'all could get dressed together and have a small ceremony. Then have the one you want," Gotti suggested.

"I like that," Troy said.

"Like her and Grandma Clemmie get dressed together?" La'Shea asked.

"Yea," Gotti answered.

"That'll be beautiful," La'Shea said.

"Where do y'all want to get married?" Gotti asked.

"I want Jamaica...I think. I'm still deciding."

"He left that up to you?" La'Shea asked.

"Yea."

"Smart man," La'Shea laughed.

The ladies discussed the wedding in more detail including them being the bridesmaids before they parted ways. La'Shea had spent yesterday with Troy and she would spend the rest of the day with Gotti before she caught her flight back to Texas tomorrow.

●●●

Eventually Gotti decided against going to Dallas for Christmas. Geechi had said he wouldn't be there, but Gotti knew he would only be doing that so that she could spend time with his family, so Gotti told him she decided to go with her mother. Even if she went to Dallas and spent time with his family, it would only make her miss him.

On Christmas day, Troy called Gotti and found out she was home alone and invited her to spend Christmas with her and Dominic's family. Gotti could tell by the music in the background that they were having a good time, so she climbed out of bed, threw on her clothes and went to Harlem for Christmas.

"I have a confession and it's killing me to hold it in," Gotti said as she sat with Troy drinking hot cocoa.

"What?" Troy asked looking across the room at Dominic as he joked, and play fought with his brothers. She loved their relationship.

"I fucked Geechi," Gotti whispered.

"What? When?" Troy screeched giving Gotti her undivided attention.

"In Saint Lucia."

"That letter got you, huh," she teased.

"I just missed him. I wanted some dick," Gotti admitted.

"You haven't fucked anyone else?" Troy asked.

"No. I'm not ready; I want to take my time...focus on my career. I know it's stupid; he hurt me, but I still only feel comfortable with him."

"It doesn't sound stupid to me," Troy said, rubbing her knee.

"You can tell La'Shea and y'all can discuss it amongst yourselves," Gotti said.

"Who are we to judge. La'Shea is doing whatever she's doing with Kyle..."

"Maybe it could work this time. If he's changed and she's changed; maybe the time apart was needed."

"Maybe...or she could get bored again," Troy said. "For me right is right and wrong is wrong. The same way I want Geechi to come correct or leave you the fuck alone, I want La'Shea to show Kyle that same respect. If she knows he isn't up to her speed, she needs to let that man live."

"What if she don't know, and she is trying to figure it out? What if her intention isn't to hurt him, but she wants to see if he is what she wants? Everybody isn't like you...we don't have all the answers," Gotti told her.

"I don't either. And don't come at me like I'm a know-it-all."

"You think you do," she joked.

"Whatever!"

"You and Dominic could have been together, but you thought you knew what would happen," Gotti pointed out.

"True. I can't even argue with you on that. But everything in God's timing. It wouldn't have worked then." Troy reasoned.

"Know-it-all," Gotti teased.

Chapter 29

Geechi: *Bruuhhh you think Karlie shitted on old girl's sheets?*

    Gotti: *No! And if she did why she keep them!*

    Geechi: *True. They doing this shit for TV.*

    Gotti: *I like Mimi's relationship.*

    Geechi: *Man she acts like she still wants Stevie.*

    Gotti: *What! How??*

    Geechi: *Why she letting him pull all on her and shit?*

    Gotti: *She was trying to talk to him. He did all that. Faith needs to put her foot in his ass because he is disrespecting her.*

"Who you smiling and texting?" Tione asked, walking into Geechi's office. They were working late because they needed to get payroll done.

A week after court ended, the shop was reopened. Koran Motors was flooded with applications with the announcement that they were hiring. After going through them, Geechi and Tione held phone interviews and invited the good candidates in for a face to face interview. In the end, three people were hired. They also invited Tina and Eric back to work for them. With the new hires and the fact that Lorenzo had pointed some of his customers in their direction, business was good. Lorenzo had been working as a middleman to assist his clientele with getting the cars they wanted and selling the ones they didn't. But he sent a few to Geechi with no strings attached. Even that didn't soften Geechi's resolve as it pertained to Lorenzo.

Outside of getting things backs running with Koran Motors and fighting for his marriage, Geechi also had to do damage control with Young Kings Academy. He had an honest conversation with his mentees, their parents, and the staff and sponsors for the non-profit. Geechi asked if they felt that he could still be a mentor and they all voted yes. Afterwards, they rented out Main Event and had a big celebration for the continuation of Young Kings Academy. He invited Gotti, and while she was proud of him, she declined the invitation.

"Hello!" Tione said, waving her hand in his face. "Who are you texting?" she asked again.

"Why you in my business?" he joked, putting his phone down and looking up at her.

"Gotti!" Tione said with a big smile. "Y'all tryna work it out?" she asked, sitting in the chair in front of Geechi's desk.

"I don't know...sometimes it seems that way. Then sometimes we're back at square one and she won't answer my texts. I don't even try to call," Geechi said shaking his head. "I just text her when one of her favorite shows is on. That's all she wants to talk about."

"That's cute," Tione said. "Why you look stressed?"

"Shit, I don't know what I'm doing. I'm trying and failing all the time. I wish I knew what she wants. If it's worth salvaging to her..."

"If it wasn't, she wouldn't ever reply. Plus, she hasn't divorced you."

"She thought she had," he laughed. "When it's just us we're good. It's just when we include the world that shit gets fucked up."

"You need to get like Jay-Z," Tione said. Geechi looked up at her with a confused expression. "Sexing the pain away, vacay the pain away, drinking the pain away, smoking the pain away," she sang.

"What song is that?"

"MaNyfaCedGod on 4:44," she told him.

"Yea, you right," he said. Geechi pulled up the timesheets and sales records on his computer, so they could get to work.

●●●

Now that the holidays had passed, Gotti was in Dallas, unbeknownst to Geechi. Gina had given her cooking lessons and while Gotti thought she wanted to learn to cook, it wasn't her thing. As long as her cooking skills were proficient enough to make sure she survived, she was good.

"Why you keep looking at the door?" Tione laughed. Gina had gone to bed a couple of hours ago and the two were drinking D'Usse and deciding if they wanted to hit a club.

"I just...I don't know," Gotti said.

"You wanna see him?" Tione asked.

"No, but I'm scared you told him I'd be here," she admitted.

"I didn't. I don't want to force you to be with him. If you want him, I want y'all together; if you don't, I want you to be able to walk away," Tione told her.

"That sounded like shade," Gotti said. To her Tione was saying if Gotti didn't want to be with him, she should cut ties completely.

"How?"

"I don't know. I never know with you; I feel like Mama Gina can be neutral; it seems hard for you," Gotti told her.

"I've never had to be neutral when it comes to him. I always got to just be on his side. I'm sorry if it comes off as shade; that isn't my intention," Tione said sincerely.

"Mama Gina never had to be neutral," Gotti teased.

"Bullshit! She had to be neutral when we fought," Tione said.

"I guess," Gotti shrugged.

"He feels like you're playing with him...'cause y'all went on vacation and he said it was good but then, you changed."

"When I'm with him I want him; when I'm not, I think that's best. That man slow danced with me at our reception and confessed all these things to me. He offered that information, he offered me a relationship, he offered me monogamy; I didn't ask for none of that shit. I could have kept it business; he didn't want to, and I believed in him. And it was all a lie, for no damn reason. So when we're on vacation and he's telling me this shit, it feels good then, but it doesn't matter when I get home because I know he'll look me in my eyes and lie," Gotti said. Tione felt every word Gotti spoke. The anger and hurt was embedded in her tone. Tione saw how Gotti fought tears as she relived their reception, and how what should have been happy tears turned into sad ones all because of what her brother did.

"I feel you," Tione said, rubbing Gotti's hand and downing her shot.

Chapter 30

Geechi: *Bruh Karlie and that lie detector test.* Geechi was going to wait until after the show to text Gotti, but Karlie had him doubled over laughing.

Gotti: *It's all a lie.* She texted back with the laughing face emojis.

Geechi: *Then old girl making fun of her daughter cause she took seven years to graduate...at least she did it.*

Gotti: *No she didn't. She is still in school...remember she said she dropped out because of the rumors. Like nah sis you just didn't want to do it!*

Geechi: *Well shit how long did it take you?*

Gotti: *4 years...my mama don't play that shit. I graduated on time!*

Geechi: *Kirk steady fucking up.* Geechi texted a few minutes later.

Gotti: *You're one to talk.* Gotti texted back. When he didn't reply after 5 minutes she texted again.

Gotti: *That was a joke.*

Geechi: *That's what I thought. Now anyway, she should be able to contact him about the child, but he should have told Rasheeda.*

Gotti: *Crybaby!*

One Week Later

Geechi: *Sierra going hard on old girl who said Karlie shitted in her bed.*

Gotti: *Her name is Pooh lol. But yea I know. I'm like are there deleted scenes that we need to know about?!*

Geechi: *Why they end the damn reunion like that?* He texted after the show ended.

Gotti: *So we'll watch next week. Karlie can't be lying though because she offered to take the test.*

Geechi: *Yea but they could do some sneaky shit to make it seem like she lying...like they did Jessica.* He was referring to Jessica Dime on *Marriage Bootcamp.*

Gotti: *You remember that lol. That's when I first got you into reality shows!*

Geechi: *Ruined my damn life!*

Gotti: *Whatever, you love them. I wonder who Karen hit...I couldn't see it.*

Geechi: *Somebody in a blonde wig.*

Two Days Later

Gotti was heading into a business meeting with a potential client when she got a call from Geechi. She silenced it and rushed into the restaurant to make sure she wasn't late. A well-known and highly successful publishing company was starting an imprint with two of their biggest authors Imago and Peachie. They wanted help making the subcompany its own entity without having to depend on the mother company. The meeting went extremely well, and they agreed to do business together. To celebrate their new partnership, they went to the bar to have a drink.

As they were wrapping things up, Gotti pulled out her phone to order her Lyft.

"We drove but we'll wait for your car to get here," Imago told her.

"Oh no," Gotti said, waving them off. "Don't worry about it. It's gonna take like 10 minutes. Go ahead; I'm good. I need to get caught up on some emails," she assured them. They hugged and the girls left. Gotti climbed back on the stool and began going through the emails.

"How you doing tonight?" Gotti heard from behind her. She turned to see a handsome man smiling at her. He was 6'2, brown-skinned and dressed in a suit.

"I'm good," she said with a smile. Gotti looked back down at her phone when she got the alert that her car was almost outside. She stuffed her phone in her purse and stood up.

"My name is Abraham," he said, extending his hand.

"It was nice to meet you," she said, shaking his hand, and then heading for the door.

"Do you have to leave so soon? How about a drink?" he said. She turned back to face him; he was really good looking.

"Oh no I have to go, but thank you," she said.

"Can I have your number?"

"No," Gotti heard herself say although she was curious about his conversation. "But again, thank you," she said bashfully and exited the restaurant.

What Gotti didn't know was that she had pocket dialed Geechi and he was talking shit on the other end until he realized she couldn't hear him. Geechi heard the man trying to flirt with her and it had him pissed. He figured she had ignored his call and was at a bar or something with Troy. Geechi quickly hung up and called Gotti back. As soon as she climbed in the back of the Toyota, she answered his call.

"Ayo put buddy on the phone," he said as soon as she said hello.

"Who?" she asked confused.

"Who were you just talking to? You on a date?" he questioned.

287

"Uh no, I had a business meeting."

"I heard dude talking 'bout 'let's get a drink' and all that bullshit," he fussed.

"I'm beautiful, Geechi," she said as the driver pulled off.

"I know that," he said a little thrown off by her statement.

"So dudes are going to try to talk to me," she let him know. Gotti figured if he heard Abraham trying to buy her a drink, then he also heard her telling him no.

"Gotti!" he roared.

"Geechi!" she retorted. He took a deep breath and paced the floor as he bit his lip. She looked out of the window on her way home. He didn't want to argue with her; she seldom answered the phone and he didn't want to spend this time talking about another man. He'd missed her and wanted to see her, so he changed the subject.

"My mama been asking about you. You don't have any plans of coming back to Dallas?" he asked.

"I was just in Dallas and I saw your mom," Gotti told Geechi knowing he was using Gina as bait to get her to come see him.

"Damn, you couldn't tell me you was coming?" he questioned.

"I don't owe you that, Geechi," she simply stated. He had a way of thinking she belonged to him; she didn't.

"What?" he questioned taken aback by her attitude. But Gotti didn't have an attitude, she just wanted him to understand the boundaries. She liked their weekly texts, but she wasn't ready to commit to anything else. Saint Lucia was great, but she didn't want him to feel like she had to call or text or answer to him in any way.

"I don't have to tell you where I am, when I'm there, who is hitting on me. You had that and you didn't know what to do with it," she told him.

"How long I'ma have to pay for that?" he seethed.

"I'm not trying to make you pay for shit. I'm just letting you know that your actions have repercussions; because you did that, our relationship is like this."

"Cool," was his only reply.

"I'll pulling up at home. I'll talk to you later," she said.

"Yea," he said and hung up.

Chapter 31

Gotti had planned her whole day so that she could be in front of her TV with food and wine when part two of the *Love & Hip Hop* reunion came on. Gotti couldn't lie, part of the excitement stemmed from talking to Geechi while they watched. He had been in his feelings since their last conversation, and she was looking forward to having fun with him.

Gotti: *Part 2 comes on in an hour! I'm excited 'cause I know my girl ain't lying!*

Ten minutes into the show Gotti realized Geechi hadn't texted back. Normally, he texted her first but today he wasn't even replying. She tried to control the anger that built inside of her, but she couldn't. She figured Geechi was still mad and therefore he wasn't talking to her.

Gotti: *You must be busy...catch ya later homie.* She texted with the deuces emoji.

●●●

When Geechi's flight finally landed he was beyond irritated. His flight had been delayed which fucked up all his plans. He wanted to be at Gotti's house in time to watch *Love & Hip Hop* with her, but the layover in Detroit ruined that. Geechi grabbed his bag off the carousel and headed for the taxi exit.

In the back of the cab, Geechi turned his phone on and saw the missed texts from Gotti. He tapped on her name and waited for her to answer the call.

"Yea?" Gotti answered.

"Chill," Geechi said. He knew she was trying to appear busy because he didn't answer her texts.

"What's up?" she said, irritation in her voice.

"My flight was delayed," he began to explain.

"Oh okay. I didn't know you were traveling," Gotti said still irritated but with less bite in her voice.

"Yea well I'm on the way to my hotel. I need to shower—"

"Cool," she said cutting him off.

"Can I come see you, Gotti?"

"You're in New York?" Gotti asked in a nicer tone.

"Yea."

"Where are you staying?"

"The Hilton," Geechi replied.

"I'll come see you. They have a good restaurant. You wanna meet me for a late dinner...10?"

"Yea; I'm hungry as hell."

"Okay," Gotti said. She had planned on spending the night preparing for her upcoming meeting with Imago and Peachie but decided she could give him a few hours. Then she would have to rush back home and pull an all-nighter.

●●●

The food and the drinks were delicious, but sex was the only thing on each of their minds. Gotti was dressed in jeans that looked painted on and a low-cut shirt. Geechi had a fresh line up; he had taken out his permanents to get his teeth cleaned but hadn't put them back in yet. His pearly whites glistened; he smelled like heaven and he kept touching her knee under the table which had her squeezing her pussy muscles and lubricating her vagina.

"Can I come see your room?" Gotti asked, taking a sip of her wine.

"Just for a minute," Geechi flirted.

"That's all I need," she said, waving the waitress over.

"I already told them to charge it to my room; we're good," he said, getting up. Gotti smiled when he reached for her. With her hand in his, they headed to the elevator.

After kissing him from head to toe and riding him until he had absolutely nothing left, Gotti crawled off Geechi and headed for the bathroom. Geechi dozed off but woke up as he heard her moving around the room.

"What you doing?" he asked, sitting up in the bed.

"I gotta go, baby," she said and smiled back at him.

"Go where?" he questioned, watching her hop into her jeans.

Gotti raised her brows and chuckled. "Home," she answered. Geechi searched for his boxers and pulled them on.

"I came all the way to see you and you can't stay? Oh," he said dramatically, "I forgot; you don't owe me that."

"No, I don't," she said unapologetically.

"Why the fuck are you acting like this?" Geechi roared. Gotti looked up at him and fire raged inside of her, flashing through her eyes. Thoughts of Ashlei, the lies at the reception and all the bullshit in his phone ran through her mind. Geechi had embarrassed her, set her up for failure by having no regard for the pain his actions would cause her, got her wrapped up in a bullshit fairytale only to be dropped on her face when reality set in. And here he was questioning her because he took a flight—once—to New York when she moved to Dallas, put more into his career than hers, changed her whole life, for him. Her face contorted. Her voice was low when she finally spoke. As the sentence progressed and more rage filled her, her voice got louder.

"You need me to remind you what the fuck you did to me! Have you forgot, muthafucka!"

Her chest heaved up and down; Geechi saw the hurt and anger in her and it humbled him. He sank on the bed with his head in his hands. She rolled her eyes and grabbed her shirt.

"I don't know what you want," Geechi said to her.

"I don't know what I want," she shot back.

"I'm trying, Gotti," he replied.

"You just showed up; you didn't ask if I had to work. You didn't ask if I was busy. You showed up and you expected me to drop everything and cater to you," she spat. Geechi didn't speak because he didn't have anything to say.

"I have to go...I have to work. You feel like I'm supposed to just be at your beck and call," she accused. Geechi hadn't thought about it like that; Gotti wouldn't come see him, so he came to see her. He never meant for it to be an inconvenience to her.

"No, I don't," he said, standing and walking to her. "It's just sometimes we're good...like Saint Lucia or even our text messages. Then all of a sudden—" he abruptly stopped talking and threw his hands up.

"Sometimes I'm good, Geechi, then I think about what you did and I'm not," she admitted.

"I'm sorry for everything I did...for just showing up. If you have time tomorrow; call me," he said. She nodded and exited the room.

●●●

"Hey," Gotti said the next day when she called Geechi. She felt bad about their argument, but she meant everything she said. Gotti knew he had come to surprise her, and it would have been fun to watch the show together again, but they weren't at the stage in their relationship where he could surprise her in that way. Geechi coming to New York meant she had to host him, and he didn't have the right to put that responsibility on her.

"Hey," he replied.

"I'm finishing up with work. Do you wanna come over; I'll cook?"

"You want me to cook, since you've been working all day?" he offered.

"I bought the ingredients for spaghetti," she let him know.

He laughed. "Cool; that's one of my specialties."

"Whatever! You've never made spaghetti," she said.

"Yea 'cause we always eat out or you make that pasta shit."

"You love that!" Gotti replied.

"Yea the first few times," he admitted.

"So that's why you want to cook because I can't?" she questioned. He laughed. "You're trying to piss me off," she laughed. "Bye!"

"Bye. I'll see you in a minute."

● ● ●

"I'm not trying to be mean to you," Gotti admitted later that night while they were in bed.

"I know...I didn't at first but now I see...you're battling yourself," he said. She relaxed in his arms because she felt like he finally got it. "I wish we could live in Saint Lucia."

"We had a good time," she agreed.

"When it's just us, we always do. But then—"

"I don't let people get in my head," she said cutting him off.

"I know; you let *you* get in your head," he joked. Gotti playfully pinched him.

"I'm just scared, Geechi," she humbly admitted.

"If you let me, I'll make it up to you," Geechi promised.

"I want to..." she said and paused. "Let you. But you gotta be sure. If you have doubts—"

"I don't, Gotti."

"I don't want to move back to Texas right away," Gotti stated. That was something she had been thinking about for a while. Gotti wasn't willing to give up her whole life for him again.

"We should travel," he suggested. Ever since Tione had mentioned it, Geechi had been looking up places, costs and considering the possibly of using their travels as a way to reconnect.

"Travel?"

"Yea...the Caribbean islands for like a month," Geechi said.

"Whatever," Gotti said, shaking her head. With his business and hers that was impossible.

"Whenever we have business that we need to handle we can fly in. But I think if we go there and it's just me and you, we can work on our shit. Build it back tight so that when we come here it's solid," he stated.

"I don't know," Gotti said as thoughts of traveling with him, making love to him and working alongside him played out in her head.

"Think about it, baby, and let me know," he said, snuggling next to her. Soon he was fast asleep but the thought of a month-long honeymoon with him kept Gotti up all night.

● ● ●

"We would have to be in Jamaica on March 29th because Troy is getting married and I'm a bridesmaid," Gotti told Geechi two days after he had returned home. She had just left a bridal shop with Troy where they picked out her wedding dress and dresses for Gotti and La'Shea.

Geechi was excited when he saw that she was calling, but he had not expected that to be the first thing she said.

"Okay. We can do that," he said, cheesing from ear to ear.

"And I need time to get my business affairs in order before we leave," Gotti said.

"When do you want to leave?" Geechi asked.

"Beginning of March?" she suggested.

"Okay, let me get with Charlette," Geechi said referring to his travel agent. "I'll have her to call you so y'all can coordinate the dates."

"What dates do you prefer?" she asked.

"I'll make whatever works for you work for me," he said.

"Okay," Gotti said with a smile.

"Okay," he replied smiling too.

"I'll talk to you later," Gotti told him.

"I love you, Gotti," he said.

"I love you too, Geechi," she replied.

Similar Books From Natalie Sadè:

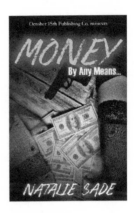

Newest Release From October 15th Publishing Co.

9 798643 013853